THE
NAKED
SPY

THE NAKED SPY

Captain Yevgeny Ivanov
with
Gennady Sokolov

BLAKE

Published by Blake Publishing Ltd.
98-100 Great North Road, London N2 0NL, England

First published in Great Britain in 1992

ISBN 1-85782-092-4

British Library Cataloguing-in-Publication Data:
A catalogue record for this book is available from the British Library.

Typeset by BMD Graphics, Hemel Hempstead

Printed by Cox and Wyman, Reading, Berks

1 3 5 7 9 10 8 6 4 2

"Men are born lying and die honest."
CHARLES BAUDELAIRE

For Danny McGrory, who initiated this book, and for Barry Wigmore who helped to make it happen.

CONTENTS

Foreword 7

Introduction 11

Prologue: Returning to the Past 15

PART ONE: POSTING TO LONDON

Sir Colin Coote's Surprises 23

Court Chiropractor 33

Millions for the Kremlin 39

MI5 on My Tail 45

Fox in the Henhouse 49

Portrait of Furtseva 57

A Lecture from Sir Winston 63

Second Russian at Cliveden 69

Failsafe Bridge with Lord Astor 75

Bastion Under the Embassy Roof 81

Compromising the Royals 87

The Charms of Christine Keeler 95

Gagarin's London Orbits 105

The Loose Cannon and the Queen's Messenger 109

Jack Profumo in the Trap 113

The Unrecruited Agent 119

The First Lady of the GRU in London 125

Pan Penkovsky, My Fellow Student 131

Farnborough Theft 143

The Berlin Crisis and Sir Godfrey Nicholson's Gin 151

Russian Steppe on the Banks of the Thames 159

Paul Getty Disappoints 165

The Portsmouth Recruit   171
Paul Richey's Basement   177
MI5 Hand Out a Fighter   183
A Flirtation with Mariella Novotny   189
The Cuban Crisis and the Lost Wager   195
Christmas in the Country   201
Kim Philby's Dispatch   207

PART TWO: THE WAY TO THE TOP
My Nomadic Childhood   215
Cadet at the Red Navy School   223
Want to Become a Spy?   229

PART THREE: MISSION TO OSLO
Visiting Haakon VII   239
The Febs   245
The Bodø Theft   255
Picnics in Oslo Fjord   261

PART FOUR: WORKING FOR THE GRU
Test by Returning   271
The Corrosion of Corruption   279
Disintegration   287

Foreword

If I hadn't gone to bed with Yevgeny Ivanov that night it is very likely that none of it would ever have happened. My love affair with John Profumo, the Minister for War, would never have developed overtones of treason. Harold Macmillan's government might not have been rocked to its socks. Stephen Ward would never have killed himself. And me, I guess I'd just be a happy mum living quietly somewhere, instead of being one of the most notorious femmes fatales of the twentieth century.

Such were the thoughts dancing through my mind in January 1994 after a journalist telephoned me to inform me that Yevgeny had died a sad, lonely, drink-sodden death in his glum Moscow apartment.

It seems so long ago that it all happened. I was a giggly teenager, barely out of school, high on the heady power I had suddenly developed over rich, powerful and handsome men. I had been brought up in a railway carriage, which had been converted into a kind of caravan. Then, suddenly, I found myself swept into the shimmering, Machiavellian world of Stephen Ward.

Stephen was an osteopath, an artist, a brilliant raconteur. And his friends were people like Sir Winston Churchill, Lord Astor, John Profumo... and Yevgeny Ivanov. Many thousands of words have been written and many learned men have pored over the significance of my relationship with Yevgeny. Yet, to this day, I still believe no-one except Yevgeny and I know the real truth. He tried to convince his Soviet masters that he had seduced me as part of some huge, brilliant, spy plan. But the truth was rather more intricate than he would like to have believed.

The incident which caused all the fuss happened after we had all spent a glorious, hot Summer day at Lord Astor's exquisite stately home, Cliveden. We had splashed around in the swimming pool and there was a crazy swimming race which involved Yevgeny, John Profumo, Lord Astor and another friend racing from the deep to the shallow end without using their legs. I'll never forget how Stephen Ward laughed and laughed at John, who cheated by walking the last bit. Of course he won the race easily. Even Yevgeny laughed when John said: "That will teach you to trust the British!"

After that we had a piggyback race in the pool, and I found myself sitting on John's strong shoulders. Most of the guests stayed on as the day cooled, but Yevgeny had to return to the Soviet Embassy in London, so he offered me a lift home. As I was about to leave John Profumo asked me for my telephone number, but I dodged giving it to him. He seemed a sight too pushy for my liking.

Yevgeny and I left early and headed off for London. He droned on and on about the glories of Russia, to the point where he almost sent me off to sleep. To him everything about Russia was wonderful, and everything about Britain was dreadful. Yet, despite his seriousness, he was darkly handsome and he was exactly the kind of man I liked to befriend. So, when he dropped me off at the house, I invited him in for a cup of coffee. Yevgeny had other ideas, however. From the boot of this car he produced a bottle.

"In Russia, we drink vodka," he said.

We drank and talked more about his country. He told me how large it was, how much had been achieved by the Party, how loyal its people were to progress.

"In Russia we don't have bus conductors, the people are trusted to pay" he told me ponderously. "We don't have homosexuals in Russia either – we do not have those kind of people."

Slowly the vodka bottle was emptied. Then, quite suddenly, Yevgeny lunged forward and kissed me. Before I knew what was happening he was holding me passionately in his strong arms and slipping me out of my clothes like a conjuror pulling a dove from a top hat. Before I knew it, and much against my better judgement, we were making love. He was a wonderful, fiery lover and I found myself reluctantly enjoying the experience. He left shortly afterwards and I felt a tremendous warmth towards him every time I saw him thereafter.

Then, all of a sudden, the good times were over. I was sent to prison, Stephen killed himself, John Profumo was disgraced and Yevgeny fled to Russia.

The whole, messy business was dragged up again with the release of the film Scandal in 1989. I thought Joanne Whalley-Kilmer, who played me, was a fine actress and John Hurt gave an impressive performance as Stephen Ward. But the story was quite a long way from being a true representation of what really happened.

In the Spring of 1993, a newspaper offered to fly me to Moscow to meet Yevgeny, so we could celebrate the thirtieth anniversary of our disastrous affair.

He had aged badly and his face was scarred by thwarted ambition, vodka and the depredations of the Russian winter. But he gave me a box of chocolates and kissed me on the cheek. Then we laughed together about the old times and about the stories contained in this book.

The Naked Spy is, without doubt, the best and most honest book ever written about the Profumo scandal. Yevgeny knew things nobody else could possibly have known about the affair. I believe, as I have always believed, that Stephen Ward was the grand master of the whole dreadful business. I am certain in my heart that Yevgeny never realised, to the end, how skilfully and ruthlessly he had been manipulated by him – just as John Profumo and I were each exploited by Stephen.

But I know that Stephen did confide to Yevgeny in a way he never confided to me. So much of the information in this fascinating and skilfully written autobiography is new.

His end was sad. He was found dead in the hallway of his Moscow flat by a friend who had called round to help him celebrate his 68th birthday.

The sun shone on the day they buried him. The army fired rifles over his coffin and he was laid to rest with a dignity denied him for the last 30 years of his life.

The last of the great cold war spies left this world as a hero.

But, to me now, looking at the way the world has moved on, all his sacrifices and schemes seem a little sad and a little pointless. Perhaps there is a lesson for all of us contained in his story...

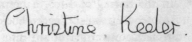

Christine Keeler, *London 1994*

Introduction

It would take a novel to do justice to the story of how this book was conceived and written, but I do not want to burden you with background information. I do have one explanation to make, however, without which the book cannot begin.

What follows is a story based on the recollections of a former secret agent who decided to tell the truth about his life and work, contrary to all written and unwritten laws. He had much to risk. Captain Ivanov did not write this book; I wrote it, with his consent, on the basis of numerous stories and recollections which Yevgeny generously shared with me and which I taped in 1988–91. These recollections contain a number of new facts about the Profumo affair and about the role of Captain Ivanov, GRU agent, in it.

I hope the reader will appreciate the courage displayed by this former agent of Soviet military intelligence who dared, in defiance of both his seniors and the censor, to remove the veil hiding the mysterious world of clandestine operations undertaken by the world's most secret intelligence agency, the GRU.

Much of what this man knew was not included in the book. Some names have been changed, and some details and facts deliberately omitted or barely outlined. Revelation of secret information is forbidden to a retired GRU officer, although the events described in the book took place three decades ago. The reason that much information remains classified, three or four decades later, revolves around security: agents recruited by Captain Ivanov in Norway in the mid-1950s, or in Britain in the early 1960s, might still be working for Moscow.

My mission as an author is to tell readers what I have learned from Captain Ivanov by carefully arranging his recollections, a process allowing me enough room for creative participation. My main priority was loyalty to the words of the hero of this book, to his manner of speech, to his style of expressing himself, because in them an attentive reader will be able to discern the personality and the will of Captain Ivanov.

The last year of my work on this book became a year of trial for Yevgeny Ivanov. His health deteriorated quickly, a consequence both of his experiences and an alcohol problem. Doctors performed miracles, rescuing him time and again from crises which made his heart, legs and memory fail him. I thank God that I had the time to collect enough factual material for the book, and am profoundly grateful that Zhenya lived to see it published.

Some people will doubt Ivanov's veracity. I can understand such doubts. The profession of spy, after all, involved Captain Ivanov in the arts of deceit and disinformation. He describes the use of these skills more than once in the following pages. I have no doubt, however, that my interlocutor was sincere and truthful – just as his recollections are. Without such faith I would not have taken up the writing of the book at all. I believe him because I got to know him well during the six years of our acquaintance, enough to understand his thoughts and sympathise with his troubles. He was no longer what he used to be thirty or forty years ago, when he carried out the orders of his Kremlin superiors without asking questions, dedicated to his mission of professional spy. In the evening of his life he decided that he should repent.

Regrettably, I cannot provide documentary evidence to prove to the sceptical that Ivanov *was* telling the truth at last: I was refused admission to any, even declassified, archives of the GRU concerned with the activities of Captain 1st Rank Ivanov as a member of the Soviet military missions in Norway and Britain. Indeed Rear Admiral Bardeyev, the First Deputy Chief of the GRU, called this book "evil and dangerous". In addition, many former colleagues of Captain Ivanov, whose co-operation I sought, refused to share their recollections with me or to speak up in the press. They did, however, provide bits and pieces of information to Yevgeny Ivanov and to me on condition that their identity would never be revealed. We have kept our word: their names will be kept secret. This may not lend our story credibility, but it will keep safe those who had enough courage to tell us about the operation of the GRU.

Ours is an exceptionally dynamic age in which major global changes occur almost daily. The defeat of the right-wing neo-Bolshevik coup in Moscow in August 1991 has, ironically, ushered in a new era in the history of Russia. The country is struggling towards true democracy. It is possible, at some time in a not too distant future, that the GRU archives will become accessible to the public, and then we shall know the *complete* truth about the "Russian connection" in the Profumo affair. For now, readers will have to content themselves with this first testimony, acquired despite many difficulties, about the role of the GRU in one of the most talked-about scandals of the century, one which led to the fall of Harold Macmillan's government.

Gennady Sokolov, *Moscow*

PROLOGUE

Returning to the Past

Time is a strange thing. It can render an old and wise man a naïve simpleton, and a beardless youngster a sage capable of foreseeing the future. But maybe it is not time but simply life that is to blame. It makes people undergo such profound transformations that they cannot recognise themselves from one decade to the next. I have always been a captive of illusions. I believed in the "great Stalin", unaware that I was worshipping a bloody tyrant. I believed in the Communist Party, "the mind, honour and conscience of our epoch", which led my country and its people to the severest of crises – political, ideological, economic and moral, leaving them without any beliefs and ideals whatsoever.

The time for awakening has come. In these troubled times I have decided to look back on my life. "What for?" you may ask. I don't know myself. Maybe the time has finally come to repent and tell the truth. Now is the time to write about the most wonderful period of my life, a time when I lived easily and had convictions, sincerely believing in the communist ideals which had been spelled out for me. But the question for me now is: through what eyes should I look back on my past? A large ideological gulf separates my past and present views. And what words can I use to describe a life which I once loved with the passion of a young man but which today, strange as it may seem, I want to expunge from my memory?

I was brought up on national pride. I was dedicated unconditionally to my country and its Communist Party. Maybe the patriotism of my green years and maturity was fallacious, built on insecure foundations, but I lived in the country of victors. We had won a terrible war against fascism. We were the first to send a sputnik into outer space. We were building communism. Wasn't it something to be proud of?

I have wanted to write my memoirs for a long time now. There is nothing easier than to persuade oneself to start writing. Just as there was an artist in every Cro-Magnon man, so there is a writer slumbering in every modern man. And when you are bored and a pensioner to boot, the slightest prompting is enough to wake up this writer. So I started writing, but soon saw that the will to write is not enough: you need at least a hint of the writer's talent. My pen stuttered on every paragraph. But of course this was natural: the core of my profession as a spy was to leave no traces. I never wrote letters. I wrote only reports and coded messages to Moscow Centre. I needed a partner. That's when I met Gennady Sokolov, who has ghost-written this book for me.

In the old USSR its publication was prohibited for security reasons. Even *glasnost* will not tolerate the revelations of an ex-spy. But the publication of this book abroad does not promise me a tranquil life either. I am not a defector who has made a good living in the West; on the contrary, I am destined to live my last years in Moscow.

Why do I run the risk, then? Am I aware of the dangerous consequences? Yes, I am, although I do not reveal a single state secret in this book.

My future critics may argue that, security reasons and state secrets apart, there are professional ethics to be considered. I have violated them. Why have I done this? Probably because there are limits to tolerance, and I have reached mine. Maybe everything is much more prosaic. Maybe I have become senile and decided to play Don Quixote, to challenge those who for years incited me to lies and forgery, theft and provocation, bribery and blackmail. Of course, not a single secret service obeys the dictates of conventional morality. There exist only the high interests of state, in the name of which crimes are committed. And a spy remains a spy only while he believes in the rightness of these interests of state, while he is convinced that he must commit crimes in the name of his country, of his people. I never lost this belief while I worked. I have woken up only in the evening of my life.

My former god has been thrown from the pedestal. The communist system, which I served faithfully all my life, is crumbling before my eyes. The people are waking from a long and unpleasant nightmare. Young people are waking up more easily, because they have their lives before them and they can choose a new way and view the future with hope in their hearts. But it is much more difficult for the old ones to wake up, because they have no future.

My last years have been painful and bitter years of awakening for me. It is terrible to understand in your old age that you had been hostage to a beautiful and inspiring idea that has proved fallacious. I have always played by the rules. But the time has come to tell everything, to let this book represent my belated repentance, to let it relate the story of an old and ailing man who once did scandalous things in Britain, Norway and Russia.

Much has been written about me in the past thirty years. Journalists have sent me to Siberia, said I have defected, and even buried me. I kept silent. I tolerated the smirks of my superiors and colleagues, and the displeasure of my wife Maya Gorkina, whom I have now divorced. My family life, too, has tumbled like a house of cards. I have remained well nigh alone in my old age, but I have preserved my memory, my recollections of the affairs of the past, known previously only to a narrow circle of officials. My name is almost unknown in Moscow, and in Norway, and in Britain I am remembered mostly by old people.

Several decades and quite a few scandals separate us from the turbulent 1960s. Much water has flowed under the bridge since then. Time has produced many new sensations. But the scandal over the Profumo affair, which led to the demise of the Conservative government of Harold Macmillan, is still of great interest and significance, because it involved politics, espionage, sex and the blighted career prospects of many senior officials.

At that time I worked in London as deputy naval attaché under the command of the Main Intelligence Directorate of the General Staff of the Soviet Army, but I was regarded merely as the man who slept with Christine Keeler, she being the girl who also slept with Jack Profumo, Lord Astor and a dozen other high-ranking officials. I was not blamed for anything else; Lord Denning's Commission stated that Captain Ivanov, who "probably" worked for Soviet military intelligence, was constantly monitored by the British secret services, and thus prevented from damaging the state interests of Britain. The honourable Lord Denning never knew how gravely mistaken he was. This book will undoubtedly be a revelation for *him*, at any rate.

Regrettably, the same can be said about other politicians, journalists and researchers, who have uncovered a number of things of a scandalous nature about the Profumo affair. A number, but not *all*: the Russian connection in that scandal has remained a secret until now.

With this book, new facts are brought to light. They help to illustrate, in their turn, aspects of the scandal hitherto buried by the establishments of Britain, Norway and the old Soviet Union. I am aware of the danger I am courting, and of the pain I shall inflict by writing this book. I know that it may be cruel and against the rules. But I have made my choice, and nobody will prevent me from doing what I have decided to do.

PART ONE

Posting to London

Sir Colin Coote's Surprises

If somebody should be blamed for the Profumo affair, that person is neither Christine Keeler nor myself – although quite a few people have accused us of being responsible for the scandal. Of course, both Christine Keeler and I played our part, but the scandal could have been avoided had it not been for the initiative of somebody else. I am not referring to Jack Profumo; in the final analysis, the ill-fated minister was only a victim of circumstances, falling as he did into a skilfully set trap. Neither do I want to make a scapegoat out of poor Stephen Ward. He has suffered enough from his compatriots. Nevertheless he, too, was merely a victim of conditions created by others.

So, who stirred up the trouble? The answer will sound incredible to those who know at least something about the Profumo affair. The trouble was stirred up, quite unwittingly, by none other than the eminently respectable Sir Colin Coote, now, alas, dead. Nobody asked him to introduce me to Ward. It was his idea. Had it not been for this introduction, I would never have visited Cliveden and fulfilled the dream of any spy by becoming a good acquaintance of all those lords, ministers, counsellors and businessmen. The managing editor of the *Daily Telegraph* gave me a unique present, something which I could not even have dreamed about: he introduced me to Britain's élite, he opened the doors of many high-ranking officials for me.

However, this was not Sir Colin's only surprise; he gave me another superb present, which earned the Soviet Union a huge sum in gold. This story will be told in its proper place, but I must now go back to March 1960, to my arrival in Britain.

Snow storms were raging in Moscow; winter did not want to leave. Week after week, snowflakes as big as apples fell down on the capital. Poplar branches broke under the burden of snow. In contrast, London enveloped me with the smell of spring. I felt it even in the exhaust fumes.

How do you begin in an unknown country? Of course, you listen and look around. You try to merge into a new way of life. However, this seldom proves simple. In Britain you feel like a deep-sea diver in his gear, which, no matter how deep you may go, prevents you from becoming "one of them"; eventually you realise that it is not easy to "dive" into the British way of life. You can only gradually absorb it, drop by drop, as a raincoat absorbs drizzle.

Britain is a kingdom of private life. This national respect for privacy poses a number of problems for a spy, but also provides quite a few dividends. Many of my colleagues could not negotiate the barriers which separated them from that kingdom. The walls that hide Britons' private life from prying eyes appear to be insurmountably high. In my first months in London it seemed to me that a veil of silence enveloped the city like a dense fog, as if an unseen sound editor had cut all sound down to the minimum. We Russians are used to speaking up unnecessarily, so much so that we no longer notice it. In Britain, people speak little, in low voices. Attempts to address strangers are as out of place in the UK as flirting with the girl in the next car at the traffic lights.

The difficulties of engaging in smalltalk, making acquaintances and establishing business relations in Britain thus became my first barrier. After the first six months, I had to admit, without much pleasure, that even if you did manage to establish contact with an Englishman, you then had to be prepared to sweat until you could steer him in the necessary direction. Simply put, even in the most hearty conversation with a Soviet, Englishmen would talk about the weather, absurd rumours, their hobbies and pastimes and what not rather than about their careers, especially if they had attained a certain eminence. This happened more than once to me, yet I continued to search stubbornly for ways to approach the Englishmen I needed.

Having visited British homes half a dozen times, I understood that the fabric of their acquaintanceship is woven around mutual likes and interests, above all those related to pastimes. When I was introduced to people at parties, I was surprised to see how quickly they withdrew once I had learned their profession and started poking about. With time, I understood that the course of conversation natural for Russians is unacceptable in Britain, that it would be better to search for a backyard entry rather than to pound on the front door. The new tactic eventually yielded its first fruit. I gathered experience of getting acquainted and scored my first result at the party in the Soviet Embassy on the occasion of the anniversary of the 1917 October Revolution, a state holiday in the Soviet Union. It was at that party that I met Sir Colin Coote.

A spy cannot employ his entire arsenal of instruments for

collecting information and recruiting without a contact of this kind; not even the most brilliant agent will fulfil his task without contacts and recruits. This is the ABC of any professional spy. Moscow Centre wanted results, answers to questions on the nuclear stockpiles of the British and West German armed forces, new missiles, aircraft and submarines. The GRU was interested in the strategic and operational-tactical plans drafted in the headquarters of NATO countries, in the military-political policy of the British government, and especially in British–US relations in the sphere of military co-operation. There were many questions, and little time in which to answer them.

The first six months of my stay in London were nearly over, yet my results were modest. I was running out of time and badly needed a breakthrough. That is why I prepared for the 7 November 1960 party at the embassy with special care. I read and reread the list of those invited to the party. For hours I studied the files on each of the nearly one hundred guests, pinpointing my victim, planning the conversation and thinking up ways to establish a reliable contact. Scenarios of approaching the necessary people had been written back in Moscow Centre, when I was prepared for the London posting. Materials which I received were put together from bits and pieces provided by different sources. They concerned not only the military-political plans of the British leadership but gave details of the specific executors of these plans. Of particular value for me was information about contacts and about the influence of prominent figures in the British élite.

It should be said, for justice's sake, that despite their permanent rivalry, the KGB and the GRU exchanged their most important materials. After my return from London I learned that a lion's share of that information was provided by Kim Philby. "The Magnificent Five", as the KGB called Philby, Blunt, Burgess, Maclean and the then unknown fifth man, ferreted out for Moscow Centre not only fundamental information but lots of data on the contacts, hobbies and weaknesses of prominent British politicians. This apparently trivial information was actually invaluable, at least for me.

I had studied with special care information, supplied most probably by Kim Philby, about the Other Club. This was a dining club founded in 1911 by Winston Churchill and F. E. Smith, a prominent lawyer and leading Conservative, and it met fortnightly while Parliament was in session. Besides Sir Colin, the then Foreign Secretary Sir Alec Douglas-Home and Prime Minister Harold Macmillan, and last but not the least, Secretary of State for War Jack Profumo were all members of that club. In any case, Sir Colin was managing editor of the *Daily Telegraph*, which was regarded, with good reason, as the mouthpiece of the ruling Conservative Party.

No wonder that I was drawn to them as a bee to pollen. But however invaluable our information about Sir Colin's contacts was, it lacked a detail which, as it turned out later, sealed my union with him. I did not know that Sir Colin hated "the Hun". I knew only that he had fought in the First World War, and quite gallantly at that. But I could not know that he had lost a lung during one of the Germans' gas attacks. That wound made Sir Colin the enemy of Germany for the rest of his life.

In London I did not miss a single important party in the

US, Canadian or Soviet Embassies, to say nothing of Buckingham Palace parties. This socialising formed a very important part of my work. How could I get acquainted with the people I needed otherwise? These parties provided an opportunity for establishing contacts in a matter of minutes, given skill and application. Nevertheless, few members of the Soviet Embassy used those official parties for developing their business contacts. Indeed some of them attended the parties only for free booze and a nap in the corner, or a talk with their hosts about the weather.

My chief, Captain 1st Rank Sukhoruchkin, the naval attaché in London, was one of these clumsy and, to be honest, absolutely useless people. It was sheer pain for him to entertain guests. Since he held the post of the naval attaché, he was nominated for the rank of Rear Admiral, because the post demanded it. I knew about this and tried to help my chief to score points, in order to curry favour with superiors and obtain the coveted stars. I offered him promising plans, but he rejected them all. It took me some time to understand that my chief was playing it safe, and was interested only in avoiding trouble. As a result, in nine cases out of ten I neither consulted nor informed him about my plans. I worked with the GRU *rezident* (fixed-post spy) in London or directly with Moscow Centre.

I regarded every party as an actor regards a performance. I had to learn my lines for every scene and play my role to perfection. I quickly introduced myself and surged on. For example, I would come up to a guest and ask: "Excuse me, sir, but what does this interesting sign on your lapel mean?" Then I would add, without giving him time to think,

"Sorry, I didn't introduce myself. I'm assistant naval attaché. And you?"

He replies, for example: "I'm manager of a flour mill."

Nothing to gain here. I bow and go to the next guest. "Excuse me, sir, I read in yesterday's papers about the change in the Tories' position on joining the Common Market. What do you think about it?"

"Both I and all the journalists of my paper believe that this position is substantiated," he replies.

Well, I think, *my* paper? "And what paper is that, if I may ask?"

"*Daily Telegraph.*"

"Oh, glad to meet you! Excuse me, sir –?"

"Sir Colin Coote. And who are you?"

"Captain Yevgeny Ivanov, assistant naval attaché."

And we have a drink to seal our acquaintance. A short exchange of niceties, and my next move: "Sir Colin, I would like to see how a British newspaper is made. Could you help me?"

"Of course," says Sir Colin.

"When would it be suitable for you?"

"Well, let's make it next Wednesday. Come directly to the editorial board."

This is how I met Sir Colin Coote. A week later he demonstrated the achievements of British printing to me. We talked at length. From printing we passed over to politics, from politics to the economy. Next, we got on to military affairs, the struggle against Germany in the First and Second World Wars...

In an hour I sensed that I had found the point of contact. Sir Colin indeed hated "the Hun". I exploited this revelation without thinking twice. Our conversation focused on the German problem. I thought it suitable to start off by saying that I believed Germany had not forgotten the motto of the Kaiser's Reich: "God Punish Britain". Next, I reminded Sir Colin that in Germany's military circles they still called Britain "*der Erbfeind*", blood enemy. "Meanwhile," I continued, "British credits, just like American ones, are still being used for the restoration of the military industries of the Rhine and Ruhr. The West German Bundeswehr," I said, "now commanded by Hitler's former generals, have become stronger than the British army!"

It was apparent to me that Sir Colin was not paying special attention to my opinions, but I continued my offensive on the anti-German front. "Even Goebbels could not have imagined in his most daring dreams that, barely fifteen years after the end of the war, Germany would have bases in the British Isles, while a German general would occupy a responsible post in the new military-political bloc and would draft strategic plans for the US and Britain," I proclaimed with sincere indignation, seeing Sir Colin's eyes light up.

I sensed that our agreement on this question was unshakable. Yet I went on, in an attempt to cement it. "It's a fact that the bulk of those who are supervising German affairs now shouted '*Sieg Heil!*' in the streets of fascist Germany twenty-five years ago. Twice in your life" – this time I directly referred to Sir Colin's bitter experiences – "Germany drew your homeland, and Europe as a whole, into a war. If we all remember this, the Germans will not ruin Europe again."

"We the British have to pin our hopes on you in the Soviet Union," remarked Sir Colin with heavy irony. "As for us," he added, somewhat embarrassed, "we can do nothing: Britain is bound hand and foot by its partner relations with America, and Washington's view on Germany differs from ours."

This introduced British–US antagonism into our conversation. Sir Colin recalled the wrangle between ex-Secretary of State Dean Acheson and Harold Macmillan. "Imagine, Captain, that Yankee dared to say in a public speech that Britain as a great power had expired and could no longer claim the role of the main US partner in Europe. That it should cede this role to West Germany!"

I readily shared the indignation of Sir Colin and quoted Harold Macmillan, who compared Dean Acheson to such bitter enemies of Britain as King Philip of Spain, Louis XIV and Napoleon of France, Kaiser Wilhelm and Hitler of Germany.

"Mr Acheson is obviously in a hurry to bury Britain," stated Sir Colin, clearly convinced that he was right. "Gravely mistaken are those who no longer see us as a great power. Britain has not yet had its final say."

Naturally, I supported this statement. The boundaries of our concord visibly expanded. We were gratified to find that we had common worries over the deployment of chemical and nuclear weapons in West Germany. The basis of a mutual understanding was laid. I did not have to wait long for Sir Colin's next invitation.

It was a meeting which any spy can only dream about: Sir Colin introduced me to Stephen Ward. He introduced us to each other in the Garrick Club. Sir Colin laid it on thick, complimenting Ward without embarrassment, giving me to understand that Stephen was a star of the first magnitude: a talented osteopath, an artist of genius, a pet of the British upper class. I understood that such meetings were not arranged without reason, and waited for an answer to the logical question: "Why should Sir Colin introduce me to Stephen Ward?" I did not get it.

Today, over three decades later, I still don't know the answer. It was rumoured that the meeting was organised by British counter-intelligence in order to push me into a trap, but this is laughable. And neither could Stephen Ward have sought my co-operation in organising his meeting with Khrushchev, whose portrait he wanted to paint. I think it was chance, pure and simple. It was Lady Luck at her kindest, arranging my acquaintance with Sir Colin. If Sir Colin had not invited Stephen Ward to the Garrick Club, I would not have met Lord Astor, nor visited Valerie Hobson in Jack Profumo's home when he had dates with Christine Keeler. It also made many other things possible, which eventually developed into a scandal that led to the resignation of many leading British politicians.

Court Chiropractor

"I can't believe it, Captain! You don't know what osteopathy is?" Ward was clearly astonished at my ignorance. "I must immediately fill in this blank. Let's go to my clinic straight away."

"But I'm in perfect health."

"Nobody is going to treat you there," Stephen assured me. "But any civilised person should know about the healing secrets of osteopathy."

"I'm more interested in military and political secrets," I joked.

"Shame on you, Captain! How dare you say such things in the presence of a patriot and gentleman? Come on."

We said goodbye to Sir Colin, thanking him profusely for the wonderful lunch in the Garrick Club, and went to Ward's clinic on Devonshire Street. On our way there I learned that there are exceptions to every rule. Stephen Ward absolutely lacked the characteristic British taciturnity and restraint. I hardly had a chance to insert a word into the monologue of my new acquaintance. Stephen was the proverbial fund of jokes and stories. It was a brilliant monologue, provided by a consummate master of oratory.

This simplified my task. In several hours I learned more about my new friend than I would have uncovered in a month if Stephen had not been such a talkative person. In one evening I not only learned about the secrets of osteopathy but, much more interesting for me, about Ward's friends. He boasted that nearly all of high society, Britons and foreigners alike, were his patients. He seated me in a soft armchair in his office and poured French brandy for us. Without any prompting on my part, Stephen started telling me about his life and its metamorphoses, its ups and downs, his past and his present. His openness and irreverence were disarming. His self-advertisement was clearly designed to impress me. Enumerating his acquaintances, friends and patients, he mentioned former Prime Minister Winston Churchill, ex-Minister of Defence Peter Thorneycroft, US President of the 1950s Dwight D. Eisenhower, Ambassador Averell Harriman, stars Elizabeth Taylor and Frank Sinatra, monarchs-in-exile and ex-politicians...

My head span. I tried to remember every name, so as to be able to write a detailed report to Moscow.

"Yevgeny, you are a military man," he went on. "Tell me, do you have osteopaths in the Red Army?" I was so stunned I didn't know what to say. "As for our army, it was my idea and it was taken up," Ward boasted. "I paved the way for them. Where did you fight in the Second World War?"

"In the Far East," I replied. "I was a cadet on a training ship in the Sea of Japan."

"And I served in a medical regiment, first in Britain and later in India. My boss there did not want to appoint me the regiment's doctor. 'What kind of medical profession is osteopathy?' he used to ask me. As a result, the regimental authorities didn't recognise my US diploma or see any need for me. This went on until I helped the regiment's commander back on his feet. He suffered from a contracture of the spine, and could hardly stand. It took me several sessions to heal him, and he helped me to launch a campaign for the recognition of osteopathy in the army. But we would have failed, if not for one incident."

"What incident was that – or is it a secret?"

"Not at all," replied Stephen as he turned on the stove and started making coffee. "Not only Englishmen but also Hindus knew that I practised osteopathy in the King's Medical Regiment in Delhi. It so happened that old Gandhi learned that, too. He suffered severely from neck contracture. I was asked to help him. I remember entering his room and him saying to me: 'So far English officers came here with only one aim, to arrest me. But they tell me you are a doctor and have agreed to help me.' I couldn't but feel sorry for the old man," Ward went on. "However, I had to work on him very hard. Later that story reached Lord Mountbatten himself. They say he whispered a word or two where it mattered, in support of osteopathy, and the attitude to me changed dramatically."

Stephen poured coffee and grinned: "But Sir Winston didn't like it that I had helped old Gandhi. He said so outright: 'Why in hell didn't you break his neck? That would have settled quite a few problems.' So, the story with Gandhi had reached the ears of the Prime Minister."

We talked and talked, unheedful of time. Ward went from osteopathy to gardening; he told me that Britain was a country of gardeners. "It's the hobby of every Englishman, from miners to stock-brokers," he said. "Gardening is our national passion. There is nothing better for me than to spend several days a week in my garden."

"And where is your garden?" I asked, to keep up the conversation, rather than because I was eager to hear the answer.

"In Cliveden, on the estate of Lord Astor. I have a small cottage on the bank of the Thames. A wonderful spot! You should visit it. I would be happy to show you my garden."

You can imagine the effect of that statement on me. I could hardly prevent myself from jumping up and down. Was this really happening to me? Or was I dreaming? "Are you friendly with Lord Astor?"

"You mean Billy?" Stephen laughed. "But of course! I saved Lord Astor from becoming an invalid ten years ago, after he had fallen from his horse clumsily while hunting and damaged his spine. I had to work to help him. And a year ago I married him to Bronwen Pugh. He did not look much like a newly-wed, though. Bronwen is his third wife, you know, and the youngest of them: she's twenty-five years Bill's junior. You won't believe it, but I organised their first date. Old Bill was as excited as a boy. Imagine, with his experience!"

"Are you married?"

"Was," he replied, not very willingly. "But I'll never repeat *that* mistake again."

Stephen lighted another cigarette. It seemed to me that the private life of my new acquaintance was not as easy as he tried to paint it. Noticing my embarrassment, Stephen said: "Freedom is my only wife. Remember how Heinrich Heine put it: Germans regard freedom as a grandmother; the French, as a lover; and Englishmen, as a legal wife. And you Russians, how do you regard freedom?"

"Englishmen are famous for their art of understatement,"

I replied. "But we Russians are not afraid of overstating our passions. We are not afraid of sentimentality. Few Russians would give up a beautiful girl for imaginary freedom, especially if they have never seen freedom."

That was how, at the initiative of Sir Colin, I met a man who not only had a wide range of friends in high places but largely shared the political convictions I held at that time. Stephen Ward told me that in 1941, the most difficult year of the war for the Soviet Union, with the Germans barely twenty-six kilometres from Moscow, he had stuck a pin into the circle marked "Moscow" on the map and said: "Russia will win."

Stephen Ward was a true find for me. He knew a great deal and was a good companion. Besides, we were drawn to each other through the similarity in our political interests. Stephen was sympathetic towards my country, although he was not a Communist.

On the day of our first meeting neither Stephen nor I could know where our friendship would lead us. Yet I was convinced that Ward's acquaintances must become my acquaintances, too.

"Start working on it, Zhenya," GRU *resident* in London General Pavlov told me when I reported to him the day after my meeting with Ward. "You must not miss this chance. Try to use that chiropractor for our purposes. Get acquainted with his friends. And report to me personally."

Millions for the Kremlin

As I mentioned earlier, Sir Colin Coote not only introduced me to Stephen Ward, but gave me another present, the true significance of which I did not fully appreciate at the time. Nevertheless, I immediately reported his information to Moscow Centre.

I learned later that the present from Sir Colin pleased the Soviet government very much. However, the resulting decorations were awarded not to the managing editor of the *Daily Telegraph* nor to me, but to the GRU chiefs.

It was just one phrase of Sir Colin's, said in passing during lunch. But the price of that phrase amounted to several millions in gold. It happened like this: Sir Colin had invited me to the Garrick again. He was deliberating about the British system of government. "Mind you, Eugene," he said, "we have the most covert system of government."

"What's so covert about it?"

"Do you know, for example, why we invented the Garrick?"

That question perplexed me even more. "Why?"

"The Englishmen invented a system of clubs for gentlemen in order to introduce a secret mechanism of power."

"You must be joking."

"Not at all," Sir Colin replied coolly. "Listen well, and you will see what I mean. Say, a gentleman comes up to me in the club and says: 'What about appointing Mr So-and-So?' I reply: 'Well, maybe. Why not?' He thanks me and adds: 'This is all I wanted to know.'"

I laughed.

"Do you see now?" Sir Colin asked haughtily. "There is no better cover for sifting the élite than London's clubs, each with its own membership rules. However, you Communists are against any élite."

After coffee our conversation switched over to newspapers.

"The director of the Bank of England complained to me the other day," Sir Colin said. "'I wouldn't dare tell you what to publish in your newspaper or how to write your commentaries,' he said, 'but the silly sensationalism with which the press describes a regular currency fever is damaging the fiscal interests of Britain.' Imagine how bad the situation is, Eugene, if the British bankers are complaining over the freedom of the press!"

We agreed that the British economy was in a deplorable state. Sir Colin began talking about some troubles in the British Treasury. I feigned interest, although the subject did not interest me in the least. It turned out that the *Daily Telegraph* chief was not averse to the world of big business. He was acquainted with quite a few businessmen. I was not much interested in Sir Colin's business adventures, but I did not stop him, giving him a chance to unbosom his problems. I was waiting for an opportune moment to steer the conversation to military-political problems. This moment came after Sir Colin said: "There is trouble. In five days, and I know this for sure, the Treasury will have to review the exchange rate of the pound as compared to the dollar."

Back from the lunch in my office at 16 Kensington Palace Gardens, I wrote a detailed report to Moscow Centre and took it for approval to the *rezident*. General Pavlov ordered it ciphered and sent to the Centre immediately. To be truthful, I did not pay much attention to that report. I knew little about finances. Only upon my return to Moscow did I learn that the General Staff was commended for that action by Anastas Ivanovich Mikoyan, then Deputy Chairman of the USSR Council of Ministers responsible for foreign economic relations.

If not for Marshal Biryuzov, then chief of the General Staff, I would never have learned that my initiative had been appreciated, or why. The marshal summoned me to his office shortly after I was forced to return from London. It seemed that he understood my sentiments concerning the trouble in London and was trying to cheer me up. Yet the conversation remained awkward. Then the marshal, brushing aside his official tone, said: "Don't worry, Captain. Every thing will be all right. You'll go to the Academy of the General Staff, which is not peanuts. In three or four years you will master all the intricacies of our profession, and then we'll see."

"Yes, sir," I said, recognising this as an order.

"Come here," said the marshal, and he took a letter marked "Top Secret" and "USSR Council of Ministers" from a file on his desk. "Read it. You probably don't know what a good present your information was for Mikoyan. If I were you I'd throw a celebration party. This involves millions of roubles."

I read the short letter from Anastas Mikoyan to Marshal Biryuzov, in which the statesman expressed his gratitude to the General Staff for the timely information about the coming review of the exchange rate of the British pound. The measures taken as a result, the letter ran, helped the Soviet Union to earn a considerable sum in hard currency.

"They should have given you an order for that, Ivanov," Biryuzov said, locking the letter away. "But your seniors in the department proved to be smarter than you. The order went to the man who delivered your report. And so they overlooked your contribution. But I'll mend this, in time. After I return from my business trip to Yugoslavia I shall bend a few ears in the Supreme Soviet."

The marshal did not bend any ears. His plane crashed outside Belgrade. The death of Biryuzov undermined my career in the directorate. Marshal Matvey Zakharov, who replaced Biryuzov as chief of the General Staff, was not inclined to assist me. I had to abandon my hopes for becoming an admiral. However, I got off lightly, compared with my brother-in-law, who nearly lost his head as the result of the crash. I am referring to Igor Konstantinov, commander of the special aviation division. His brother Anatoly and I were married to sisters and both served in the GRU. Anatoly himself had worked in London, but before my time and as air force attaché. (Some British publications, incidentally, erroneously call him Igor, and list him among the 105 Soviet secret service agents deported from Britain in 1971. This is a mistake. At that time Anatoly Konstantinov worked in Indonesia as the air force attaché of the Soviet Embassy in Jakarta.) Igor, because of his position in the special aviation division, saw his life hanging by a thread until a search party found the "black box". It then transpired that despite the Yugoslavs' recommendation that the plane should land at the nearest airfield because of foul weather in Belgrade, which was closed to incoming planes, Marshal Biryuzov ordered the crew to land only in the capital. The plane's commander had to comply with the orders of the marshal, but lost his way over mountains in zero visibility and crashed.

After Marshal Biryuzov's death I never brought up the story of Sir Colin's million-rouble present, although I naturally wanted to know how our accountants had managed to turn my information from London into money. In the end, caution stilled by curiosity, I asked an acquaintance, who for many years worked in the hard-currency department of the USSR Ministry of Foreign Trade, how money can be earned with this kind of information. To understand it I had to listen to a tedious lecture on the history of currency operations. I am not an expert in this field, and besides, the system of currency regulations has changed radically since then. But in my time it was based on the agreements of the 1944 Bretton Woods international conference, where the dollar was proclaimed to be the basis of the world currency system. It acted, on a par with gold, as the gold standard for all other currencies, including the pound sterling. Exchange rates were closely tied to the dollar. They were allowed to deviate from the established norm by no more than 1 per cent either way. This narrow margin of fluctuations in the exchange rates of foreign currencies insured US goods and investments against troubles on the world market. It precluded major drops in the exchange rates as a result of the reduction of the gold content or of dwindling buying capacity. Yet fluctuations within the limit of 1 per cent were possible.

These fluctuations, if somebody were forewarned, provided fantastic possibilities for effective gambling on the stock exchanges and for daring operations with banking capital, transactions of greatest benefit to countries with a centralised system of managing currency and financial resources. The Soviet Union is one of these. Taking this into account, the Soviet leadership back in Stalin's time used fiscal espionage in order to reap profits from Western currency markets. A special group of experts was set up for the purpose, and they bought or sold currency, shares and securities on the world's largest exchanges upon receiving reliable information about planned reviews of the exchange rates.

My snippet of information from London, so unexpectedly received from Sir Colin, was relayed to Soviet brokers in Zürich, Frankfurt-am-Main, London and New York in the form of orders to buy this currency and sell that one. The gamble earned the Kremlin government millions in free profits.

MI5 on My Tail

The spring of 1961 promised quite a few changes for the better in my difficult work, but the long-awaited results were slow to materialise. I attributed this to the particular problems involved in working in London, and redoubled my efforts to develop new and useful contacts.

The situation in my country and the rest of the world seemed favourable to me. In April Yuri Gagarin became the first man to orbit the Earth. Some time later I worked with him during his visit to Britain. Yet Gagarin helped me in my work even before he came to London: being a compatriot of the world's first cosmonaut was more effective than any personal recommendation. In short, the popularity of the Soviet Union was growing. I was in a hurry to exploit it. But my activities did not go unnoticed by British counter-intelligence. I sensed them shadowing me more and more closely that spring. It was becoming more difficult to evade MI5. Of course, this preoccupation of the British secret services with foreigners of my stripe was natural and understandable. Nevertheless, I needed to break out of their stifling embrace.

My superiors and I had to think hard about how we were to dispel the suspicions of Sir Roger Hollis, then chief of MI5. I did not know then the real reason for the heightened MI5 attention to my person. I thought that I was simply too active for their liking. Only after I returned to Moscow did

I learn, at the trial of my classmate Colonel Oleg Penkovsky, that he had been recruited by British intelligence and the CIA at approximately that time and had revealed to his new bosses everything he knew about my humble person. Anyway, the unceasing attention of counter-intelligence and the thirty-five-mile rule made me search for ways to move about the country with apparently innocent intent.

It is common knowledge that Soviet diplomats, journalists and other officials living in London could travel no farther than thirty-five miles from the capital. Every trip beyond this limit called for special permission, to gain which you had to present to the Foreign Office the plan of your trip and then get confirmation from the hotels where you intended to stay the night. This information had to be typed into special forms marked "Travel Notification" in five copies. One copy was for yourself, the second copy for the embassy, and the other three had to be sent to the Foreign Office no later than forty-eight hours before your trip – plus holidays. Each form had also to be signed by the first secretary of the embassy, otherwise the notification would be considered invalid. Similar, but much stricter procedures existed in the USSR for the officials of the British Embassy there. While preparing for such a trip, we all – both in the East and in the West – waited impatiently for the phone call that would allow or prohibit it.

"Look here, Zhenya," General Pavlov advised. "Give a couple of lectures. A quiet, respectable job. Give MI5 a break. Hopefully, this will allay their suspicions. Besides, you will be helping the embassy. They are drowning in requests for lectures! What has happened to the British?"

Indeed, the embassy was receiving large numbers of requests inviting Soviet experts to discussions, meetings and other functions. The traditional British lack of interest in foreigners – and Soviets were no exception – suddenly and unexpectedly gave way to a sincere interest in the Russian way of life. I cannot say that being Russian in London at that time offered any privileges. The Englishmen traditionally look down on foreigners, apparently regarding them as children in the company of adults. They certainly treated me in this way. They invited me home and regarded my rather direct behaviour with amused tolerance, evincing surprise that I spoke English fluently and was not shy about demonstrating knowledge.

I therefore stopped my espionage activities for a time and started giving lectures. My first lectures taught me what questions to expect, whether they were at meetings of Young Conservatives, associations of housewives or Rotary Club functions. Such lectures were usually held in a large room in a local hotel, and were given after a satisfying dinner. They reminded me very much of third-degree interrogations. Each question was a kind of a comprehensive political statement, a small speech intended to trip you up, but they only made me brace myself, and some of them were actually amusing. These questions nearly always contained anti-Soviet attacks, detailing the violations of human rights and aggressive designs of the Kremlin. I expected them. And I was prepared to rebuff them, never taken by surprise.

Strangely, these absurd attacks, as I saw them, those persistent, double-edged questions, did not depress me. On the contrary, they exalted me, and my listeners could not but feel this, and as a result, each lecture ended well after midnight in the living room of a local dignitary, filled to overflowing with members of the local Rotary Club, or tipsy Young Conservatives, or whoever.

Strangely enough, it was in my capacity as a lecturer that I succeeded in accomplishing what I could not do while performing my professional duties: I recruited a promising agent. Reading a lecture about the Soviet Union in Portsmouth to a local association, I became acquainted with a man who asked the strangest of questions, naturally stirring my interest. This gentleman was a certain "Captain Souls" of the Coast Guard. During our second meeting, in London, he agreed to work for Soviet intelligence. I will go into more detail about this contact in its appropriate place, later in my story.

Fox in the Henhouse

Gradually, and without my noticing it, my London life began to look up. It had been busy even before the meeting in the Garrick, but now I planned all kinds of meetings and trips, keeping me busy until the beginning of 1962.

It would be tiresome to enumerate all of my plans here, but I shall mention some highlights. I wanted to visit Scotland, Holy Loch in particular, for this was where Britain was establishing a fleet of nuclear submarines armed with Polaris missiles. My visit was of crucial importance for monitoring the development of the British deterrence forces, and the story of how I obtained permission to circumvent the thirty-five-mile rule is told later, in the chapter dealing with MI5. For the moment, suffice it to say that I managed to visit Holy Loch and, with MI5's help, I also went to Lossiemouth to see the new aircraft at the RAF base there. In addition, I frequently visited Portland, Portsmouth and Southampton to watch, photograph or film these major naval centres, or to get other information.

Trips to Britain's largest radar station in Fylingdales, in Yorkshire, were made to determine the frequencies of that radar. Each time I went there, the technicians of the GRU *rezidentura* in London gave me a "black box" crammed with electronics. This box was fixed in the boot of my Humber Super Snipe and monitored the radar's frequencies while I wiped the car's windscreen or checked its plugs or tyres. I also attended the Farnborough air fairs, usually accompanied by specialists from Moscow Centre, with the express aim of technological or industrial espionage.

The autumn and winter sessions of Parliament and the traditional Prime Ministerial Guildhall policy speech usually engendered hectic activity in our *rezidentura* on the political front. In those periods I would work non-stop to acquire government documents on military politics and development from all available sources.

There were also the annual conferences of the political parties, the forums and congresses of various associations and organisations directly concerned with military policy, the traditional lectures in Chatham House, meetings of the association of London-based military attachés, parties, soirées, discussions, first nights, races, festivals, regattas and holidays. All these functions offered me opportunities to fulfil the tasks set by Moscow Centre. My life was thus planned months ahead. An ancient sage once said: "If you know your life in advance, should you bother living it?" Indeed, a life planned a year ahead leaves no room for romance and adventure. But it also leaves no room for surprises. My connection with Stephen Ward disrupted all these plans. I had to review them, cramming more tasks into an already packed schedule. When Moscow Centre charged me with special tasks, which was quite often, my life became a nightmare without a moment to stop and think calmly.

In the first hundred or so days of our acquaintance Ward had introduced me to two or three dozen high-ranking officials from the British corridors of power. Operating in high society placed new demands on both my time and my manners. Nothing offends the English more than indifference to the wide gamut of social differences, let alone an arrogant neglect of them. The British élite regards itself as a class on its own, one which it thinks is best prepared for governing the country courtesy of heredity, traditions and education. If I did not want to be a *rara avis* among them, I had to learn their laws, their complex system of social etiquette.

This role also called for additional spending. If I had lived solely on my official salary, I could not have played my new role satisfactorily. But, being a GRU agent, I spent as much money as I wanted. All my cheques were signed and paid by the embassy accountants without so much as a word. The GRU had impressive credit in London. That's why I wore shirts and shoes from Barkers, suits and ties from Harrods, and colognes from Christian Dior. I had to dress as well as my new acquaintances. And I could not invite them for lunch at the local Wimpy Bar. One of the wardrobes in my office in Kensington Palace Gardens was filled with crates of vodka, caviar and souvenirs. I had only to reach out to get a present for my new acquaintances.

In the two years that I knew Stephen Ward, he took me to nearly all the clubs in Pall Mall and St James's. I also visited the Connaught Club in Marble Arch, and other small card clubs. British clubs are the hub of establishment, power, information and secrets. Could a man of my profession be prevented from talking about these subjects in passing, over a glass of wine? These establishments were respectable buildings for respectable gentlemen, where ladies (and then far from all) were allowed only twice a week. Each club had its own rules and membership. The Carlton was the hideout of high-ranking Conservatives. The Travellers' was the backyard of medium-rank Foreign Office officials. High society gathered in the Garrick or White's. These clubs had a select membership, and decisions taken over brandy in White's, founded in the late seventeenth century, were sure to be passed also at 10 Downing Street and Westminster.

"Gentlemen relax here in body and soul," Ward used to say, introducing me, dressed in my Sunday best, to the habitués of the Garrick or the Carlton. "Only here will you find such a wonderful, cordial atmosphere. It takes years of close association by people from the same circle to develop. They can differ in age, interests and even in professions, yet they've got one thing in common – they belong here."

Visits to those respectable clubs, evenings over bridge at Ward's apartment in Wimpole Mews, weekends at Spring Cottage in Cliveden half a mile from the mansion of Lord Astor, lunches in expensive restaurants, and dinners in the flats of high-ranking officials eventually helped me to identify my targets. It was impossible to maintain relations with everybody. I needed trusting, stable and promising contacts. By the summer of 1961, I had made my selection. There were six top-priority acquaintances, four of them linked by Stephen Ward.

At the top of my list were Secretary of State for War Jack Profumo, to whom I had been introduced in July, and his wife Valerie Hobson, with whom I maintained relations after we met in Cliveden. Next came the Astors, who promised to become good contacts. Third on my list were Princess Margaret and Antony Armstrong-Jones. I was introduced to them by Ward, who also equipped me with certain details about their life, because he loved gossip and had known the royal family for years. This connection held out the possibility of getting information through provocation and blackmail. The fourth was billionaire Paul Getty, a man whose business connections could lead me to arms producers and sellers, who interested me a great deal at that time. Fifth place was occupied by two men connected with the press, Sir Colin Coote and Paul Richey, both invaluable sources of information. And the last was Captain Souls, whom I recruited.

Details about each will follow. For the moment, however, I want to tell you only one thing: five of my six attempts succeeded. Only Paul Getty resisted me; all the rest yielded, with favourable results.

My name became known in London circles. To believe Ward, all of his friends regarded me as a pleasant and clever chap, a man who made a good impression on them. I did not behave in any special way, flattering nobody and always offering my frank opinion. I did not try to force it on others, although there were quite a few debates and arguments. This wide range of acquaintances added to my importance. Photographs in the press did their bit, too. Besides, the popularity of the Soviet Union was soaring. It became fashionable to invite Russians to functions, and I was always at hand, an easy-going man, ready to talk. I did not try overmuch to create a good impression or to attract attention to myself, but sometimes this happened without premeditation on my part.

Explosive as all Kutuzovs, I sometimes did foolish things. Once, at a party in Lord Astor's manor in Cliveden, a tipsy actor by the name of Paul Carpenter, a Canadian famous for his heroic roles in second features, started pestering me.

"Hey, Mister Molotov," he mumbled, right into my face. "Let's have a cocktail."

I tried to evade him, but the tipsy actor became more and more arrogant. In the end, he said rather loudly: "You Russians should not be believed at all. You always lie. Why do you say, for example, that Gagarin was the first man in space? Several fliers died before him, attempting to conquer outer space. Did Gagarin orbit the Earth at all? This needs checking."

I knew what he meant. The British yellow press was circulating rumours to this effect at the time, alleging that the first Russian cosmonaut was the invention of the Kremlin rulers, nothing but the old lying Red propaganda. I flared up. I grabbed the poor actor by the lapels, pushed him against a wall and, remembering my boxer's past – I was middleweight squadron champion during my service in the navy – made a fist, and punched the wall an inch above his head, so hard that plaster fell.

"When we are not sure in Russia, we hit the wall," I told him.

The frightened actor retired speedily from the room.

As the Russian saying goes, "There is no smoke without fire." Five years later, I attended the Academy of the General Staff together with cosmonaut number two German Titov, and he told me that pilot Valentin Bondarenko, who was to become the world's first man in space, had indeed perished in flames during a training session in the altitude chamber. Paul Carpenter had been right after all.

Later, Stephen gave me a talking to: "Eugene, you behave like a Russian bear in a British forest. Keep your wild temperament in check. Otherwise you'll frighten away all of Billy's friends."

I promised never to hit the palace walls again.

Portrait of Furtseva

The year I met Stephen Ward was exceptionally fruitful for
him as an artist. He had his first one-man exhibition in the
Leggatt Bros art gallery in Duke Street. I naturally visited
the exhibition. Other guests were Dr Ward's famous
patients. It was the best possible exposure for an artist. As
a result of this event, his simple drawings done many years
before in Paris, pleasant but mediocre sketches of Ceylon
and India, portraits done in the US and Britain, all were
lauded to the skies by the critics.

Ward was not a stupid man, though he was very vain.
The press's reception of his modest works pleased him
immensely. He was not bad for an amateur portrait artist,
but he was not in the first rank as an artist, despite his
acquaintances presenting him as such, perhaps because they
thought this praise might help their backs to be cured by
the healing hands of the osteopath.

Anyway, the fortunes of my friend visibly improved.
In one year, Ward was requested to paint the portraits of
the then Prime Minister Harold Macmillan, Sir Winston
Churchill, Foreign Secretary Selwyn Lloyd, Chancellor of
the Exchequer Derick Heathcoat Amory and Labour leader
Hugh Gaitskell. The apotheosis came when the magazine
London Illustrated asked him to do portraits of the royal
family. But this was not all. Sir Colin Coote did not forget
his friend and doctor, either, and sent him on a trip to

Israel, to attend the trial of the Nazi war criminal Adolf Eichmann, about whom the world press was writing every day at the time. Ward did a series of drawings at the trial, published by the *Daily Telegraph*. Back in London, the osteopath discovered that he was more famous as an artist than as a doctor.

At this time I got a chance both to help Ward in his striving for recognition and to satisfy his vanity as an aspiring artist. Soviet Minister of Culture Yekaterina Furtseva came to London on a short working visit. The morning of her arrival, I was woken up by a call from Stephen. "Eugene, you simply must help me," he panted. "You alone can do it. Nobody else can."

"I don't get you," I mumbled, still half asleep.

"Arrange my meeting with Madame Furtseva, please." Stephen was so excited that I forgot about sleep. "I must do her portrait. Just imagine, a Russian woman minister poses for me and gives me an interview. Editors will be after me. Well, what do you say?"

What could I tell him? That Comrade Furtseva would not even talk with me? Of course, I did not try to dissuade him, but neither did I promise him anything. I said only that I would think about it. I knew that Soviet leaders did not meet journalists other than at official press conferences. Besides, their personal lives were strictly off-limits. Even in post-*glasnost* Russia, thirty years later, this remains so, although press freedom increases daily. Besides, Yekaterina Furtseva was not just a Minister of Culture, but a member of the Presidium of the Central Committee of the Communist Party, an influential person in the communist hierarchy. She was orthodox. Our attempt was surely doomed to failure. That is why I did not promise Ward anything. He was offended by my apparent lack of interest in his request.

Nevertheless, I understood that success in this undertaking would increase my influence on Ward better than anything else. I owed him a lot, and one should repay one's debts. If I could organise a meeting with Comrade Furtseva for him, my contact with Stephen could develop into a close, even bosom friendship. It was vital for my work. Besides, I liked Stephen as a person and tried to help him whenever I could.

Without thinking twice I rushed to the embassy, to Mrs Furtseva's headquarters. She did not expect such arrogance, of course, and from a naval officer to boot! But I was pressed for time; I could not wait for an opportune moment. Without waiting for a reprimand, I launched an attack, engaging all of my oratory and what remained of my charm. I employed numerous arguments to persuade her to meet with Ward, to allow publication of an interview in the British press, and commission a portrait. I blocked her retreat. After a short resistance, she gave up. Tired by my persistent pleading, and perhaps a little curious about her portrait, Furtseva said: "All right, let him come. He can do my portrait. But he can have no more than half an hour."

The fortress had fallen, and I, inspired by my unexpected victory, phoned Ward immediately. "She agreed!"

Silence.

"Steve, are you there?"

"You are a true friend, Eugene. I never doubted you," he said, drunk with happiness.

At the pre-arranged hour I brought him to the embassy.

Comrade Furtseva had just returned from a party at Lancaster House. She greeted us and I introduced Steve. They shook hands and settled themselves in armchairs at the window, facing each other. Ward took out some paper and started drawing, occasionally asking Furtseva questions. I translated.

"Is this your first visit to London? How do you like it? Do you like pictures? You don't like modern painting? You look wonderful. How do you manage it? Do you play tennis? You don't use make-up? You don't wear jewellery?"

In half an hour the portrait was ready.

"Well, let me look at it," Furtseva said. "Not bad. What do you think, Yevgeny Mikhailovich, is there a likeness?"

"I think so," I lied, not wanting to offend the artist or his victim.

I actually thought that Ward had failed dismally in catching her likeness. Madame Furtseva looked younger and prettier in her portrait, more like a coquettish middle-aged woman than a minister. But I did not say this, of course. Madame Furtseva liked the portrait, presumably because she did not look like a minister in it.

We left our hostess in high spirits. "Please, don't forget to send me the publication in the diplomatic pouch, Yevgeny Mikhailovich," she said, bidding us goodbye. "Mr Ward, please come to the Soviet Union. I will be pleased to continue our acquaintance."

Hardly had we left the embassy building when Ward rushed to his car, saying he was in a hurry to file his copy. "I must write at least thirty lines for the portrait for tomorrow's issue," he told me, already sitting in his car.

In the next day's *Daily Telegraph* I saw the portrait of

Furtseva and a small item by Ward. I had not expected this. Sir Colin Coote had probably been forced to remove some other article to publish Ward's material. He could not turn down his protégé.

There was some time left before Comrade Furtseva's departure, and so I went to Heathrow to fulfil my promise and give her the newspaper, which she most probably did not expect so quickly. Seeing me with the *Daily Telegraph*, she said regally, "The embassy officials have been talking about this article and the portrait since early this morning. I had the article translated. Not bad. Short and to the point, without any foolishness. Give my regards to your friend."

The British invited Mrs Furtseva into the government plane. "I should introduce your artist to Nikita Sergeyevich. Let him do his portrait, too. What do you think?" she said by way of goodbye. She climbed into the plane.

I did not place much faith in her words at the time, regarding them as a joke. But later I realised I could use them all the same. At that time Premier Khrushchev was the world's most popular and least predictable politician. Western journalists virtually hunted him during his foreign trips, expecting him to give them another shock. The shoe-beating in the UN in the autumn of 1960 made headlines worldwide. And his famous "We shall bury you!" delivered from the balcony of the Soviet Mission at the corner of 68th Street was similarly famous. Today such escapades appear wild, but they were prompted not only by Khrushchev's ideological mind-set, his pre-programmed thinking, but by the world situation. This was a time when history seemed to be working for the Soviet Union. The colonial system was disintegrating.

The USSR had become the first space power. Statistics reported an annual production growth of between 10 and 15 per cent. It seemed that the Soviet Union, having shed the fetters of Stalin's personality cult, was on the verge of making a great leap forward. Khrushchev proclaimed that we would overtake the US in the production of meat, milk and butter by 1970, and build true communism ten years later. Just like many of my compatriots, I lived in a world of illusions and militant arrogance, based on self-deception and ignorance. The gung-ho spirit was at its highest then, but many regarded it as something real. Khrushchev stirred minds. Meeting him was the dream of every journalist.

I decided to play this card. I went to Stephen's Spring Cottage in Cliveden (Ward had invited me to drop in any time I wished) and told him: "Madame Furtseva is absolutely happy with your publication. I am to convey to you an invitation to visit Moscow and do a portrait of Khrushchev."

After a minute of dead silence, Stephen roared "Hooray!" His guests joined in. I opened a bottle of Stolichnaya and toasted his success. Ward's eyes sparkled green, like the eyes of a cat in darkness.

A Lecture from Sir Winston

It was Sunday and Steve and I were going to Cliveden after lunch. He called me an hour before our departure. "Eugene, I may be a little late. I have to go to a patient whom I can't refuse. He has been my patient for a long time. Do you understand?"

"Of course I do. Let's go together," I suggested.

The day before I had sent my car for a service and Steve knew about it. He had suggested that we go to Cliveden together in his Jaguar.

"Right," he said. "Pick you up in fifteen minutes."

Presently I was sitting in Ward's love, his Jaguar, which he treated like a woman. I had noticed that cars were another of his fads. The beautiful machine sped as if on wings along London's weekend-empty streets.

"Where are we going?" I asked Steve, taking out a pack of Winston from my pocket.

"To Winston," Steve grinned, flicking the pack.

It could be only one man. "You don't mean Sir Winston?!" I was petrified.

Steve nodded. "He's been my patient for five or six years now," he explained. "It's the old man's back. I visit him from time to time, as today."

"I'll wait in the car," I said, unwillingly, when we stopped at Sir Winston's home. I had to say this, if only not to appear imposing. But conflicting desires were ripping me apart. On the one hand, I wanted to see Sir Winston. On the other, I could not put Steve in an awkward position by asking him to take me along.

"What the hell!" said Ward carelessly and arrogantly, sensing my embarrassment. "Let's go. You can wait for me in there."

"Well, in that case we should take along a bottle of the universal medicine for your patient," I said, taking a bottle of Armenian brandy from my bag. "Somebody told me that Churchill is not averse to Russian brandy."

People in the Soviet Union and other countries differ in their attitude to Sir Winston, but no matter what they say about the legendary British premier, millions of Russians, including me, will always regard him as a great politician, our ally in the life-and-death war against Hitler. Sir Winston was, of course, an opponent of the system for which I worked throughout my life, but he was a worthy opponent. I still remember one of his phrases. He once said, about Russia, that it is "a riddle wrapped in a mystery inside an enigma". I found this brilliant.

When you had to deal with the unpredictable, contradictory and treacherous policy of Stalin, you were bound to regard Russia as "a mystery redoubled", but there is nothing mysterious about my country or its people. The riddle was invented by those who staged a revolt in Petrograd in 1917 in order to implement a bookish dream. That inhuman plan, which Stalin sealed with the blood of millions of my compatriots, could not but frighten reasonable politicians. Churchill was outraged by Stalin's atrocities and could not understand the tolerance and forgiveness of Russians. That was what he must have regarded as the mystery of the Russian character.

"Who is that with you, Steve?" We heard the voice of the master of the house. "Ask forgiveness of your companion, but I'm not dressed. Please come here. The small of my back is bothering me again. I need your help. I have an invitation for tomorrow which I cannot turn down. But I can hardly move."

Steve told me to remain in the living room while he went to treat Churchill. I gave him his portable orthopaedic table and he disappeared with it inside the house. I was left alone. A servant looked in, asked what I would like to have, and brought me a whisky and soda. I looked around at the rows upon rows of old books, massive paintings, antique furniture. There was an open box of Havanas in aluminium wraps, Armenian brandy in the bar. This confirmed my suspicions: the old man liked Armenian brandy. I unwrapped my bottle of brandy and put it on the shelf among the other bottles.

There were papers on the table at the window. I lighted a cigarette and approached the window. I was alone in the room. The papers were letters and documents, probably sent to Sir Winston for information, possibly to ask his advice. They included reports on fiscal, economic and political problems, and some personal correspondence.

I caught myself thinking simple but criminal thoughts: these papers could be of great interest to us, and nobody can stop me from stealing them. There are so many of them that the disappearance of two or three documents would surely go unnoticed. But then, why steal? It would be enough to photograph. Why hadn't it occurred to me before? I had visited many homes of high-ranking officials, and each of them had his mail and documents lying around, a treasure-trove for a spy! The only thing I lacked was a miniature camera and custom-made pockets in my jacket. I must rectify this mistake immediately, I decided, looking at the documents in front of me and trying to remember their most important paragraphs.

My eye was caught by a letter from a military leader who was writing about the new attitudes to NATO policy in Europe, namely, the concept of "forward-based defence", which I had not heard of then. Under this concept, West Germany was assigned the role of a buffer zone, a theatre of operations in the hypothetical war against the Soviet Union. It entailed arming the Bundeswehr with nuclear weapons, apparently as a deterrence factor against the potential aggressor, the USSR. The letter did not provide detailed information, yet it was clearly of great interest. I tried to remember it as best as I could, so as to be able to relay it to the Moscow Centre later.

"Well, where is your Russian?" a hoarse voice inside the house said. The door creaked.

I retreated to the bar. The famous man, his girth as substantial as his reputation, stood before me in all his splendour, eighty years of a rich life furrowing his brow.

"The patient is better," proclaimed Stephen proudly, "and I have allowed him to drink a brandy."

It was a signal for me to retrieve my bottle of Armenian brandy from the shelf and present it to Churchill. Sir Winston looked at the label, nodded appreciatively and asked me to pour a shot for us all. We drank to the health of the master of the house, who was smoking a Havana.

"Good brandy indeed. You Russians are masters of

surprises," the old man said. "But try to understand me and don't take offence – you are still barbarians for us. Not in the bad, but in the *true* sense of the word: like in ancient times, when Greeks and Romans regarded everybody else as barbarians. And we are their descendants. Anglo-Saxons are of the classical culture. We represent two great qualities, lucidity and a sense of proportion, better than anybody else in the world. These two qualities are dimmed in other nations, including Russia. Otherwise you would not have uprooted your traditions. That is why I cannot but regard you as barbarians. Russia has no other way than to follow the example of Europe," Sir Winston went on. "Any Briton will tell you that Leo Tolstoy is the greatest writer of the nineteenth century. We regard him, and hence also Russia, as a friend. The tragedy is that revolution tore Russia away from its historical way and turned it into our enemy. Russia is ill, and her disease is highly catching. I could not help you to combat it, but I am sure that others will be luckier. And don't take offence at my forthrightness, Captain. One shouldn't take offence at old men."

This was easier said than done. I was outraged. Ward, who knew my temperament and sensed that I was going to explode, hurried me away. He was right to do so, because I had been on the verge of proving to Sir Winston that Russians can indeed be regarded as barbarians.

I did not recover from the blow dealt at my people and me for a long time. Steve listened patiently to my furious tirades, waiting for me to calm down; he had to wait till Cliveden.

Today, when I recall Sir Winston's words, I can only say that the old man was right in calling us barbarians and in saying that the events of 1917 were a national tragedy. But at that time I did not, and could not, share his views. Relentless brainwashing had cleared my brain of any vestige of doubt. I believed in our communist rectitude. And the lecture of Sir Winston's only strengthened my conviction.

Throughout that evening I tried not to forget the contents of the letter about the new NATO strategy. I also understood that I had to prepare and equip myself for such trips, since they were becoming more and more frequent, thanks to Ward. I had to be able to photograph the documents I happened to see.

On the following Monday morning I handed the *rezident* a report on the materials I had seen in Sir Winston's home, ordered a miniature camera from the *rezidentura* technician, and asked my wife to add inside pockets to my jackets.

Second Russian at Cliveden

My weekend visits to Ward's Spring Cottage could not remain unnoticed by Lord Astor. I was sure that sooner or later we would meet, and patiently waited for that moment. I did not need to stalk the famous master of Cliveden; I knew that we were bound to meet anyway.

The eldest of the Astor sons, Lord Astor had inherited the beautiful manor and 400 acres of land on the bank of the Thames ten years previously. He lived there with his young wife, former French mannequin Bronwen Pugh.

Preparing for my eventual meeting with the Astors, I read several books on them borrowed from the local library. I learned that the Astors were aliens, if I might put it like that, because their forefather was a Spanish butcher who settled in Germany in the eighteenth century and sent his sons into the wide world to trade and earn money. They succeeded. One of these rich descendants of the Spanish butcher, William Waldorf, decided to settle in Britain at the end of the nineteenth century. He bought the Cliveden mansion from the Duke of Westminster and started a family. He was the father of the current owner.

Money earned by the Astors abroad attracted the attention of prominent people. Monarchs and premiers, ministers and ambassadors flocked to the Cliveden mansion. Eventually the Astors associated themselves with British politics, William's wife Nancy becoming the first woman to sit in the House of Commons, and Cliveden becoming a meeting place in the 1930s for those favouring appeasement of Nazi Germany. The rich family were thus rocketed to the heights of political power, but the Profumo affair was to send them plummeting into the abyss no less quickly.

General Pavlov, who read my detailed reports as the London *rezident* and my boss, used to say: "Zhenya, remember that what is said in Cliveden today will become official policy and practice of the Tories tomorrow. You must take root beside the Astors."

I understood this no worse than the general did, otherwise I would not have cultivated contacts at Cliveden for nearly two years. Indeed I would have worked there longer, had it not been for the scandal, and achieved even more spectacular results. Instead, the fateful quarrel between Christine Keeler and Lucky Gordon in the autumn of 1962 leaked to the press and eventually brought to light all the characters in the scandal. Lord Astor had to eject Steve Ward from his cottage in Cliveden, Profumo had to resign, and I had to flee to Moscow. But it was nearly eighteen months till that fatal day, and our spy network in London was hatching grandiose plans.

"Yevgeny Mikhailovich, you are the second Russian in Cliveden," the *rezident* told me. "Before you, only Ambassador Maysky managed to get there, but that was before the Second World War. This luck can happen only once in a blue moon. You must not miss this chance."

Only one man, head of Soviet military intelligence in London, General Anatoly Georgiyevich Pavlov, knew about my contacts in Cliveden. I had wonderful business and personal relations with the general. Nobody else knew, or had a right to know, about my work with Ward. It was the decision of Moscow Centre: all my reports on Ward or Astor went directly to the GRU *rezident*, bypassing the military mission.

I soon realised that Lord Astor and Stephen Ward were linked by a long-time friendship. I was able to reconstruct the history of their relationship – including intimate details – from Ward's stories. Steve had quite a few pretty girl-friends who visited him in his country cottage. I first met Christine Keeler and Mandy Rice-Davies there in June 1961. After that we saw each other quite often, not always in front of witnesses. I will expand on this in the chapters which follow. But there were also other girls, and it was clear that they came there by arrangement. They were "delivered" to the guests of the nearby mansion. Lord Astor and his high-society friends were not averse to enjoying young, pretty and easily available girls.

On Saturday evenings Steve often left Spring Cottage for an hour or more to visit Lord Astor. One of his young girlfriends usually accompanied him, although it is true that sometimes Steve went there as a doctor, because Lord Astor liked to "treat" his guests, especially ailing ones, to his "court osteopath" who lived nearby. After such visits Steve returned to the cottage and he would tell all those present – without any prompting whatsoever – about who was visiting the Astors, and why. Sometimes I managed to get him in a talkative mood and on those occasions Ward told me about the subject of their talk. This was invaluable information, because these were quite often secret visits, not only of a family nature, but business meetings, the political results of which transpired soon afterwards.

After one of these short visits to the mansion Steve relayed to me Bill's invitation to dine with them.

"Who else is invited?"

"Nobody, which is strange. You may regard this as a personal invitation. Billy has been wanting to meet you for a month now. I know it for sure. But he was waiting for a day when there would be no other guests, which doesn't happen often. I hope you won't turn old Bill down?"

How could I?

The Cliveden mansion makes an indelible impression on all those who see it. Before that dinner I had quite often walked in the park and enjoyed its majestic beauty. It reminded me of Peterhof, outside St Petersburg (then called Leningrad). But Peterhof is a museum, while the Cliveden mansion was a private home. My brainwashed mind could not grasp the immensity of that thought. For me Astor was an alien being, something which we did not have back home and which simply could not exist in a communist society, the only just and correct one.

We entered the house and found ourselves in a vast hall. Everything was on a grand scale in that mansion: high ceilings, giant windows, an immense table and fireplace, with huge bronze figurines of nude women standing nearby.

"Look how their bronze tits shine," Steve told me. "Old Billy must be polishing them every day, or else why do they shine so?"

We were touching the figurines' bosoms when we heard Lord Astor's voice behind us: "Got you, you old lechers! Don't worry, you are not the first or the last. Not a single man in this house can resist the temptation of fondling my bronze lasses."

Steve introduced us. Some time later, Lady Astor invited us to dinner. There were no servants; she herself served us. We soon started talking and seemed to like each other. After cigars and brandy came politics. Lord Astor was a strange man. Even the few things that he said were important and interesting. On that day he was preoccupied with the possibility of Britain's joining the Common Market, in particular the economic consequences of this step, such as the immigration of cheap labour, since at that time labour on the continent was cheaper than in Britain. In his opinion Britain's joining the European Economic Community was a two-edged weapon. On the one hand, the EEC could help the Tories to control the trade unions, which had become excessively independent. On the other, it could send unemployment soaring. The former was good, while the latter was not acceptable.

Suddenly Lord Astor asked me: "Well, and what does the Kremlin think about it?"

I said that Moscow regarded the problem from a political rather than an economic perspective, believing that the creation of the Common Market would split Europe into East and West and provoke confrontation with the socialist countries. I knew that my orthodox statement held nothing new for Lord Astor, so I added that I had a personal opinion on the integration processes in Europe.

"Well, and what is it, if I may ask?"

"Indeed, Eugene, what do you think?" Ward echoed.

We settled at a small table by the window, where Lady Astor brought coffee. I went on: "As a military man I regard the Common Market as a strategic, rather than as a fiscal problem. It is designed to create a third political force capable of becoming an equal of the US and the Soviet Union. I know that it is not in my interests to help you, but if Britain does not join the Common Market, it will become merely an isolated island deprived of any political influence on world developments."

Lord Astor liked my statement. I had managed to show him that I could think independently of my government, although I was its military diplomat. In this way I established relations, and friendly ones at that, with Lord Astor. I was asked to visit him without invitation. Understandably, I accepted gratefully.

Failsafe Bridge with Lord Astor

"Yevgeny Mikhailovich, why do you take bridge lessons? I can understand learning the language or driving, but bridge? And on government money at that?" I shall never forget that direct question from a young diplomat at the Soviet Embassy in Norway, to whom I was assigned as an official tutor. The young man was clearly put out by my conscientious study of bridge. The inquisitive young man learned from the embassy's accountant the cost of those lessons, and when he heard the sum he was profoundly shocked. The young Pinkerton regarded bridge-learning as an anti-governmental fad, and set out to unmask me.

By that time the great Stalin was dead, but the ways of his loyal assistant Lavrenty Beria, executed soon after his master's death, were still alive in some young lads, who suspected enemy intrigues and the treacherous designs of world imperialism everywhere. I had to stand that test of the super-vigilance of my colleagues. It was very difficult to explain to the young official with KGB leanings that I, Lieutenant Captain of the Navy on the Soviet military mission in Oslo, was learning to play bridge not because I wanted to indulge myself with bourgeois pastimes in Oslo's seedy spots, but because I needed the skill for my job. While playing cards you can talk, establish the necessary contacts, and hence get the required information.

The boy was surprised by my revelations, but soon came

to believe in the importance of an older comrade's task, and highly respected my work there. That vigilant youngster, Volodya Grushko, whom I patronised in Oslo in the mid-1950s, became First Deputy Chairman of the KGB thirty years later and questioned KGB Colonel Oleg Gordiyevsky, who was suspected of treason yet continued actively to work for British intelligence. Grushko even planned to torture Gordiyevsky in the Lubyanka cellars, but the double agent escaped, with the assistance of the British, across the Finnish border. Eventually, Grushko's Bolshevik zeal cost him dearly. He and his chief, Vladimir Kryuchkov, were arrested and tried for participating in the failed coup d'état of August 1991.

But back to my efforts to improve my bridge skills: bridge helped me quite a few times in Norway, and proved to be useful in Britain, too. I could have missed many important meetings, and my superiors would not have obtained a number of interesting bits of information had it not been for my passion for that popular card game.

Ward thought that I played quite well, but not well enough to become famous. This made me a reliable partner. Stephen was the first to appraise my mediocre skills, and he never missed an opportunity to invite me to a game of bridge with his guests, either in his Wimpole Mews flat in London or in Spring Cottage in Cliveden, where I often spent my weekends.

The second man to want to test my talent for bridge was Lord Astor. He was an experienced card player, and after he had satisfied himself concerning my abilities, my further participation in evenings over cards in Cliveden was assured. The calibre of my partners can be easily imagined:

insignificant people were not invited to Cliveden.

With each new visit to the Astors I felt more comfortable in my new surroundings. Famous names ceased to bother me. I felt more at ease in the palace, getting to know it, learning the layout and the purpose of its numerous rooms. Naturally, I was most interested in Lord Astor's study, his library, correspondence, documents and materials with which he worked at home. It took me some time to get my bearings there, to learn the rules, understand Lord Astor's behaviour with his guests, the Astors' routine, and the rituals of having meals, talking and playing bridge. I reported the essence of these talks with Members of Parliament, ministers and foreign guests in the Astor mansion, but Moscow Centre was most interested in Lord Astor's mail, which I perused and photographed, employing maximum caution. My miniature Minox camera was always with me: a small flat trinket hanging around my neck. It was easy to take it from under my tie at the opportune moment; one click and you had a picture.

The microfilm was removed by the embassy technician, who also fed fresh film into the camera. The microfilm was then immediately sent to Moscow by diplomatic pouch. In some cases, when the material I wanted to photograph was too bulky and there was not enough time, I put it in my inside pocket. In other words, I stole it, not an innovatory spying technique, but there were so many documents on Lord Astor's table that the disappearance of one of them could easily go unnoticed.

What kind of material was it? I had little time to study it, a few seconds at most. I would try to determine the nature of the material I saw and then decide if it was worth photographing. I could work only while the master of the house was on the telephone, seeing off a guest or going to the kitchen for another bottle of sherry – he always served his guests personally, without servants. I managed. An hour later the material in question would be in the embassy and it would be sent over to Moscow the day after.

I still remember the contents of some of those documents. There was, for instance, a letter from Lord Astor's American acquaintances, who had connections in governmental quarters and Congress, which mentioned the delivery of US Skybolt missiles to Britain. In the autumn of 1961, over a year before Washington officially dropped the project, Lord Astor's friends wrote to him about the probable demise of the Skybolt programme.

Since Skybolt was a US, air-launched missile usable in British V-class strategic bombers, supposed to prolong their life as an effective weapon for a nuclear attack, it is small wonder that Prime Minister Harold Macmillan pinned special hopes on the programme to replace the fixed-site rocket, Blue Streak. Thanks to Lord Astor's well-informed sources and my bridge games in his Cliveden mansion, Moscow learned about Washington's intention to back out in good time. The military and politicians know the price of such information. It was a major turn in Anglo-American military plans. It gave the green light to the programme of equipping British submarines with US Polaris missiles, with nuclear warheads produced in Britain.

This zig-zag in the policy of the White House actually deprived the British government of independence in the creation of its own deterrence forces. The change of plans played into Moscow's hands, although it was conceived in Washington: it undermined the unity of the NATO nuclear powers – the US, Britain and France. Britain did not have a constructive policy to offer, was unable to stand up for itself and relied on the possibility of establishing special relations with the US, while France was shocked by the American unilateral action and did not believe in the reliability of Britain as a partner.

GRU archives now contain quite a few materials which I acquired in Cliveden during my bridge games with Lord Astor. I thought of these as "failsafe" games, since no matter who won at the card table – I lost more often than not – I always gained invaluable material there, much more important for a spy than bridge winnings.

With time, Moscow Centre's tasks became more complicated and varied. Sometimes I could not understand their purpose. For example, the GRU *resident* persistently demanded from me a detailed plan of the Astors' mansion and a description of its interiors and furniture. "Where is Lord Astor's study? Where do you play bridge? Where does he talk with his guests? Where are the telephones?" General Pavlov asked me again and again. I drew plans, explained where rooms were situated, and where guests usually met. Years later, back in Moscow, I learned from my colleagues that Moscow Centre was pondering the possibility of bugging Lord Astor's home – with my assistance, of course. The conditions for this were just right. The only thing I lacked was time, because the scandal caused by the Profumo affair closed the doors of the Astors' home to Ward and me.

Moscow Centre also paid special attention to my numerous reports about the sexual preferences of the hosts and guests of the Cliveden mansion. It is an open secret that the GRU and the KGB actively used all available means (even blackmail and bribes) to obtain the materials they needed. In certain conditions, information about the scandalous habits of MPs and high-ranking officials (such as homosexuality – then illegal in the UK – drug abuse or greed) could be used to discredit the highest echelons of power in Britain. This could easily be done by leaking the information to the press, which ensured a scandal. Knowing the acquaintances of Stephen Ward and Lord Astor helped me to obtain detailed information of this kind, and in abundance. I can only guess how Moscow Centre used it, but one thing was clear: had it not been for the Profumo scandal, my bridge games in the Cliveden mansion would have ensured Moscow an even greater prize.

Bastion Under the Embassy Roof

Rezident and *rezidentura* are words often mentioned in this book, but most readers will not know what they mean. A brief digression is therefore necessary here to explain my position in the Soviet Embassy in London, my relations with the heads of its services, and the nature of my work.

The Soviet Embassy in Britain, as in any other country which has diplomatic relations with the Kremlin, incorporated three independent structures: the embassy as such, headed by the ambassador and supervised by the USSR Foreign Minister; the KGB *rezidentura*, headed by a KGB *rezident* and supervised by the KGB chairman; and the GRU *rezidentura*, headed by a GRU *rezident* accountable to the GRU chief.

The *rezidenturas* operated independently of each other and were not subordinate to the embassy, although they worked under its roof. However, not all workers of these *rezidenturas* were on the embassy staff; many of them held executive posts in the USSR trade mission in London, newspaper and news agencies' bureaux, Aeroflot, Intourist and other missions. But no matter where they worked officially, they were accountable to the *rezident*, who, in his turn, received orders from Moscow Centre.

To imagine the power wielded by the two *rezidenturas*, one has to know the following facts: in my time they had more personnel than all other Soviet establishments and organisations put together. The KGB *rezidentura* had two and a half times the number of staffers of its GRU counterpart. Their vast budgets were simply in a different league from those of the embassy or the trade mission, and could be increased, if needed, at any time by more allocations from the state budget. The *resident* had only to request money for bribing an official or buying secret information, and he automatically received the required sum.

In some cases the functions of the two *rezidenturas* overlapped. For example, both collected military-political information and recruited agents, although the GRU *rezidentura* did more in the military field, naturally, in view of its interests. But there were major differences, too. Thus, up to a half of KGB agents engaged in counter-intelligence and acted as bodyguards as well as political police. This work involved controlling their compatriots working abroad, especially those with access to secrets who communicated with foreigners. The scope of this work was truly formidable. Each Soviet person, even those working for the *rezidentura*, felt the heavy weight of this "attention". Although Stalin's dictatorship was a thing of the past, its residues were still present in the early 1960s, during the so-called Khrushchev thaw. Pathological suspiciousness, blind communist orthodoxy and aggressive intolerance of dissent formed the creed of the KGB *rezidentura*. Military intelligence, on the other hand, had always taken pride in the fact that it did not engage in political police work. That was probably why it had always been valued more highly than the KGB by professionals.

The GRU *rezidentura* in London included professionals in different spheres, above all specialists of the three services. They worked in the military mission, with the leading expert on ground forces being General Yefimov, the Soviet military attaché. Aviation was the responsibility of the Soviet air force attaché Colonel Rumyantsev and his assistant Major Belousov. The navy was monitored by naval attaché Captain 1st Rank Sukhoruchkin and his assistant, that is, myself, Captain 3rd Rank upon arrival and Captain 2nd Rank upon departure from London.

I found it easiest to work with air force men. Fyodor Seliverstovich Rumyantsev, the air force attaché, was an old and good friend, a fighting pilot decorated as a hero of the Soviet Union and Yugoslavia. He received his hero stars for rescuing Marshal Tito from encirclement by flying his plane under heavy Nazi barrage. His assistant, Tolya Belousov, and I were bosom friends. Near my home in Regent Street lived a cat whom I called Murka, Russian-style. Every morning when I left for work the cat was out on its morning walk. One black morning I learned from its master that Murka had died under the wheels of a passing car. Tolya and I had a wake in memory of that cat. We went to a pub and drank beer, pint after pint, till our table was full of empty glasses. Tolya loved that pub because it was owned by a former RAF pilot.

The pub's customers asked the barman: "Who are those guys? Do they want to make it into the *Guinness Book of Records*? To break the beer-drinking record?"

"They are Russians, commemorating a neighbour's cat. It was killed by a car today," replied the barman.

The customers looked at us sympathetically and clinked glasses to our Murka, too. The barman respected us even more after that. He also loved cats.

But to return to the matter at hand: apart from Anatoly Belousov and Fyodor Rumyantsev, I was friendly with our *rezident* Anatoly Pavlov and two journalists – Vladimir Osipov of *Izvestia* and Yevgeny Gurnov of *Komsomolskaya Pravda*. And, of course, Anatoly Gromyko, the son of our legendary Foreign Minister. Anatoly often acted as the boss at 13 Kensington Palace Gardens in the ambassador's absence. My life would have been gloomy so far away from home without them and their friendly support.

But to get back to the GRU: it included a group of top specialists in telecommunications, photography, codes and ciphers, radio interception and electronic reconnaissance. Posted in various Soviet establishments were field workers of the *rezidentura* – its heart and mind. They recruited agents and maintained contact with them, ferreted out secret information and collected non-secret data, and engaged in visual reconnaissance and secret operations throughout Britain. I was one of them. Field workers seldom knew each other, although they worked for the same organisation. But this is the law of undercover work, and none of us could ask each other questions pertaining to our profession. It was absolutely forbidden. As a result, the only person who knew everything about the operation of the *rezidentura* was the *rezident* himself.

I had met our *rezident*, General Anatoly Pavlov, at the Academy of the Soviet Army in the early 1950s; he was one year my senior. Officially, Pavlov was scientific counsellor to the Soviet Embassy in London. He was a fine man. Regrettably, his wife did not often visit him, preferring to live in Moscow and coming to him during her vacation every year, for two or three months at the most. She was engrossed in her work and had little liking for the comforts of life in London, unlike most of the other wives. Pavlov's wife was a doctor of chemistry and the only daughter of the famous military leader Mikhail Frunze, hero of the Civil War. After her father died while still a young man (it is rumoured that he was murdered), she was brought up by Defence Commissar Kliment Yefremovich Voroshilov, a close friend and associate of Stalin. Such family ties and connections were bound to help the Pavlovs in their careers. Anatoly came to London as Lieutenant General and left it as Colonel General. Upon his return to Moscow he was appointed deputy chief of the GRU. His wife became a leading specialist in experimental chemistry and the chief of a major secret research centre.

The GRU's special concern was undercover agents, my colleagues who were infiltrated into Britain under assumed names. They were without official protection, unlike the rest of us; if a *rezidentura* agent is uncovered, he can be expelled from the country at the most. But if an undercover agent is exposed, his or her fate is settled by enemy counter-intelligence, and they are usually sentenced to long prison terms and can wait only for a chance to be exchanged for an enemy spy, at best. This is why work with undercover agents was a secret even from *rezidentura* officers. Only the *rezident* knew about them, while all the main links of control over undercover agents were held by a small group in Moscow Centre.

GRU tasks were usually sent to the *rezident*, who, knowing what each field worker was engaged in, apportioned tasks accordingly. I usually got my tasks from General Pavlov. He used to summon me to his office, explain to me the task demanded of us by Moscow Centre, and say: "Now that you have all the necessary information, you are free to act as you see fit." Sometimes these tasks were relayed to me by my immediate superior, Captain 1st Rank Sukhoruchkin, who got them from the *rezident*. Correspondingly, I sent my written reports to the *rezident* or to the naval attaché, who forwarded them to Moscow Centre in a coded message or by diplomatic pouch, depending on their urgency. Only non-secret information was sent in the ordinary way.

I had only to ask to receive all the technical and material assistance I needed. Allocations on business lunches, trips, clothes and the like, let alone payments to agents, were managed by the accounting office, which in these cases acted without the usual red tape. If the fulfilment of a task by agents of the *rezidentura* was too risky or difficult, we were often helped by our colleagues from the Czechoslovak, Bulgarian or Romanian embassies. Incidentally, there was no thirty-five-mile travel limit for them. That is why if I needed to visit Holy Loch again, I would ask the Bulgarian military attaché in London, Nikolai Ivanovich Krivlev, to go there for a day or two. And he would comply, because my request was tantamount to an order from his superiors for him. He would go to the base, put up a tent there and play badminton with his children, simultaneously collecting the information I had requested. Upon his return he sent me a detailed report, which I forwarded to Moscow Centre.

The *rezidentura* employed specially trained people sealed by an iron military discipline and cemented by a common ideology of struggle for communist ideals. It was a formidable force.

Compromising the Royals

This "formidable force", the GRU, never tired of telling me that any spy operating in a foreign country should be familiar with local realities. Britain has more than enough institutions of power, each with a place and role of its own. Specialists in my field are bound to set their sights on the government, Parliament, the army and the press. I had to know about all major changes in these institutions of power, to understand their machinery down to the tiniest of their cogs.

The only institution of power which I was allowed to overlook was the royal family. Why? Because the monarch reigns but does not rule, as they say. Any school student knows that the rights of the British Queen are formal rather than practical. She can convene or adjourn Parliament, appoint the Prime Minister or accept a resignation, approve a law adopted by Parliament, or make somebody a peer or a knight – but then only upon advice from her premier or Parliament. The real power of Elizabeth II, both back in the 1960s when I was in Britain and at present, is practically non-existent. But her influence on life in Britain, on the decisions of other institutions of power, can hardly be overestimated.

Captain 1st Rank Golitsin, who gave me many a lecture before my departure to Britain and who had worked in the UK as a GRU man for many years, used to tell me:

"Zhenya, remember that monarchy is not just ceremonies and processions in a gilded carriage escorted by dragoons. No matter where the Queen is – in Buckingham Palace, Windsor or Balmoral – the red box with all the vital state documents and government information is delivered to her regularly and on time. The Queen is the second best informed person in Britain, after the Prime Minister."

Everything seemed clear to me. The obvious conclusion was that a military spy should welcome information from any source, including the reigning house, although the difficulties of infiltrating it appeared to be insurmountable. But we seamen are an obstinate breed: the more difficult a task, the more stubbornly we attack it. In Norway, about which I will write more later, I became an accepted figure at the court of King Haakon VII, the first Norwegian monarch after the dissolution of the Swedish–Norwegian union in 1905. In Britain I attained an even greater success: I laid my hands on information about the royal family. It is kept in the GRU archives, ready to be used at any moment. Perhaps by revealing this information, I shall protect the United Kingdom against possible provocation in the future, which could conceivably be orchestrated so as to do the greatest possible harm. By revealing its existence now, I might deprive the KGB and the GRU of the chance of using it.

In my three years in Britain I became convinced that respect for monarchy is one of the pillars of the country's way of life. Nothing that has happened in that country or beyond its borders has so far rocked this pillar of British society, which, although varied and heterogeneous, is united in its respect for and loyalty to the British throne.

I think, therefore, that attempts to spy on this august institution reflect badly only on myself and my superiors, but not on the royal family itself.

Everything began with Ward's commission to do portraits of the royal family, which he received soon after our meeting in the Garrick, from Sir Bruce Ingram, editor of the *London Illustrated News*. Sir Bruce knew the royal family and often went to Buckingham Palace. By that time Ward's artistic talents had become widely known in London's high society, yet the commission surprised many people, including Stephen himself. But it was a pleasant surprise and Ward liked to discuss it with his friends. "You know, Eugene, this commission was not quite unexpected," he once told me. "Prince Philip and I are friends of long standing. We have known each other for fifteen years, since I returned from India and started practising in London."

By talking for the first time about his acquaintance with the Queen's consort, Ward gave me a chance to return to it again and again, under different pretexts but with the same aim of ferreting out whatever Ward knew about the royal family. It turned out that he knew quite a lot.

In 1961 Stephen did his series of portraits of the royal family, in particular Prince Philip, Princess Margaret and Anthony Armstrong-Jones. I met them later, not at official ceremonies and parties, like the annual tea party in Buckingham Palace, but more personally. I had material on each of them, as well as on the Queen herself.

My face-to-face meeting with Prince Philip was organised during the visit of Mikhail Mikhailovich Somov to Britain. Prince Philip was chairman of the Royal Geographical

Society, which made Mikhail Somov an honorary member and awarded him a prize for his outstanding contribution to the exploration of the Arctic and the Antarctic. In the 1950s Somov had headed the first Soviet North Pole drifting stations, and founded the first Soviet Polar station. The Royal Geographical Society was bound to appreciate his research on the ice crust of the Polar seas and on ice forecasting, which is vital for navigation along the northern sea route linking the industrial centre of the European part of Russia with Siberian mining centres. Somov was thus an outstanding practical worker worthy of international recognition. Since then his name has been engraved on a bronze plaque in the hall of the Royal Geographical Society, alongside other honorary members of the society.

I arranged to become Somov's aide and interpreter during his visit to Britain, since I knew that in this capacity I was bound to meet Prince Philip. The board of the Royal Geographical Society gave a dinner in honour of Mikhail Somov, with Prince Philip as chairman. Somov sat on the Prince's left and I on his right. Somov was a simple person who had spent his life in Polar expeditions, and such ceremonial functions were torture to him, as he himself once admitted to me. But he kept up a brave appearance, despite the evening dress, toasts and speeches and other formalities. His lengthy silences at the table gave me a chance to fill these pauses with questions and short sentences, addressed mostly to His Royal Highness. As a result, the subject of physical geography soon gave way to political geography. I tried to involve Prince Philip in an exchange of opinions on international affairs, but he cautiously evaded my bait. He was not moved either by the

German question, or the nuclear arms race, or the prospects for the Common Market, or any other subject I introduced.

We were served coffee in a small room adjacent to the banquet hall. Somov remained reticent, while I did my best to seal our acquaintance by inducing His Royal Highness to talk about such everlasting human values as peace, concord, understanding and co-operation. Prince Philip listened politely, sometimes saying: "You think so?" but then he turned his attention to his guest: "How did you like London, Mr Somov?" I realised that I would never squeeze the tiniest scrap of valuable information from Prince Philip, but at least I had tried. If the head-on attack had failed, I might try more subtle means.

In a few days I relayed my impressions to Stephen Ward. "Just imagine," I complained, "His Royal Highness proved inaccessible, although I sat next to him. It was a conversation of two deaf-mutes."

"The Duke of Edinburgh and Philip Mountbatten are two different people," Stephen replied. "I remember him before he married Her Majesty the Queen. I know him as he is now. I can compare these two people. You talked with a statesman who tried to appear wise and cautious. The thing is, for many years he lived by different rules, easily and without concern. Now he is no longer Prince Hal, the carefree youth. That is why the Duke of Edinburgh tries to dominate Philip Mountbatten. He probably managed it at the dinner in the Royal Geographical Society."

"Power changes people in any country." I agreed with Steve. "But what exactly do you mean?"

"Remember that photo album?"

"Of course, but what does it have to do with Prince Philip?"

"Look at the photographs again and you'll understand," replied Steve significantly. "You'll see there Prince Philip and his cousin David and the rest of our merry bachelors' company."

I recalled the album and the candid photographs, which I had not thought important when I saw them. Steve showed me the album, identifying the people in the photos. "This is Antony Beauchamp, the husband of Sarah, the daughter of Sir Winston Churchill. This is Arthur Christiansen, editor of the *Daily Express*. Prince Philip and his cousin David. This is Nichole. And this is Maggie, I think.

"Nice girls they were." Steve sighed and went to the kitchen to make coffee, leaving the album behind. I did not dare steal the photographs. But I had my Minox camera with me, and so I photographed five or six of the snapshots. When Steve returned with coffee I started talking about the pastimes of Moscow big shots. In return, Ward told me how Prince Philip, his cousin the Marquess of Milford Haven and he had enjoyed themselves in Soho pubs, about parties at their friends' homes and visits to clubs for the select few.

Later in the day I sent the photographs and my report to Moscow Centre.

I met Lord Snowdon and Princess Margaret during the ceremony of their wedding in St Paul's. We also spent quite a few amusing hours at Ascot and at the Henley Regatta together; each time I added new information to my initial data. The *rezident* demanded that I should establish closer contacts with Lord Snowdon and Princess Margaret, and I complied. I once went in for rowing myself, and it turned out that Lord Snowdon did, too. He used to be a coxswain,

probably because he was a smallish man. One of th[e] Soviet eight-oars usually attended the Henley Regatt[a] this gave me a chance to develop my friendship[ ] Princess Margaret and Lord Snowdon, who never mi[ ] regatta. Afterwards they usually invited me to their[ ] Once, I told Stephen about my conversation with Pr[ ] Margaret and Lord Snowdon during such a voyage[ ] the Thames. In return I heard new information abou[t] royal family. The court artist and osteopath was a fu[ ] information.

In this way I collected material on the royal fa[ ] Relaying this information to the *rezident*, I asked hi[ ] Moscow Centre was annoyed with me for suppl[ ] information so far removed from military intelligence.[ ]

"We are doing the right thing, collecting this in[for]mation," General Pavlov reassured me. "Eventually it [will] be used by the GRU or the KGB. It is invaluable. And [my] superiors in the General Staff, as you know, are not ave[rse] to trading information with the Lubyanka."

As I learned back in Moscow, the GRU chiefs – Gene[ral] Serov and many of his deputies, let alone rank-and-f[ile] agents – could not do anything for the KGB at that tim[e] The treachery of Colonel Oleg Penkovsky, who had acces[s] to the highest levels of the organisation, undermined trus[t] in the GRU and even caused a temporary paralysis. Many[ ] links were disrupted. But the main thing was that the highest[ ] Party leadership no longer had confidence in the GRU. It took military intelligence years to restore its prestige.

While I was collecting this information in London, however, British intelligence delivered the GRU a deadly blow through Penkovsky, thwarting many promising plans.

The Charms of Christine Keeler

Christine Keeler, a semi-literate, naïve provincial girl with loose morals, first appeared in Stephen Ward's company in the spring of 1961. I met her in April or May in Steve's flat, where she lived for some time. At first I thought that she was his lover. She was not very refined, I thought, but she was devilishly attractive; I concluded that this was enough reason for Stephen to let her live in his flat. After his divorce Stephen lived alone, although he was by no means a monk, so the appearance of Christine Keeler did not surprise me at all.

But then another girl settled in Wimpole Mews: Mandy Rice-Davies, also very attractive and also with loose morals. As it turned out, both girls had started working relatively recently, dancing semi-nude in the variety show in a shady London nightspot. This made me think twice about Dr Ward's tastes and intentions. Was it a *ménage à trois*, or simply the charity of a gentleman who had decided to set two young lost sheep on the right track? I pondered on the problem for a long time, and would not have resolved it had it not been for Stephen himself. "If you think that I sleep with them, you are gravely mistaken," he once told me after the girls had bade us good-night and retired to their bedroom. Steve and I were playing cards, drinking whisky and talking about the meaning of life. There is nothing better than philosophy when you are tipsy and everything seems right with the world. Steve was in just such a mood and he tried to explain to me why he hated family life and the duties of a husband, why he would never marry again and why he had let two loose girls live in his flat.

"You see, I want them to get what they want from life: money, love, and happiness. I can help them get it. I shall introduce them to influential people. I can help them believe in themselves. Then it will be their party. You won't believe it, but I feel attached to them, especially to Christine."

I did not understand Ward completely at that time, but I believed him. I valued his sincerity in his relations with me. At that time I could only guess that he was very vulnerable and unstable himself.

There was some magic in Christine, and this immediately caught my eye. Steve might well have thought her just another girl from the provinces, simple and naïve, but he certainly felt at home with her. What Steve did not notice was that Christine was a dangerous creature, sly and treacherous. Her eyes told me that: they shone with passion, sensuality and cunning. Like a small furry animal, she was graceful and enchanting, but she was also a predator. These traits were soon fully revealed.

I have many reasons to hate that spoiled but enchanting temptress. Had it not been for her marijuana-influenced love games with Lucky Gordon, my posting in London would have yielded much better results. As I later learned back in Moscow, Moscow Centre had been prepared to sanction the blackmail of Jack Profumo with the aim of getting confidential information from him. If he had refused to comply, information about his liaison with Christine

Keeler, complete with all the piquant details, would have been leaked to the press. This blackmail failed thanks to Christine, because her lover's shoot-out in Ward's flat exploded the GRU operation. There were reasons to believe that it would have been immensely successful. Profumo could hardly have agreed to a public scandal and humiliation. He would surely have agreed to co-operate, not with the Soviet secret service, but with somebody who would have appeared to be a nice, respectable businessman or a smart dealer, but would actually have been a Soviet undercover agent in Britain. The minister would have been kept in the dark about *that* unpleasant detail. Such a "businessman" could have used blackmail to get invaluable information from Profumo. But Lady Luck turned her back on us.

There is yet another reason for me to hate Christine. One question which I could not answer for a long time concerned the delivery of US nuclear warheads for Pershing missiles deployed in West Germany. Moscow Centre bombarded me with demands for this information. Piqued by my lack of results, I asked Ward to help me get it. "You will agree, Steve, that the Germans must not be allowed to gain access to nuclear weapons." I tried to convince him. "Haven't the bitter lessons of the past two wars taught us anything?"

Ward was easy to convince as regards Germans. "Eugene, I promised to help you and I shall do it," he replied. "You can rest assured. I shall get this information for you."

He kept his promise, and as a result, information on the number of warheads and the schedule of their delivery to West Germany went to Moscow Centre. I shall expand upon this in a later chapter.

But Christine Keeler later spread the rumour that Ward had asked her, on my behalf, to extract this information from Profumo. Steve would never have done such a stupid thing, which was bound to place him under suspicion. Why should Christine present Ward as a simpleton? No, the truth must be told, all the more because Christine has sinned enough – including with me, although I was not unwilling, of course – without also having to shoulder the responsibility for this outrageous lie.

It all began on 9 July, if I'm not mistaken. It was a Sunday, and I decided to visit Steve at Spring Cottage. I did not know then what had happened the day before, but Steve told me immediately upon my arrival. On the Saturday evening Christine decided to swim, in her birthday suit, in the pool situated next to Lord Astor's home. The Astors' guests saw her climbing out of the pool, a Venus emerging from the sea. Jack Profumo was among them. Throughout the next day, he could not take his eyes from Christine, despite the sobering presence of his wife, Valerie Hobson. He swam in the pool with her, apparently beside himself, stroking her hands from time to time. In a word, he was flirting outrageously with the young girl. He even placed her on his shoulders in the pool, and they fought like this against another couple.

On that day, however, I was more interested in another guest of the Astors, the Pakistani President Ayub Khan, who came to Cliveden in the company of his assistants. He stopped there for a short rest on his way to Washington, where he intended to discuss with the US President the Berlin developments, which did not promise a tranquil life for diplomats either in the West or in the East. Four months later, the Berlin crisis set the Soviet and the US armies against each other, but at that time politicians were still trying to avert the dangerous turn of events in Berlin.

German affairs were therefore on my priority list, so I spent that Sunday trying to lure information out of the high-ranking guest of the Astors. I wanted to know what he thought about the West's position on the German question, but I was unsuccessful.

When I was leaving, Steve asked me to take Christine along with me. "Please, take her away," he whispered into my ear, "or else Jack will lose his head completely over her. God forbid that Valerie should suspect anything. Then I couldn't hide anywhere from her, because it was I who had the bad luck to bring Christine to Cliveden."

I had nothing against taking such a pretty passenger. Steve's request suited me well. So Christine and I set off for London. She was clearly pleased with her success with Lord Astor and Jack Profumo. Christine's instincts as a woman told her that both gentlemen were now in her power. But I noticed with surprise that she was also trying to use her charms on me. This fitted my plans perfectly. We talked about meaningless things, enjoying the beauty and the coolness of the summer evening.

Her hand touched mine. Next she stroked my hand and my arm, eventually getting to my shoulder and neck. I pretended not to take any notice, but it was getting more and more difficult. We kept silent for the last part of the journey, each thinking about what to do next. When I stopped the car in Wimpole Mews, Christine said: "We could have tea, if you like?"

I suggested having something stronger, but to my shame

it turned out that there was nothing in the car. We had drunk everything in Cliveden. I had to go to the nearest pub for a bottle.

What happened next became the subject of speculation for many years afterwards, as if it mattered as far as the Profumo affair was concerned if I had slept with Christine or not. I am prepared to admit now that I did. I allowed Christine to seduce me. That devil of a girl could seduce anybody! Besides, she seemed to like me. I knew that the fair sex in general liked me, and could expect to win Christine's affection, too. Besides, I could use her in my work.

We had hardly had a drop before a veritable battle ensued. It was a good thing that the furniture in Ward's flat was solid, otherwise the material damage resulting from our love play could have been considerable. We devoured each other like two animals. In what seemed like seconds, Christine stepped out of her dress. She looked very sexy that night, with something of both satin and velvet in her. She had both the firm lithe line of a slender woman, and a provocative ripeness. Her eyes were dark and moist, her mouth glowed, her flawless skin reflected the light.

When I took her to bed I was fascinated by that whiteness of her skin, the beauty of her breasts, her slender waist. She was irresistible.

Christine's caresses had a strange quality, at times soft and melting, at other times fierce. There was something animal-like about her hands which she spread over each part of my body. She behaved like a cat, inspiring a desire, but beholden to no one.

As she moved in our hot rhythm of passion, she gave me

the feeling that the whole world was shut out and only this sensual feast existed. For a moment, just for a moment, I felt that there would be no tomorrows, no spying – that there was only this room, this night, this bed and this woman, the mistress that matched me perfectly, the lover who was equal to my strength and vigour. She responded to my every move. Her hair was wild, her eyes drugged. She made me feel I ruled her as a king, making her pleasure subordinate to mine. Her body, panting and malleable, became even softer under my fingers. I searched every nook of her, leaving nothing untouched.

We were two hungry beasts that night. Christine followed my passionate rhythm, moving up and down with sighs of almost unbearable pleasure, until at last our passion was spent. For a moment we lay cupped like twins, Christine's body soft as gossamer alongside mine.

I left late at night, when Christine was asleep, congratulating myself on having gained an ally. I was wrong. It took me a further, last passionate night to understand that my attempts to turn Miss Keeler into an accomplice had failed dismally, for by that time she was engrossed in the possibilities of her other new love adventures. We spent that last night in Steve's flat. Tired after a long day, he fell asleep on the sofa. It was then that Christine invited me to her room, and I yielded to her charms for the second time, still hoping to use her, but to no avail.

Yet the very fact that Christine had been both my and Jack Profumo's lover was a potential trump card in any possible future game involving the ill-fated Secretary of State for War. Sex has always been, and will most probably remain, a powerful weapon of political blackmail and espionage. The GRU did not use it as frequently and successfully as did the KGB. In this sphere the Lubyanka was the undisputed champion. It suffices to recall two cases. One concerns William Vassall, a British military diplomat and homosexual who was recruited by Moscow Centre and worked for the Soviet secret services for seven years, from 1955 to 1962. The other case I have in mind involved the US Marines who guarded the entrance to the US Embassy in Moscow in the mid-1980s. Their mistake was that they let in their Russian girlfriends, who strove less to satiate their sexual needs than to fulfil the orders of their KGB superiors.

In both cases the Lubyanka showed unbelievable ingenuity, to the chagrin of its Western counterparts. In the case of Vassall, the KGB used Moscow homosexuals to collect the necessary compromising material and so induce him to work for the Soviet secret services. As a result, the British Admiralty, which employed Mr Vassall after his Moscow mission, worked not so much for the benefit of HM Navy as in the interests of the Kremlin. That operation was orchestrated by General Ivan Serov, then chairman of the KGB, who became the GRU chief in 1958.

Thirty years after Mr Vassall's recruitment, the US Marines fell to the charms of Russian girls. What they did not know was that their beautiful lovers were not ordinary promiscuous girls but priestesses of love in green KGB stripes. The all-American Marines did not just mellow in their arms but also allowed inquisitive KGB boys to roam in the secret rooms of the embassy.

In both cases the opposite side's losses were immense. My amorous involvement with Christine Keeler yielded good results, too: the Conservative Macmillan government, which did not suit Moscow, resigned and the Labour Party took its place at the helm. The Kremlin expected to have warmer relations with it.

Gagarin's London Orbits

July 1961 was a scorcher in London. Asphalt melted, car engines coughed and stalled. Londoners sought refuge in the shade, in air-conditioning, in ice-cold drinks straight from the fridge and refreshing showers in their bathrooms.

Evenings did not bring respite: the temperatures were more appropriate to Madrid, Rome or a Finnish steam bath than to London. Londoners did not like it, and everybody who could do so left the city, some on holidays, others to their country houses, or to their relatives and friends anywhere outside London, which had become a stone furnace.

I changed my sweat-drenched shirts and took showers several times a day. The faces of the embassy staff shone with perspiration, but also with excitement, for a Soviet trade and industrial exhibition was soon to open in Earl's Court. Yuri Gagarin was also to come to London, but how many Londoners would remain in the city? Only tourists and visitors roamed its empty streets. Who would come to the exhibition? Who would meet Gagarin? The hellish heat would thwart an important propaganda function, embassy officials complained in Kensington Palace Gardens.

But all our worries proved groundless. Londoners flocked to the exhibition – God only knows from where they appeared. And the arrival of Yuri Gagarin filled London with crowds desperate to get a glimpse of the famous man.

The official programme of the visit was overturned at once. Improvisation was king. People were overwhelmingly curious to see the Russian who was the first human in space.

The British sent a white Rolls-Royce convertible with numberplate Y1, as if specially ordered for the occasion, to meet Gagarin. I asked an official: "Where did that limousine come from?"

"It was simple to get the car, and the plate we leased from a lady from Manchester. Actually, she offered it to us herself."

I accompanied Yuri on nearly all his trips and to all the parties held in his honour. I grabbed at the opportunity for self-publicity. I willingly posed for photographs, embracing Yuri. I helped him to answer journalists' questions. My smiling face was to be seen more and more often in newspapers and television shows devoted to Gagarin's visit.

The visit ended with a big party in the Soviet Embassy. On behalf of the ambassador I sent official invitations to Stephen Ward and to Jack Profumo and his wife, with whom I hoped to develop my acquaintance. I failed to establish a friendship with Mr Profumo, who talked with me in a reserved manner, but I did establish a rapport with his charming wife, whom I had met in Cliveden.

No other official Soviet party attracted so many guests as that in honour of Gagarin. Despite its being summer and the time for holidays, the halls of the embassy were filled to overflowing. I talked with the guests, swapping impressions or discussing the latest international events. I did not seek the acquaintance of any special person, since I knew nearly all of the guests, and knew to whom I should pay attention and whom I should pass by. My real target was the Profumo couple.

It had been just a week since I had seen the indisputable evidence of Jack's infatuation with Christine, in the Astors' swimming pool. I had only to learn how to exploit that weakness. It transpired that Valerie Hobson loved hats and drank spirits. I saw my chance and jumped at it.

My conversation with Jack at that party did not go well. Although we asked each other question after question, our answers suggested that we were only feigning a conversation. Political subjects were bypassed, while personal questions remained unanswered. I did not expect anything better, though, and was satisfied even with this semblance of a conversation.

No matter where I went and with whom I talked that evening, I sensed the eyes of Lord Denning on my back. I didn't know then, of course, that he would later investigate the Profumo affair. At that time he was for me merely someone whom I often met at affairs of this sort.

"Where is your charming wife, Captain?" he asked. The question had become a tradition.

Lord Denning had met Maya only once and was never able to meet her again, however hard he tried. He did not know that she worked in the radio intercept group of our *rezidentura*, and that, as a result, embassy parties often coincided with her shift.

Ward pestered me all through that evening, because he wanted to be photographed with Gagarin. I found one of the photographers working at the party and asked him to take the picture. Steve then decided that he would leave the embassy and enter it again, so that the photographer could perpetuate for posterity the moment when he met Gagarin. He complied, and soon Ward, happy and content, settled near me in an armchair. "You know, Eugene, he noticed that I had come up to him for a second time!" Steve laughed heartily. "How did he remember me? I don't get it. There are so many people in the hall. Impossible!"

"You have an outstanding jacket," I joked. "Nobody has another one like that. Look at the lapels! The latest Paris fashion."

"Stop being a fool, Eugene." Steve was angry. "You don't understand anything. He is a genius, I tell you. A simple genius. See? You know what he told me when I approached him for the second time? He told me: 'Second time in orbit, pal? Well, let's meet again. My name is Yuri Gagarin.' That's what he told me, and we shook hands. And he smiled. What a smile he has! Even film stars cannot smile like that."

The Loose Cannon and the Queen's Messenger

Jack Profumo's affair with Christine Keeler played into my hands. He was seldom at home, using every spare moment to meet his lady love. When my chief learned about the Secretary of State for War's affair with the Keeler girl, he was so surprised that he unlocked his safe and took out a bottle of vodka. After we had downed our glasses, Pavlov grunted and said: "Well, what a turn of events! We should think about it calmly. You understand that we must not miss this chance. Draft your proposals, and I will ponder mine. I think that we can stir up fantastic trouble."

Of course, spying is a complex and subtle game of bluff and counter-bluff, and it is reasonable to suppose, therefore, that our British equivalents were, at this time, also plotting to ensnare me through my connections with the more raffish elements of high society in general and Stephen Ward in particular.

My high public profile, coupled with my well-known predilection for the trappings of capitalist life, may well have encouraged MI5 to suppose that, with a little discreet manipulation of my contacts – especially Ward – I myself might be made a suitable candidate for entrapment.

Indeed, in the 1980s it emerged that what had previously been regarded as a relatively unimportant relationship between Ward and MI5 had probably been seen by Ward himself as rather more than this. Never one to underestimate his own significance, he seems to have thought that he could fulfil a long-cherished dream – to mediate between hostile Cold War governments to their mutual benefit – by cultivating both his relationship with me and co-operating with British intelligence.

Unfortunately, the plans of both the Soviet and British intelligence services were brought to nothing not only by the shooting in the mews involving Lucky Gordon and all its attendant publicity, but also by the unreliability of Ward himself. Frankly, a less suitable candidate for intelligence work would have been difficult to imagine. Indiscreet, gregarious, prone to fantasy and delusions of grandeur, Ward was simply a loose cannon careering wildly across the deck of contemporary intelligence, demolishing the carefully assembled plots and counter-plots of each side indiscriminately.

Far from being the "thoroughly filthy fellow" or the "wicked, wicked creature" painted by prosecuting counsel Mervyn Griffith-Jones at his trial in July 1963, Ward was merely a tremendously insecure fantasist, eager to please both sides for his own self-glorification.

An ironic footnote to Ward's involvement in the murky and dangerous world of espionage was precipitated by his having persuaded the Duke of Edinburgh and a number of other aristocrats to sit for him. Fearing taint and compromise, the Queen's private secretary, Michael Adeane, commissioned a public servant discreetly to buy the resultant sketches when they were put on show in Mayfair. This task was performed by a man himself subsequently famous for his involvement in intelligence matters: Anthony Blunt.

But despite my uncertainty regarding the counter-plots

of MI5 and the unpredictability of my friend Stephen Ward, I continued to accumulate material of use to the GRU plot to compromise Profumo. I'll roast in hell for my treachery and slyness, but what else was I to do? These are the drawbacks of my profession, and I hope my victims can forgive me.

Eventually, Moscow Centre ordered me to cease operations in this quarter, regarding the risks involved as too great, and in any case acknowledging that they had already received enough information to put the blackmail plot into operation. It only remained to hone the details and to begin the entrapment of the Secretary of State for War. Had this proved successful – and there is good reason to suppose that it could easily have done so, given Profumo's subsequent unwillingness to reveal the truth about his affair with Christine Keeler to Parliament itself – an endless flow of information to Moscow Centre from the hapless politician could have resulted. But this scenario, which would have been the crowning achievement of my career, fatally ignored the existence of that loose cannon, Stephen Ward.

Jack Profumo in the Trap

When I had scanned GRU files before leaving for London, reading up on Macmillan's government, I could not help but notice John Profumo, a rising star now Secretary of State for War. Specialists predicted a brilliant future for him. I could not imagine that I would ever stand in his way, even hold his fate in my hands for a while. He was just an official for me, John Profumo – not Jack, as his acquaintances and friends used to call him.

I saw him two or three times, at the most, in Lord Astor's manor in Cliveden and in the Soviet Embassy. He could hardly suspect that a diplomat from the Soviet military mission, a certain Ivanov whom he hardly knew, could be so closely connected with him. Yet it was so; I held the ace of trumps and waited only for an opportune moment to begin the decisive game with him.

Everything began with our meeting in Lord Astor's home on that July Sunday in 1961. From that day onward Mr Profumo became Jack for me. On that hot July afternoon in Cliveden, Jack and I staged a mini-competition. We were to swim without using legs. Jack was losing when, eager to impress Christine, he broke the rules and finished first, to the applause and laughter of the audience.

"It will teach you a lesson, Captain," he told me condescendingly. "Next time you'll think twice before trusting an Englishman."

It was just a swimming race, but Jack was so pleased that his unscrupulousness had brought him victory over a trusting Russian bear who couldn't make head or tail of British intrigues and treachery. I lost that race, but I won the competition. Jack Profumo had underestimated me.

It was his first mistake.

Contrary to the code of conduct of high-ranking government officials, Profumo yielded to passion. That breach of the rules was not as innocent as the one in Lord Astor's swimming pool.

It was his second mistake.

Being a man, too, I can understand Jack. The hot blood of his Italian ancestors had kindled a passionate love in his heart; he could not resist Christine's charms. I myself fell for her, although I intended to use our affair for my own purposes. Profumo made a much more serious mistake: he thought that nobody, apart from Stephen Ward, would know about his affair with Christine. He had been friendly with Steve, introduced to him by Lord Astor, for six years. Profumo trusted Steve, and one can hardly blame him for that; he could not know that Steve told me almost everything. But he should have known that Christine would not keep silent about their love affair.

It was his third mistake.

I have seen a number of defence ministry officials who had a weakness for the fair sex, and not only in Britain. Take my compatriot, Marshal Grechko. He was appointed Defence Minister by his great friend Leonid Brezhnev in 1967, and headed the Soviet military department for ten years afterwards, till he died. The marshal had a mistress, a young stewardess from his personal plane. Trying to massage the ego of his vain and ambitious lover, who did not have a higher education, the Defence Minister ruled that girls should be admitted to the Institute of Military Translators. His girlfriend visited the institute rarely, going there in the minister's black limousine solely to pass exams. Naturally, she got the highest marks despite her lack of knowledge, and eventually received her diploma in record time. Nearly everybody in the General Staff knew about the minister's passion, but he was not afraid of resignation. The Soviet press wrote only what it was ordered to write, while posts were given not to knowledgeable specialists, but to those who stood close to the helm.

Jack Profumo could only envy the stability of the Soviet Defence Minister's position, for while life was not all milk and honey for Moscow marshals, their love affairs did not bother anybody.

When I became acquainted with Profumo, he – as I have already admitted – behaved cautiously with me, both in Cliveden and at the Soviet Embassy party in honour of Yuri Gagarin. We talked only about matters that were public knowledge. Jack loved to recall his trip to the Soviet Union back in the 1930s, to talk about the difficult life of servicemen and the trials of our joint struggle against fascism, but he never talked about rearmament plans for the British nuclear forces, or prospects for strengthening the military might of West Germany. On the other hand, I never tried to steer our conversations into dangerous waters either.

My _modus operandi_ with John Profumo became more and more clear. Willingly or unwillingly, Ward provided me with information about Profumo's liaison with Christine. I tried to write down all the details of their affair, as part of my ongoing plot to provide myself with enough material to mount what would undoubtedly have been a formidable blackmail assault on the Secretary of State for War.

Moscow Centre had to add only a few finishing touches to the plan of operation, which provided for approaching Profumo through one of our undercover agents with compromising materials. Our agent would have had only to talk with Jack about several details of his affair with Christine and to show him copies of secret documents which I had stolen from his desk to render him co-operative. Profumo would never have known for whom he was working. It was not in GRU interests to reveal themselves. At least that was how I envisioned the continuation of my operation.

During my pre-Christmas leave in Moscow, I sensed that the GRU leaders were preparing the plan painstakingly and secretly. It was clear that its realisation would be entrusted not to me but to the GRU *rezident* in London and an undercover agent. It was not by chance that Captain 1st Rank Ivlev, then department head in the GRU, summoned me several times for a talk, checking and rechecking information on Mr Profumo.

This was done in conditions of top secrecy, so as to avoid the slightest risk of a leak. Actually, nobody talked with me about the plan proper. It was touched upon indirectly. I could guess about the outlines of the operation only by the questions I was asked, by the situation around Jack Profumo, and by the logic of possible actions in such circumstances. But I knew hardly any concrete details about it.

It was years afterwards that my first chief in London,

Colonel General Talokolnikov, who later became first deputy head of the GRU, told me about the planned operation against Mr Profumo. But the operation was called off before the preliminary stage was complete. It was not what we wanted, but a major scandal was engulfing Jack Profumo and Christine Keeler. A wave of revelations sweeping Britain – quite contrary to our desire – soon resulted in the resignation of the Secretary of State for War, and later of the Prime Minister himself. The Profumo scandal actually removed the Tories from the helm for many years, and brought the Labour government of Harold Wilson to power.

"If not for that slut and her jealous lover, we could have brought off a brilliant operation in Britain, with your assistance, Zhenya," Talokolnikov once told me. "In the event of success you would become a Hero of the Soviet Union, indeed, and a Rear Admiral to boot."

A pity, of course, but it could not be helped. Should I have leashed Christine to prevent her from frequenting pubs? I clearly could not have done this, because Christine was like one possessed.

It appears that a strictly limited group of people knew about the GRU operation: no more than two or three people at the top of Soviet military intelligence. Had it not been for this secrecy, Oleg Penkovsky would have learned about it and alerted the British. He apparently did not know anything, otherwise information about the Profumo operation would have gone straight to British intelligence and the CIA. On the other hand, Colonel Penkovsky could have heard about the operation from the GRU chief Serov, who was friendly and trusting with him. He could have reported it to British counter-intelligence, and they might have decided to keep it secret, say, till 2015.

The Labour Party and its leader Harold Wilson came out as the only winners in the scandal. It was not merely fortuitous that the new premier's first visit was to Moscow, and that one of his first requests was to meet Captain Yevgeny Ivanov. Mr Wilson informed Nikita Khrushchev of this request in the Kremlin. The latter then called the GRU chief and ordered him to keep me on red alert. I donned my parade uniform and went to the Kremlin, where I waited for several hours, in vain. Nobody called me in. After a meeting of some kind, Harold Wilson left for Leningrad. I held myself in readiness for several days more, until the Prime Minister returned to Britain, but we did not meet nor have the promised photograph taken. Later my superior told me: "When Khrushchev learned about your heroic deeds and your role in the Profumo scandal, he ordered that Wilson's programme should be packed so tightly as to leave him not even a minute for a meeting with you. That's exactly what was done."

So Harold Wilson did not meet his benefactor. I am not actually sure that he really wanted to meet me. The only thing the Kremlin photographer and I regretted was the waste of time.

The Unrecruited Agent

Apart from the skill involved in the gathering of intelligence data, the art of recruiting agents is probably the core of spying in any secret service across the globe, and the GRU is no exception. All GRU agents are taught the art of recruiting from the very beginning, at seminars in the Academy of the Soviet Army. The years of service in the GRU hone this skill, because it is possible to recruit an agent from one's very first trip abroad. Not everybody succeeds, of course, but recruiting one's own agent is the aim of all GRU agents.

It was the same for me, both in Norway and in Britain. Yet each time I succeeded I could not but feel repulsion towards those who had agreed to betray their own country. It is becoming more and more rare to find people willing to work for a secret service out of political conviction or selflessly to serve an ideal, however naïve or utopian it may be. Idealists are becoming rare birds in this world. The most frequent motive for intelligence work is money, and money is most often used to "buy" an agent. Thirty pieces of silver, however you may look at them, are blood money.

Spies will never hesitate to use any information at their disposal to get what they want. In this sense the CIA and Mossad, the KGB and STASI are all alike. They are all prepared to blackmail and to bribe, to commit forgery and to steal – even to kill – in order to achieve their goals.

I must admit that the moral aspect to my profession did not bother me for many years. My conscience slept, while my belief in the justice of the communist cause was limitless. I would do anything to guarantee the necessary result, be it lie or bribe, blackmail, forge or steal. Paradoxical as it may seem, I have become aware of the immorality of my profession only now that my life is nearly over.

I am sure that my colleagues, both in the East and in the West, will castigate me for my naïve moral casuistry and my criminal revelations. The profession of spying has its own rules: it is not done to wash our dirty linen in public, or to talk about morality, because there is hardly any in the profession. Everybody knows this, but few discuss it openly. Why? Because espionage is still necessary in this sinful world. It was, it is, and it will be necessary always. So morality has to give way to pragmatism.

During my two trips abroad, which lasted eight years taken together, I recruited three agents: two in Norway and one in Britain. I shall tell about them in their appropriate place, in later chapters, although they seem more or less clear-cut cases: paid agents who wanted money and who got it by selling their country's secrets. This may be despicable, but it is as old as the hills.

My relations with Stephen Ward were quite different. "Prepare yourself concerning his recruitment," the GRU *rezident* once told me. "It's a clear case. He is asking for it." The general was right in one thing: Ward indeed helped me willingly, and even fulfilled some of my requests which I thought I could not fulfil single-handed. But recruiting him would have destroyed my relationship with him.

I managed to convince my superiors of this. Steve's recruitment was therefore removed from the agenda. It was a situation where the usual rules did not apply. On the one hand, Steve was *not* a recruited agent. On the other, he *was* an agent of sorts.

Judge for yourself. Who introduced me to Lord Astor and Jack Profumo, as well as to other high-ranking people? Who told me about the guests of the Cliveden manor and the problems discussed there? Who supplied me with material about Members of Parliament, the government and even the royal family? Who offered me his services in obtaining classified information from his high-ranking patients?

Of course, much of what I learned from Steve by chance or design could not properly be called secret information. Take the phrase he dropped one day about Jack Profumo leaving London with Christine Keeler. What was so criminal about it? Apparently nothing, especially if I did not know about their burgeoning love affair. But it was Steve himself who told me about it, and that information was clearly compromising and could be used in any conceivable way.

Lord Denning's report on the Profumo affair drew the firm conclusion that Ward's connection with me did not in itself threaten national security. I was allegedly monitored and Ward was allegedly controlled. Indeed, he *was* controlled. But what they should have done was sever all of my connections with Ward. In that case they would have prevented the information leak. But British counter-intelligence thought that my relations with Ward did not threaten national security. How perfectly wrong they were!

It was probably to cover up this mistake that they spread the rumour that Steve worked for MI5. This is nonsense. The trouble is, Ward did not work for anybody, not for his own or for any other country. He lived by his own rules which few could understand. Already in his green years he began building up a reputation for himself. But his every attempt met a wall of rejection, at school, where he was ordered to keep silent about a crime committed in his presence; in the army, where his superiors used his medical skills but did not admit this officially; and in his family life, with his egotistical wife wanting only money for more clothes. He had reason enough to become disillusioned in life, and he was prepared to cut short his existence twice. The third time, he made the fatal decision and took an overdose of sleeping pills during his trial.

His tragic life was a protest against a society which he loved but which rejected him again and again. He climbed to considerable heights in his life, but there were also a number of falls. His main problem was that he could not find a foothold. He had many acquaintances, but no friends. He had many talents but no cause, many hobbies but no passion, to give him strength, hope and confidence.

He was a man who loved people and found what little happiness he could in numerous acquaintances, meetings and contacts. My friendship with Ward was one such life-saving contact. He tried to please and help everybody, rich and poor, vile and innocent, friend and foe alike. But when he really needed help, there was nobody around.

Once in his Wimpole Mews flat he told me what he had heard in the Astors' home, in particular about the financial crisis. His information was precise and to the point, as usual: a month later, in July 1961, Parliament approved the so-called emergency budget. I listened to Stephen carefully. Suddenly he fell silent. After a while he asked me: "Eugene, what would they do to a person who was friendly with an Englishman in your country?"

I answered him honestly: "He would be summoned to the KGB sooner or later. Why do you ask? Are the rules different here?"

Stephen seemed disappointed by my answer. He said, with childish passion: "We don't have political police here. And you shouldn't have them either. You have proclaimed your noble goals for the whole world to hear. They cannot be achieved by dirty means."

I did not contradict him and tried to change the topic of conversation. But it kept nagging at him, for some reason, and a few days later he returned to it. "You know, Eugene, you were right when you told me about Big Brother. I was invited to MI5 today."

"Nothing strange about it." I tried to calm him down. "You'll listen to what they have to say. It may even be interesting. Will you tell me about it?"

In the evening I came to Wimpole Mews again, listening to Steve's impressions of his interlocutor at the meeting. "He seems to be a nice boy, surprisingly correct and polite. Asked me about you and our relations. Hinted that our relations do not bother MI5. They are even glad that a Russian and an Englishman meet quite informally. But they wanted to know what information you tried to get out of me. I calmed them down by saying that you are not such a fool as to ask me treacherous questions. That was it."

Steve showed me his pass into the Ministry of Defence

where his meeting with MI5 took place, a small yellow piece of paper with the time of the meeting, the number of the room and the name of the official who had summoned Ward upon it. "I kept it as a souvenir." Steve grinned. "Do you want it?"

I took the pass and added it to my report to Moscow Centre. It is probably still kept in their archives.

The Profumo scandal removed both Stephen and me from the game. I say this confidently, because it was rumoured that other members of the Soviet Embassy worked with Steve after I left London. This is not true. While I was in London, nobody from the Soviet secret services was allowed to approach Steve. It is one of the rules of the game, and professionals know this. I was Ward's only control. Moscow Centre decreed this. It would have been foolish and senseless to maintain contacts with Ward or, worse still, establish contact with other people, during his investigation and trial. As professionals say, by that time Ward was exposed. The game with him was over.

Captain Yevgeny Ivanov sketched by his close friend
osteopath Stephen Ward.

Portrait of a teenage vamp. Christine Keeler's beauty
overwhelmed Secretary of State for War John Profumo.

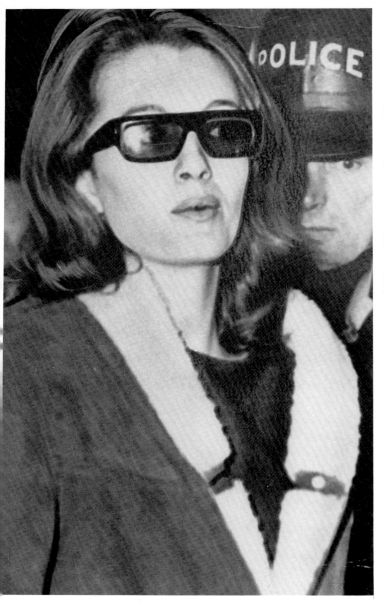

The end of the party. Christine Keeler pictured at the height of the crisis in March 1963.

T TRANSFERABLE
HENLEY ROYAL REGATTA, 1962
UMPIRE'S LAUNCH TICKET
SATURDAY

ADMIT BEARER FOR RACE

No. 12

Passengers in the Bows are particularly requested not to stand up

Top: Princess Margaret and her ex-husband Lord Snowdon became friendly with Yevgeny Ivanov after a meeting at Henley Regatta in 1962.

Right: The Duke of Edinburgh failed to succumb to Ivanov's charm.

Right: John Profumo built a new life for himself after the scandal and continued to enjoy the respect of Her Majesty the Queen.

Below: John Profumo with his wife, former actress Valerie Hobson. She supported him throughout the scandal.

Left: 1953. Maya Gorkina, daughter of the Secretary of the USSR Supreme Soviet, on honeymoon with Ivanov. Taken shortly before their departure to Norway.

Below: Her Majesty the Queen even invited Ivanov and his wife to attend a Buckingham Palace garden party.

EⅡR

The Lord Chamberlain is commanded by Her Majesty to invite

Captain 3rd Rank Evgeniy M. and Madame Ivanov

to an Afternoon Party in the Garden of Buckingham Palace on Thursday the 21st July 1960, from 4 to 6 o'clock p.m. (Weather Permitting)

Morning Dress or Uniform or Lounge Suit

The scandal spelled the end for the Conservative
Government of Harold Macmillan.

The First Lady of the GRU in London

"Zhenya, forget about your own business for a few days and help our guest," General Pavlov said, introducing me to a pretty middle-aged woman and a teenager, apparently her daughter. That was how, in the summer of 1961, I had to help Madame Serova, the wife of our GRU chief, and her daughter. They came to London with a delegation of scientists, but, naturally, had nothing to do with their mission. Their stay in London was purely a Soviet ruse, whereby the USSR government could send abroad the wives and children of high-ranking officials who, by virtue of their work, could not live abroad but who wielded enough power to organise such trips for their nearest and dearest.

I was not overjoyed at my new task. I had quite a few things to do that July. The Berlin crisis was in the making. The establishment of bases for nuclear submarines was in full swing in Britain. My visits to Lord Astor in Cliveden had begun yielding good results, and Ward was supplying me with ever more interesting information from his knowledgeable friends.

I simply did not have the time to take Madame Serova and her daughter around. Besides, I never was a toady, which hindered my ascent on the professional ladder in the corrupt GRU system. But I was not going to change myself, and even if I wanted to, I could not do it. But an order is an order for a military man. For two hot days in July I therefore escorted my high-ranking charges, whom I did not like at all. General Serov, whom I had met several times in the GRU corridors and about whom I had heard from my father-in-law Alexander Fyodorovich Gorkin (Chairman of the USSR Supreme Court for over fifteen years), was an odious figure. I remember old man Gorkin giving me one piece of advice over and over again, obviously forgetting that he had given it to me before: "Zhenya, keep away from your chief. He is a veritable hyena." Alexander Fyodorovich was a man of discipline and never throughout the time I knew him (thirty-five of his ninety years) did he allow himself to use foul words. But it was very difficult for him to keep from using them when speaking about Serov.

"Ugh, that Ivan, he . . ." he would splutter, trying to keep his emotions and his outrage in check.

Once he told me during a walk at his *dacha* in Snegiri, outside Moscow: "There was a meeting in the Kremlin today. That son of a bitch your chief" (son of a bitch was the harshest invective ever used by Alexander Fyodorovich) "behaved as if he were the commander and we his inferiors. He wouldn't listen to anybody, issuing commands hither and thither. Well, you know him, Zhenya – small, slight, with a thin peeping voice that keeps breaking... And imagine him jumping up all the time and dictating his will to everybody around. I had to stop this. I told him: 'Comrade Serov, please respect us. Why try to give commands to us?' Do you think this stopped him? Not at all! He went on as before. I stopped him a second and then a third time. Only after that did he calm down."

"Alexander Fyodorovich, you are biased. Why?"

"You ask me why!" The old man looked me in the eye. "Do you know who executed Tukhachevsky and Yakir in 1937? Who ordered the shooting of Polish officers outside Katyn? Who ordered the murder of Raoul Wallenberg and who pinched his belongings? And lastly, who tortured the supporters of Racosi in Budapest? It was him, your dear Serov!"

General Serov knew that Gorkin hated him. Frankly speaking, I worried that my chief would learn about my relation to Alexander Fyodorovich. That would be it, I thought. But it turned out that General Serov had known about my relation to Gorkin since he came to head the GRU in December 1958, when I returned from my five-year posting in Norway. I avoided passing the chief's office and tried to appear before him as rarely as possible. Once, when he saw me retreating in the corridor, General Serov said: "Where are you running to, Captain? Drop in for a minute."

I went into his office as one goes to the gallows.

"If you choose to retreat, you should do it properly. If the enemy see you retreating, you are doomed: there will be no salvation. You shouldn't make a show of avoiding me, Captain. Are you afraid of punishment? If I wanted to, I could have punished you for your unauthorised return from Oslo. But I have signed an order assigning you to the British department. I wish you success, Captain. And don't rush to write me off as your enemy. We are in the same boat. Do I make myself clear?"

"Yes, Ivan Alekseyevich," I mumbled. Actually, I did not understand what my chief meant.

In the evening I told Gorkin about my meeting with Ivan

Serov. He smiled slyly: "What a rascal! Playing with us, isn't he! He has posted Anatoly Konstantinov as the air force attaché in London, and now he is getting ready to send you, the husband of my second daughter, there, too. The best way of defeating your enemy is to lull his vigilance. Never forget about it, Zhenya, especially with such people as General Serov!"

I remembered that phrase, although I worked under Ivan Serov in Moscow for barely two years. When I returned from London, he had been replaced by Pyotr Ivashutin, removed from the political scene by Colonel Penkovsky's revelations.

But now, July 1961, was eighteen months before that fatal hour, and Serov's wife and daughter were enjoying London, with my assistance. It turned out that my charges were well-read and intelligent, which is why they chose untraditional routes in London. I was surprised to learn that the Houses of Parliament, the British Museum and the Tower of London held no interest for them. They had been there before, during one of their previous visits to London. I noted Madame and Ms Serova asked me to take them to the corner of Tottenham Court Road and to Covent Garden. It appears that the famous Eliza Doolittle sold flowers there. Next I was ordered to stop at Charing Cross. Serova, Jr explained to me that it was from Charing Cross that Mr Phileas Fogg began his eighty-day trip around the world. After that we walked on Waterloo Bridge. Madame Serova recalled the film of the same name, with charming Vivien Leigh in the staring role. In Baker Street I was ordered to find the building marked 221B, where the world-famous detective Sherlock Holmes once lived.

Next day we visited the London of Dickens, Shakespeare and Galsworthy. It remained only to visit Pinewood Studios to crown our tour when my charges suddenly asked me to take them to a pornographic film. Charmed by their previous interests, I was unable to understand this sudden metamorphosis, but I took the Serovas to a pornographic film. Thank God, it took them barely ten minutes of watching the writhing naked bodies to understand that they could not see the film to the end. Their inquisitiveness was satisfied. But embarrassment remained written on their faces after their departure. It must have taken great courage for them to put such an unusual request to me, but, as we in Russia say, "Desire is stronger than compulsion." They could not resist the temptation.

The last day of their stay in London was devoted to shopping. I was surprised by their taste and moderation in an occupation generally so tempting for women. They did not display any particular interest, maybe because the Serovas had all their demands met by the breadwinner, without going to Marks and Spencer or to Barkers. They bought only several modest blouses, sports suits and tennis rackets although, judging by their fat purses, money was not a problem. In fact, they had much more money than is usually given for business trips. What stopped them was that they already had whatever they wanted. This deprived them of any interest in things which would have been a dream for many of their compatriots.

The Serovas got from abroad whatever they wanted, by that time I knew it for sure. The situation sometimes became absurd, with couriers delivering to London requests from Serov for tights and make-up for Madame Serova, medicines for himself, toys for their relatives and friends, and what not. The *rezidentura* coder was no longer surprised by reports which mentioned consumer goods for senior GRU officials and their families. Since my superiors knew about my absolute inability to kowtow to big shots, these "tasks" were usually assigned to anybody but me.

I bade goodbye to the Serovas before their departure and sat down to work. I went to the military mission to read the latest reports from Moscow Centre. In the corridor I met Captain Sukhoruchkin, the naval attaché in London and my direct, though mediocre, superior. Trying to avoid unnecessary questions, I reported that for several days I had been busy with the Serovas.

"Yes, I know," he replied with feigned indifference. "Oleg Penkovsky dropped by yesterday and told us about Madame Serova."

"Penkovsky? What does he have to do with this? Is he in London?"

"You must be joking. Didn't you know that it was he who brought Madame Serova to London?"

I was stunned. I had an old score to settle with Oleg Penkovsky.

Pan Penkovsky, My Fellow Student

Two days after the Serovas left London, Anatoly Pavlov unexpectedly walked into my office. Usually, when he needed me he just summoned me, or, more often, an officer on duty in the embassy called me and relayed his summons. Nothing changed the established routine until that day. That strange visit put me on my guard. Had something happened?

The chief seemed to be worried. "Zhenya, are you busy now?"

I didn't like the strange tact of that question. "Not now, the first business meeting is scheduled for eleven," I replied. "I have some time left till then."

"Then let's go outside. It's so hot today. Right?"

We went from the embassy into the cool alleys of Kensington Palace Gardens. There were few people around at that early hour. We walked along empty alleys, lulled by the cool greenery, until General Pavlov, as if unwillingly, said: "Have you known Oleg Penkovsky long?"

"For at least ten years," I replied, alarmed by this strange beginning.

"I have known him for many years, too. Do you know that he likes to kowtow to superiors?"

"Of course I do!" I grinned. "He was born like that."

"Exactly. Then why did he ask me to find an escort for the Serovas? Why didn't he himself escort them?"

"Maybe he was busy with the delegation?" I prompted a possible answer, although I was surprised by Oleg Penkovsky's behaviour, too. It was unbelievable that such a toady as Colonel Penkovsky could leave the wife of his chief to somebody else, when it was such a good opportunity to kowtow to Serov.

"No, I asked around," General Pavlov told me. "Oleg did not have much work with the delegation. If he were too busy, as he told me when he asked for an escort for the Serovas, where then did he find the time to visit many of our people in the embassy and in the trade and military missions? At least ten people have reported to me that they met with Penkovsky. Why?"

"Me he did not visit, Anatoly Georgiyevich," I noted. "On the other hand, why should he? We were not the best of friends in the academy."

"All right, he did not visit you. This is understandable. But he visited others, which means that he had time to spare," General Pavlov said thoughtfully. "But he used it for some obscure reasons. Right?"

"Yes, it does seem strange," I agreed.

"But for what reasons?"

"We have long been at loggerheads with Pan Penkovsky," I replied, "so I cannot be objective. Who knows? Maybe he decided to show to everybody that he is better than we thought? Or maybe he has quarrelled with Serov and that's why he decided to keep away from his wife?"

"No, Zhenya," my boss retorted, "boys from Moscow Centre told me that he has wonderful relations with General Serov. He enters his office without knocking. Besides, it was not by chance that Madame Serova and her daughter were on the delegation. Ivan Alekseyevich must have requested this personally."

Suddenly, Anatoly Georgiyevich changed the subject: "Well, enough about him. Your head must be spinning with my problems. Besides, this is not what I wanted to talk about. My wife is arriving from Moscow today. You know that I haven't seen her for a long time. So, please get Maya and come to dinner. We'll be glad to see you."

Regrettably, Maya went to the Pavlovs alone. I had something urgent to do. But that conversation kept nagging at me.

Some fifteen months later, in October 1962, I learned from Anatoly Pavlov that Colonel Oleg Penkovsky had been arrested. His treason was the biggest blow to the GRU in its entire history. General Pavlov's doubts had proved justified. Colonel Penkovsky betrayed everything he knew to the British and the American secret services, disrupting the work of the GRU for several years afterwards.

Oleg Penkovsky, who offered his services to the West voluntarily, was a godsend for their secret services. But it also turned out to be most humiliating for them, because the "agent of the century" was quickly caught. Penkovsky had worked for his new masters for less than two years when he was arrested. To this day analysts from the CIA and MI6 wonder why Oleg Penkovsky was exposed, and accuse each other of the loss of the super-agent. As far as I know, they did not co-ordinate their actions in monitoring Colonel Penkovsky, and in general acted foolishly. Yet it was Penkovsky himself who brought about his exposure by being too engrossed in his new role, too careless, conceited and hasty. This could not but attract attention to his actions. Thus, General Pavlov started suspecting him back in London. It was he and I who were the first to report our suspicions concerning Oleg Penkovsky to Moscow Centre. As a result, the colonel was "tailed".

I first became acquainted with Oleg Penkovsky in the Academy of the Soviet Army. We studied at the same department. He was a good-looking boy, clever and easy-going, and he soon established good relations with his fellow students. At the beginning of the academic year he was elected course leader. Several of my friends and I voted against this. (These friends nominated me, but I did not get the required number of votes. After that I was suspected of envying Oleg Penkovsky his popularity.)

That's how I "quarrelled" with him. We became rivals, never missing a chance to drive each other into the corner at seminars or during discussions. The better I came to know Oleg, the less I liked him. He was vain and conceited. He kowtowed to superiors, trying to anticipate every wish of the course chief. He shamelessly praised heads of the academy at meetings, criticised those who were blacklisted and eagerly helped to get rid of them. He acted as a true follower of the great Stalin, fighting secret cosmopolitans, spies and other enemies of the people.

But he also had a noticeable weakness. He sometimes lied outrageously. Naturally, he was occasionally caught lying. Once he even landed in a mess which should have cost him his career, but our superiors helped him out. Penkovsky's connections and patrons saved him from being expelled from the academy, and, ironically, for later work with MI6.

While at the academy, Oleg got acquainted with a singer from the Moscow Concert Society, a young, pretty and carefree girl. This infatuation made him forget about his wife, who was the daughter of Marshal Varentsov. The girl, knowing that her lover was a married man, did not think of marriage but demanded money and entertainment. Oleg, unable to resist his passion, decided to pull a trick. He told his wife that he was leaving for a business trip to Poland. Instead, he took leave of absence from the course chief and took his lover to the Crimea. In the meantime, his wife called the academy, asking if there was any news from her husband in Poland.

"Poland?!" the course chief was astonished.

It was a scandal. After Oleg had begged forgiveness and his friends had convinced the marshal's daughter that it was not in her interest to stoke the fire, Penkovsky's wife "believed" that her husband had gone to the Crimea with an important person on whose benevolence hinged his future career in the military intelligence. The academy's leaders decided to hush up the scandal and avoid washing their dirty linen in public. It was decided to forget about it, to pretend that nothing had happened. Yet the scandal with Oleg Penkovsky became public knowledge. He was not re-elected course leader at the next meeting. This was my doing. I took the floor and spoke my mind. I even added – in order to neutralise my enemies at the course – that I did not seek election myself. After the voting, it transpired that Oleg had not been supported even by his former friends.

We gathered in the smoking room to discuss the situation. I could not prevent myself saying what I thought about him. "Well, Pan Penkovsky has had it! He has been to Poland, now he can sit at home!"

I did not know that Oleg was standing behind me, eyeing me with white-hot hate.

This was in 1951, and Penkovsky's reputation as a leader was greatly undermined. Nevertheless, he was not expelled from the academy, which was something of a surprise to us.

After that, I became Penkovsky's enemy. Oleg avoided and even feared me, remembering my difficult nature. That is why I was not surprised that he did not visit me in London in 1961. The old score was not settled, although he must have had reason to see me. British counter-intelligence must have been interested in me, and Penkovsky's acquaintance with me gave him the chance to try to talk me into revealing certain information useful to the British. Yet he did not do this. Probably he decided that it was too risky. I think he was right.

Back home, I learned that Colonel Penkovsky offered his services to British intelligence about the time I met Sir Colin Coote in London. In November 1960, as Penkovsky made his first contact with the Canadian Embassy in Moscow, I met the managing editor of the *Daily Telegraph* at the embassy party on the occasion of the October Revolution anniversary. In the spring and summer of 1961, while I was actively working in Cliveden, Penkovsky came to London several times to meet his contact in MI6, each time bringing a cache of invaluable information to his new masters. It was at that time that British counter-intelligence tailed me especially busily, probably at Penkovsky's prompting. He knew about the range of my interests in Britain, and obviously passed this information on to the British.

If General Pavlov had been more energetic and decisive in July 1961, when he first sensed something amiss in

Penkovsky's behaviour, the latter would have been exposed a year earlier. Pavlov only needed to tail Penkovsky, at least in order to establish why he did not have the time to escort the Serovas, to have discovered the secret addresses in London where CIA and MI6 agents spent hours debriefing the colonel.

Even the little General Pavlov did do was enough, however. He informed Moscow Centre about his suspicions concerning Colonel Penkovsky. Our counter-intelligence did not ignore his report and started tailing Penkovsky (although belatedly). But it took them more than a year to catch the double agent red-handed. By that time he had already done immense damage to the national interest.

At first nobody in the KGB or GRU wanted to believe that Oleg Penkovsky was a double agent. Our counter-intelligence did not have unequivocal proof of his treason for a long time. They simply did not try hard enough to get it. Although they had indirect proof of Penkovsky's flirting with Western secret services, General Gribanov, then chief of the Second Main Directorate of the KGB (Counter-Intelligence), and General Ivashutin, chief of the Sixth Main Directorate of the KGB (Military Counter-Intelligence), refused to believe in the colonel's treachery and could not master enough courage to take the resolute action necessary to expose him. They were paralysed by the fear of making a mistake and thus bringing down on their heads the fury of their superiors who patronised Colonel Penkovsky. The Lubyanka did not have any compromising information on him other than Pavlov's and my reports from London and pictures of Penkovsky's meetings with suspect foreigners.

It was only many months later that KGB chief Vladimir Semichastny decided to order a search on Penkovsky's flat in Moscow. The surprise and chagrin of the KGB men when they found a hiding place filled with espionage equipment such as mini-cameras, dictaphones, money, ciphers, instructions and so on, can be imagined. This find sealed Penkovsky's fate.

General Ivashutin was commended for this operation and appointed chief of the GRU, replacing the disgraced General Serov. At least a third of GRU agents were replaced with new men, because such a major betrayal necessitated a thorough cleansing. Most of the new men came from the Lubyanka, dealing a deadly blow to the prestige of military intelligence.

At that time, in the mid-1960s, Soviet propaganda did its best to gloss over the importance of the information which Colonel Penkovsky had delivered to the British and American secret services. But these vain efforts deceived only simpletons. The damage done by Oleg Penkovsky could not have been covered up even by a triple dose of propaganda. Damage assessment done on the orders of the country's leadership showed that Penkovsky had revealed to the CIA vital information about Soviet missile forces, and this at the height of the Cuban crisis, when Soviet–US military confrontation was an actuality.

He had, in addition, exposed dozens of GRU and KGB agents working abroad, legally and under cover. British and US counter-intelligence also learned the names of their citizens who were working for us, supplying Moscow Centre with secret information of great importance to the Soviet military and political leadership. This great damage was made possible largely because Colonel Penkovsky had the cosiest of relations with Serov, because of the corruption and bribery which flourished in the GRU at that time. The GRU chief's patronage of Penkovsky opened many a door into offices and secret archives for him. There he could read documents sent from our foreign *rezidenturas* to the country's leadership. These documents were highly sensitive and should have been sacrosant; instead, Colonel Penkovsky read and even copied them, sending the most important of them to the West. In some cases Oleg Penkovsky did not even have to learn the names of agents recruited in Britain or the US. He had only to report to his new masters that the GRU had a document with such and such markings on it to enable them to identify the source of the leak.

But the GRU files were not Penkovsky's only source of confidential information; he also worked in the USSR State Committee for Science and Technology, where he was responsible for economic and technological co-operation with Western countries. In GRU parlance this means that Oleg Penkovsky was responsible for military-industrial espionage under the roof of the Committee for Science and Technology. Work in that committee gave Colonel Penkovsky great opportunities for obtaining secret information about Soviet economic, technological and military capabilities. His status as an adviser gave him access to the leaders of major military plants and design bureaux, as well as to high-ranking ministry officials responsible for the armaments industry.

Another major source of information was Penkovsky's relatives. His father-in-law was none other than Marshal

Sergey Varentsov, Missile and Artillery Forces. Over tea or *borsch*, Marshal Varentsov supplied Penkovsky with priceless information about the real state and technical characteristics of the latest Soviet nuclear missiles, the effectiveness of which was not as impressive as official propaganda claimed. To lose such an agent at the height of Cold War was a severe blow to the Americans and the British.

I did not attend Penkovsky's trial, but I heard all about it from Gorkin. As Chairman of the USSR Supreme Court, he knew all the details of Penkovsky's case, although it was actually the responsibility of the military procurator's office.

"How does he behave at the hearing?" I asked.

"As if nothing has happened. Very impudent. Answers questions condescendingly. He probably thinks that he'll get no more than ten years, and that later the Americans will exchange him for one of our agents."

When Oleg Penkovsky was sentenced to death, this did not surprise anybody but him. Here is how Gorkin described the last minutes of the trial: "When your Oleg heard the words 'capital punishment', he broke down. He hid his face in his hands and did not move for a long time. He did not expect such a sentence. All his hopes were shattered."

But Penkovsky's sentence was also a sentence on the GRU. General Serov, who had ruled the Soviet secret services for nearly twenty-five years, beginning as the SMERSH chief and moving on to the top of the KGB and GRU, paid for his favourite's treason with his career. The General of the Army was pensioned off before his time and subsequently lived in oblivion for twenty-eight years. The exiled general died in Moscow in 1990, without even receiving an obituary or a funeral ceremony befitting his rank. Nearly all other GRU leaders were removed from office or even tried in 1963. Many agents were hastily recalled from their missions abroad – too late for some of them. Several promising operations were aborted. Many contacts were lost for ever.

A second blow of similar magnitude was delivered to the Soviet secret services by Penkovsky's namesake, KGB Colonel Oleg Gordiyevsky. But this was twenty-five years later, and affected the KGB, not the GRU.

Farnborough Theft

In September London resembles a disturbed ant-hill, with the holiday period over and work beginning again. Members of Parliament return to the capital for the next parliamentary session in Westminster. Cinemas show the new mind-boggling adventure starring James Bond, made the previous summer. Theatres invite you to yet another sensational première. And the football season begins.

During my posting in London, I ignored football, theatres and the cinema. There were exceptions, of course, but they were few. I simply lacked the time for the joys of life. If I had a minute to spare, I usually went to the forest. September in Britain is a long, sunny and warm Indian summer; in short, completely unlike the same month in Russia, which ends before you notice its beginning. At this time, British forests resemble mushroom plantations. The British, however, recognise only field mushrooms and never pick other species, probably because they are afraid of mushroom poisoning. But we Russians, coming from a wild forest nation, cannot live without mushrooms, from ceps to chanterelles. Fried or pickled, they provide the best imaginable complement to Russian vodka. Yet only Russians seem to understand this; I never saw a Brit picking mushrooms in the forest. I went for mushrooms to a small – by Russian standards – town some fifteen miles outside London down the A3.

In September I traditionally complemented mushroom-picking with the collection of information about the exhibits at the Farnborough international air show, which is more complicated than picking mushrooms. The several days taken up by this show's work were probably the most difficult of my year, because each item involved a new industrial or technological espionage operation for Moscow Centre or the *rezidentura*. I was never assigned the main role in these operations. My superiors must have thought that I had other priorities, and hence could not risk diverting me from those. This "inferiority" kept nagging at me. Sensing my discontent, a senior official of the *rezidentura* said to me now and again: "What could you do at the air show, Zhenya? You have a queue of British counter-intelligence boys a kilometre long tailing you!"

Indeed, I had always been followed, thanks to Sir Roger Hollis.

"Do you imply that I cannot lose them?!"

Yet my services were usually firmly rejected: "Yevgeny Mikhailovich, do what you are supposed to do at the show, that is collect information, talk with businessmen, and report any interesting bit of information you get. But leave the serious business to other people, who have nothing to do but get samples of the technology we are interested in."

It was not easy to acquire the necessary information about the tactical and technical characteristics of combat aircraft or about the enterprises producing them. I had to twist and turn to get it. I drank till I was blue in the face to loosen the tongues of businessmen. I still cannot understand how my liver stood the trial of those immense doses of alcohol.

Andrey Nikolayevich Tupolev, the leading Soviet aircraft

designer, came to one Farnborough show. Civilians know him as the designer of a series of passenger planes, beginning with one of the world's first passenger jets, the Tu-104. Servicemen know Andrey Tupolev as the Colonel General who gave birth to several generations of medium and heavy bombers, including strategic ones, such as the Bear or the Blackjack, as they are called in NATO parlance.

At that time the USSR did not bring military aircraft to the Farnborough show, by this omission demonstrating the allegedly peaceful nature of our aviation construction. This was propaganda pure and simple, of course. In the Soviet Union, all possible and impossible priorities have always belonged to the military Moloch, and the constant hunt for Western samples of military aircraft at Farnborough by Soviet experts (both official and secret) demonstrated our true interests in this sphere.

The Soviet Union was represented at this particular Farnborough show by several more or less modern civil planes and helicopters, with the giant intercontinental liner, the Tu-114, the highlight of the Soviet exhibition. At that time few people knew that this plane was a modified version of the first Soviet strategic bomber, the Tu-95, speedily created by Tupolev on orders from Khrushchev for the delivery of nuclear bombs across the ocean. The plane could cover 12,000 kilometres without mid-flight refuelling. Its only drawback was its inadequate (for a bomber) speed of 800 kilometres per hour. It was not flying, it was crawling, and would provide an easy target for the Americans. Derivatives of the turbo-prop bomber are still flying today, but its modification was used to produce a passenger liner for non-stop trans-Atlantic flights in the early and mid-1960s.

I was assigned to escort Andrey Tupolev at Farnborough, although he was already accompanied by two men from Moscow. The designer inspected Phantoms, Volcanoes, Mirages and Starfighters, in particular their individual parts set out for public examination. On his orders I asked businessmen about their aircraft and translated their characteristics to Comrade Tupolev. Suddenly he stopped short at one stand. His assistants stopped, too. I came up closer.

"This is it, Andrey Nikolayevich, this is it!" said one of the assistants.

"We have one crash after another because of this part, yet it is working in their aircraft!" said the other aide. "If we could have it for only one day, Dmitrich would learn what's wrong with ours." He was nearly crying.

Tupolev listened calmly to his assistants and then barked at them: "Use your brains for once! Isn't it time you stopped stealing other people's ideas?! Can you no longer think independently?"

Andrey Nikolayevich moved on to the next exhibit. I approached the stand which had provoked such an emotional outburst and looked at the dream of Soviet designers. It was a blade for a turbojet engine, one which was expected to work faultlessly at temperatures of several thousand degrees Centigrade. By all accounts, "capitalist" blades were obedience incarnate and played their role perfectly, while their Soviet counterparts were a headache, refusing to work at all. A small and apparently unimportant detail like this prevented a huge machine from taking off. It was a crisis in Soviet aircraft-making.

I decided to help the homeland overcome this problem. Leaving my charges alone for a while, I remained at the stand and waited till there was nobody in sight. Looking around me cautiously, I took out my penknife, inserted it between the glass and the stand so that I could slip my hand in, and quickly removed the blade. I found Comrade Tupolev and his assistants in the next hall. Since they had seen the coveted blade they had lost any interest in the other exhibits. I sidled up to Tupolev and silently showed him the inside of my jacket: "Is this the detail you wanted so much, Andrey Nikolayevich?"

Tupolev was paralysed: "Oh God, how did you manage that?!"

One of his assistants craned his neck and peered inside my jacket. Seeing the blade, he whistled and virtually dragged me out of the hall: "Let's get out of here quick, before they get us."

Our delegation left Farnborough in a matter of seconds. A minute later, we were heading for London in my Humber Super Snipe.

"Zhenya," Tupolev addressed me sombrely, "this calls for a celebration. Stop somewhere, you know these places better than we do."

We stopped at a quiet cafe off the highway.

"Let me kiss you, Zhenechka," said Tupolev, deeply moved by my exploit. "You don't even know what you did for us. My stupid boys have been racking their brains over this blade for over four months now. All in vain."

"We'll succeed now, Andrey Nikolayevich," said one of his unfortunate assistants. "We shall copy this blade and that will be it. I guarantee you the required result. I'll be damned if we don't!"

"I don't want you damned, you fool!" the chief designer replied. "Better order us a drink."

The assistant turned to the young barman, but the latter, however hard he tried, could not make head or tail of the Moscow engineer's English.

"Zhenechka, help this oaf, please, or else he'll keep us here till the second coming, trying to maim the English language all the while," Tupolev said.

I joined the negotiations. The unfortunate man turned to me: "How do you tell him to pour us three portions of 150 grammes of vodka?" He was clearly shocked by his own inability to get himself understood. "Tell him what we need."

"They don't say that here." I tried to explain the English system to him. "They order singles or doubles, with a double being approximately 150 grammes."

"I see, Zhenya," said the designer and would-be linguist and, pointing to the empty glass, he told the barman: "Double, double and double."

The barman, grasping this sliver of information, poured a double for each of us, which we drank immediately.

"And now, *répétez*," said Tupolev in French – he did not know any English. "To you, Zhenechka! To your health!"

The barman refilled our glasses. We had another three doubles.

We returned to London happy and carefree. Tupolev, whom the vodka had made merry, promised me a state decoration for my exploit. "My dear Zhenechka," he assured me, "your chief will learn about this from me personally, as soon as I return to Moscow. I have known Ivan Alekseyevich since the war. He will not turn down my request. You'll get an order."

I didn't get the order, of course, but it doesn't matter; I had helped my homeland. As I learned back in Moscow, the blade had been delivered to the famous design bureau of Nikolai Dmitrievich ("Dmitrich") Kuznetsov, the chief Soviet expert on aircraft and missile engines. The boys claimed that the present from Farnborough had not only helped them to finish the aircraft engine over which they had been racking their brains, but had also been used in the new missile engine N-1, created at the Kuibyshev engine factory for the aborted 1965 flight of Soviet spacemen to the Moon.

The chemists at Kuznetsov's design bureau ran a component analysis of the alloy from which the blade had been made. At that time turbojet engine-making was at the dawn of its development and aircraft designers on both sides of the Iron Curtain – in both the Soviet Union and the US – were sweating to improve the form and composition of the blades, especially those used in strategic bombers. The designers' task was rather complicated: at once to increase heat resistance, to bring down weight and to guarantee stability of the blades' size in different work regimes. Experts therefore believed that the composition of the alloy was the key to success, so they tried a number of different combinations and technologies. Each success was paid for dearly.

As I later learned, the blade I stole in Farnborough was made of materials which Soviet specialists had not thought of trying. If I remember correctly, it was a multi-component alloy that included chromium and carbon, which greatly increased heat resistance and guaranteed the invariability of the blade's size in different work regimes. The blade itself, that is its composition, was not enough: you had to be familiar with the technology. Yet at that time, knowledge of the blade's composition was an important contribution.

The day after the visit to Farnborough I was summoned to the *rezident*. "Well, Zhenya Mikhailovich, you must have lost your mind! Stealing an exhibit right from the show! And what would have happened if you had been caught red-handed?"

"Sorry, Comrade General, I'll never do it again," I replied. "But those academicians wanted the blade so much, I thought I should help them."

"Yevgeny, I am beginning to think that you could have been a first-rate, world-class criminal if you had not been a spy."

"Did I do it for my own benefit?!" I was outraged. "I tried to serve the homeland!"

"All right, all right, I was only joking." General Pavlov tried to pacify me. "It's small potatoes anyway. Our boys stole the engine of a new German tank from West Germany. They installed it on a yacht they bought for the purpose and went home on it. That's theft for you!"

"Well, I can steal an engine, too!" I was burning to go. "All you need to do is order it."

"I shall give an order to you, Zhenya," General Pavlov replied seriously. "Let's get down to German affairs. The situation in Berlin is worse than ever. It's time we acted."

The Berlin Crisis and
Sir Godfrey Nicholson's Gin

Now that the Iron Curtain which divided Germany for four and a half decades has been lifted, it is all too easy to talk about political mistakes and miscalculations. But in the autumn of 1961 the mistakes which both the White House and the Kremlin had made in the fifteen years since the war had brought Europe to the verge of another disaster. As befits a patriotic zealot, I saw only the mistakes of the Western powers, while the policy of my country appeared absolutely correct and justified to me. It took me some considerable time to understand that I was wrong.

Tensions over the German question grew, and I remember the main stages very well. As part of the Marshall Plan inaugurated in 1947 a new currency was introduced in the three Western zones of Germany by the Allied Control Council in 1948, which exploded financial and economic contacts between the two parts of the country. Moscow replied to this separate money reform by sealing Berlin. In 1949 the Federal Republic of Germany was officially proclaimed, and the German Democratic Republic (GDR) was formed.

In 1952 the Bundestag rejected the initiative of the GDR People's Chamber on elections into the National Assembly, and in 1953, when the first anti-governmental revolt in Berlin was suppressed by Soviet tanks, Vyacheslav Molotov turned down the proposal of his British counterpart Sir

Anthony Eden concerning free elections in both parts of Germany.

In 1955 John Foster Dulles rejected, no less resolutely, the Soviet initiative on the unification of Germany as a neutral state. As a result, West Germany joined NATO, while East Germany became a member of the Warsaw Pact. Both parts of Germany were hastily militarised. Khrushchev proclaimed a time limit for eliminating the occupation regime of West Berlin by presenting an ultimatum to the former Allies. He demanded that the three powers withdraw their troops from the western part of the city within six months. In reply, West Berlin was included in NATO's sphere of defence. Khrushchev retaliated by signing a separate peace treaty with East Germany.

On 13 August 1961 Berlin was divided into two parts by a 160-kilometre-long wall. This most visible symbol of the Cold War, which cost East Germany 870 million marks and eighty lives of brave people killed trying to escape to the West over it, lasted twenty-eight years and eighty-eight days. The Berlin Wall has now been removed, but in August 1961 it divided Europe quite straightforwardly into friends and foes.

Throughout the three years of my stay in London I, in common with other *rezidentura* staff, was bombarded with requests to report on the British government's attitude to the German question and on the delivery of chemical and nuclear weapons to the Bundeswehr, not just because the situation was unstable, but because suspicion and mistrust of the Germans had almost become a part of the Russian character. This was not surprising, given the tremendous sacrifice and suffering by my people in both the 1914 and 1941 wars against Germany.

The temperature of the dispute was also raised by the tactlessness and directness of Khrushchev's numerous political actions with regard to Bonn. The Soviet premier called Chancellor Adenauer a "senile degenerate". What agreement could be expected after that? As a result, the task of Soviet military intelligence was extremely complicated: we needed to avert a new war, a nuclear catastrophe, and to find a common language with the Western powers.

Since there was no Moscow–Bonn dialogue to speak of, and East–West understanding over the German question was nil, Moscow Centre offered GRU *rezidenturas* in the leading Western capitals the use of all available contacts in order to establish direct channels of communication with high-ranking state officials. Such channels were to be used in crisis situations for guaranteeing quick and safe dialogue between the leaders of states interested in the peaceful settlement of conflicts. In view of my contacts, I was entrusted with the establishment of such a channel in Britain, at my own initiative.

That "hot line" was established and used twice during my stay in Britain, during the Berlin and the Cuban crises. In both cases London was perceived as able to play a special role in maintaining Moscow–Washington dialogue. However, for several reasons, London's mediatory abilities were not used, either in 1961 or in 1962.

Moscow Centre acquired more effective channels of communication. One of them was established by an agent of Soviet intelligence in Washington, Georgy Bolshakov, who worked there under the cover of the Novosti Press Agency and had direct access to Robert Kennedy, brother

of the then US President. There were also other channels,
both in the Old and New Worlds. But the unofficial yet
trusting dialogue between Khrushchev and John Kennedy
was established in 1961 and 1962 thanks solely to
Bolshakov, and it greatly helped to relieve Moscow–
Washington tensions in that crisis-ridden time.

My contact in Britain, who was supposed to guarantee
London's mediatory role by orders from Moscow Centre,
was Sir Godfrey Nicholson, a prominent Tory backbencher.
Sir Godfrey was an old friend of Lord Astor and Sir Colin
Coote, as well as an acquaintance of Stephen Ward, which
greatly simplified my task. I should say, for justice's sake,
that Sir Godfrey Nicholson was not chosen by me. By all
accounts he was authorised to establish contact with me
by the then Foreign Secretary Sir Alec Douglas-Home,
because my initial proposal concerning London's mediatory
role was addressed to him via Stephen Ward, who did not
hesitate to help me. If Ward is to believed, the positive
answer was precipitated by Lord Astor, through his
contacts with Sir Alec. The Foreign Secretary assigned Sir
Godfrey to maintain contact with me, which the latter did
to my satisfaction. We met regularly for consultations and
exchanged letters, which despite containing a number of
empty words and hackneyed phrases, also put forward some
valuable ideas, advice and recommendations. The Soviet
Embassy analysed them and informed Moscow Centre. Yet
these contacts were nothing but preliminaries for possible
later action. Both Sir Godfrey and I patiently waited for that
time to come, but it never did.

In addition to paving the way to London's possible
mediatory role in settling the Soviet–US conflict, Moscow

Centre also wanted to get information on the deployment of nuclear weapons in West Germany. Hardly a week passed without our military attaché sending relevant information to Moscow, even if it was unchecked and insignificant. I also contributed to this effort. In this task I was greatly assisted by Sir Colin Coote and Stephen Ward. I always knew that our anti-German "alliance" with Sir Colin was bound to bear fruit, and I was not mistaken in this belief.

"The Bundestag has approved a new military budget," I once told the managing editor of the *Daily Telegraph* over lunch in a small restaurant in Leicester Square. "It has topped 27,000 million marks, is nearly two-thirds of that country's total expenditure. Another interesting fact: German servicemen have been re-enlisted. How do you like that?"

Sir Colin was not amused, of course.

I kept on lashing out at him: "And what do you say to this: General Hans Speidel, Allied Land Forces, Central Europe? Germans everywhere! It only remains to give the Bundeswehr nuclear weapons and they will grab control of everything!"

"This will never happen, Captain," Sir Colin retorted.

"How do you know?" I asked, eager for this vital information.

"The question has been settled, Eugene, believe me," my interlocutor assured me.

Sir Colin was cautious and tried not to reveal confidential information, all the more so because I was his potential enemy. But his answer was confirmed by another, far more authoritative source, which I immediately reported to Moscow Centre. This source was provided by Stephen

Ward, who complied with my request and asked one of his new and well-informed acquaintances about the deployment of nuclear weapons in West Germany. This new acquaintance was none other than the US Ambassador David Bruce. His portrait was commissioned by the editor of the *London Illustrated News*, Sir Bruce Ingram, who had also requested Steve to make a series of portraits of the royal family for publication in the magazine. Steve's acquaintance with the US Ambassador continued, because the artist and the ambassador obviously liked each other.

When relations between Stephen Ward and David Bruce reached a certain plateau of trust, Steve decided to ask him about the nuclear missiles. Immediately after that conversation – it was at the height of the Berlin crisis – he hurried to inform me that he had obtained the information which I wanted so much. "I told you that I would get it," he said. "But you doubted my abilities."

After lavishly praising the undeniable talents of my friend, I asked him to tell me about the conversation in detail.

"I began by saying, in so many words, that the US should not give its nuclear weapons to the Bundeswehr, that Bonn is not to be trusted in such matters," Steve recited. "But he replied that they would never allow the Germans to control their nuclear arms. He actually cut me short," Steve complained, "but I refused to stop. Would you allow them to control chemical weapons? I asked. The answer was again a resolute 'No'."

It was invaluable information, although I later learned that I was not the first to report it to Moscow Centre. My information only confirmed what the

Soviet leadership had already heard from other sources.

In the autumn of 1961 the Berlin crisis reached its peak, and in late October Soviet and American tanks faced each other at Checkpoint Charlie. One wrong move could have destroyed the fragile balance of East–West peace. The Soviet military reported to Khrushchev that the Americans intended to use tanks to break into the Soviet zone. War and peace hung by a thin thread which the Kremlin leader could cut with one word.

"Order our tanks to leave that checkpoint," he said. "The Americans will leave, too, if they don't want a third world war."

The American tanks did leave and the threat of war was averted, only to resurface in October 1962, during the Cuban crisis.

A week after the settlement of the Berlin crisis I met Sir Godfrey Nicholson at the party in the Soviet Embassy on the occasion of the anniversary of the October Revolution.

"Congratulations, Captain." My partner in the Washington–Moscow mediation addressed me.

"What do you mean? The anniversary of the October Revolution?"

"Oh no, Mr Ivanov. I mean the peace that has been restored. Now we can rest."

"As for me, I cannot rest yet," I replied. "I am going to Scotland tomorrow. Business."

"Did you say Scotland? Fine. I have a small factory there. You are welcome to drop by."

"What factory?"

"Well, a vintage enterprise. Here is the address. Come and see for yourself."

I happened to pass through that town and decided to "see for myself". It was a brewery, and I was made tremendously welcome when they learned that I was "the Mr Ivanov". The brewery that Sir Godfrey owned produced gin, not inferior to the famous Gordon's. I did not resist when my hospitable hosts put about five boxes of it into the boot of my car.

The following weekend most of the Soviet Embassy staff tasted Sir Godrey's gin, because I treated everybody I knew to it. I must say that after that, the quality of my contacts with British parliamentarians was assessed extremely favourably.

Russian Steppe on the Banks of the Thames

The closer my contacts with Stephen Ward became, the more I wished to please my benefactor, for however high my opinion of myself and my achievements, it was undoubtedly none other than Steve who laid the foundations for nearly all of my achievements. He opened the homes of his friends and acquaintances to me and showed me the way into the British corridors of power. Naturally, I wanted to cultivate him, to cement our relationship, to preserve Stephen's interest in me. Sometimes this led to curious happenings.

Once – it was at Spring Cottage in Cliveden, one of the many weekends I spent with Stephen Ward and my new friends – I asked Steve: "What would you say if I violated the British order in your garden and made it look a little Russian?"

"What do you mean?" Steve was surprised.

"Well, you know, I will go away eventually, but this garden, redesigned to look a little Russian, will remind you of our friendship," I explained, well aware that I was becoming sentimental.

"Wonderful idea!" exclaimed Steve. "Let's do it. From now on I shall call this plot of British land 'the Russian steppe'. What are your steppes like?"

I told him everything I could remember from my school geography and botany lessons. Inspired by my explanations, Steve suggested what we should buy and where, what soil to use and where to buy it, how to redesign the garden, etc. Our combined efforts on behalf of small landholder Stephen Ward (he leased Spring Cottage from Lord Astor for a peppercorn rent of one pound sterling a year) I expected to cement our friendship with sweat and calluses, but conscious that the British value law above all else, I suggested that we should ask Lord Astor's permission before redesigning the garden.

"To behave properly," I said, imitating Billy, "a man should know the rules that concern him, as well as his rights. Only an acute awareness of one's rights can be called a truly British trait."

The smile on Ward's face told me that my performance was successful.

I went on: "It is written on the British emblem, '*Dieu et Mon Droit*', although God only knows why it is in French. This shows that the meaning of rights and the meaning of rules are inseparable. Freedom of expression and respect for law are two sides of one coin."

Steve assessed my performance highly but advised me never to mimic Lord Astor again. "I would not want to lose this cottage because of an impudent wit, and a Commie to boot," he told me jokingly. "Thank God Billy's not here. If he heard your witticisms, Anglo-Soviet relations could be threatened."

I promised him to concentrate on gardening, rather than performing. "Actually, it is you who are taking me to theatres all the time and teaching me to take up the traits of your actor friends. I could not help learning from them," I justified myself ironically.

Indeed, not long before this conversation Steve had dragged me to the Comedy Theatre at the corner of Leicester Square and Panton Street. He had been asked to help a guest actor who was down with back trouble. Ward restored the ailing star to life after a half-hour session, to the joy of the troupe. While Steve worked I was entertained by the best comics of the theatre, who taught me the simplest elements of parody. After that we watched a satirical show. I think it was called "An Evening of British Junk", or something like that. After the show, Steve and I simply could not talk because we had laughed so much that our jaws ached.

But back to my gardening project: the same evening Lord Astor gave his permission to conduct the experiment in the Spring Cottage garden, and I started learning the ABC of a new profession. During the couse of my activities as a gardener, Steve came to like me even more – or at least so it seemed. To be honest, I also became drawn to him more and more, although I have never liked gardening.

I dug up Steve's garden with a spade and a mattock, then I scoured garden centres in search of the saplings and pebbles we wanted. I discovered, during this process, a truth I did not know before but which is very well known in Britain: gardening is a national craze. When you see Britons' trimmed lawns, neat rose bushes and hedges, it is clear that everything humanly possible has been done to keep them spick and span. I don't know what it is – middle-class respectability, a desire to escape their problems, or simply love of nature – but it is a fact that the English are crazy about their gardens. Stephen was no exception: he spent every free minute in his little garden, encouraging me in my Russification of Lord Astor's land.

Ward's friends and acquaintances soon learned about our enterprise. It gave me yet another pretext for visiting Cliveden, but I had to work as best I could in order to keep up the prestige of Russian gardening. I had my reward in the form of new acquaintances and more proposals for the "Russification" of other gardens.

"He is *my* gardener," Ward would reply to such requests, protecting me from local landholders. "I cannot lease him to you until he is finished here. Let's resume this discussion at the end of the year."

Judging by the amused irony with which Steve performed on such occasions, he liked his new role as lord of the manor, disposing his workforce.

"Come to me next week and we shall discuss our deal," one of Steve's guests invited me. "Agreed?"

"Let me introduce you first," Steve interrupted. "Captain Ivanov, a Russian friend. Paul Getty, the richest gentleman in Britain and the greatest sinner."

"Hello, Captain," said the old man, who was clearly doing his best to look younger. Mr Getty did not shake hands with me. "My only sin is that I still tolerate your bad manners, Steve. Honest to God, I should have spanked you long ago for your impudence."

"And who would help you with your back then?"

"There are other merciful people in the world. I'll find myself another chiropractor, a better and a cheaper one."

"No, you won't."

"I bet you five pounds that I will. Well?"

As I watched this wrangle, I was thinking all the

while that my garden was yielding its first fruit. Getting to know Paul Getty suited me perfectly.

"All right, let's forget it. Better have a lunch with me, yes? Quite informal. Just another business meeting. OK?"

Would you turn down an invitation from a billionaire? We didn't.

Frankly speaking, the desire to get to know a live billionaire, a "Capitalist monster", a money-bag with a human face, could be compared only to the desire of a child to get to know Santa Claus on Christmas Eve. Any rich person in Britain is as famous as the British Museum or the keeper of the Tower keys. Britain is the cradle of millionaires and billionaires. They originated in that country and later proliferated throughout the world.

I waited for that meeting with keen anticipation not only because I was intrigued, but because Mr Getty had enviable connections in the business communities of Britain and the USA. His petrodollars ran quite a few businesses, but the unquestionable jewel in his crown was the armaments industry, the one that worked for the rearmament of the British and American strategic forces. That was the sphere where my interests intermeshed with those of Paul Getty.

If I am lucky, this acquaintance will answer many of the questions of Moscow Centre and the London *rezidentura*, I thought, preparing for the meeting. I did not – and could not – know then that it would become the greatest disappointment of my London sojourn.

Paul Getty Disappoints

Stephen Ward and I were invited to Paul Getty's home in June 1962, on the eve of Ascot. The mansion and grounds of Britain's richest man were suitably decorous, spotlessly clean and dignified wherever you looked. We walked to the house along an asphalted path. Stephen was gesticulating nervously as he drew my attention to various architectural niceties.

At the entrance we were met by a large fellow in civilian dress who showed us into the hall. Inside, the walls were hung with beautiful old tapestries and marvellous pictures.

"Admiring my pictures?" We heard the host's voice. "Good afternoon, gentlemen. Fine weather, isn't it?"

"Nothing out of the ordinary," Stephen replied sulkily; he had been in a bad mood all morning. "Could be better."

"At my age I must be thankful for every day I live," Mr Getty said sadly. "I am over seventy, you know. And how did your Russian gardener find my garden?"

"Oh, Eugene is overwhelmed." Steve hurried to speak up for me.

"I liked your garden, yes, especially the bluebells," I remarked.

"You must be a romantic, Mr Ivanov. But I am a pragmatist, and want order and precision in my garden. If you can combine your romanticism with my pragmatism, I could hire you as a gardener. Will you accept?"

Ward just had to interfere. He told Getty that I was not a gardener but a military man in the employ of the Soviet Embassy in London, and that my idea of redesigning Steve's garden was just an amusement for our weekends, nothing more.

"You strike me more and more as stupid, Steve," Paul Getty said calmly but resolutely. "Do you really think that I want to employ a Red officer? Don't you understand jokes? You are finished, then."

While Getty and Ward wrangled, I asked for permission to call my wife, who had not felt well that morning.

"The telephone is by the door. Call whomever you like and return to the living room. We shall have our lunch," Getty said in a commanding tone.

I went to the entrance – and couldn't believe my eyes. Hanging on the wall was a pay phone. A pay phone in that billionaire's vast house, with its park and airstrip for sports aircraft! Installed specially for visitors and guests. I was shocked.

Back in the living room I told Steve about my find.

"Nothing to shout about," he replied calmly. "It may seem strange to you, but I have known this character for many years. Put a penny on the table in front of him, and he will tremble until he gets it."

Within half an hour the rest of the guests had arrived and we began our lunch. Steve told me that Mary, who served us, was Getty's housekeeper. She turned out to be a Russian émigrée. We whispered a few words to each other as she served me. It was not difficult serving Paul Getty: his lunch consisted of three very ordinary courses. The exquisite old set of dishes in which the food was served was too good for the simple salad, purée, chicken cutlets and mineral water we were given, a strange menu for a special lunch. I am not a gourmet, but I left the table hungry.

Seeing my disappointment, Mary whispered: "Next time you are invited to lunch here, eat well before you come." She knew him of old, of course.

On the other hand, I had not come to see the billionaire merely to eat. I therefore tried to strike up a conversation with him, but failed miserably. Mr Getty asked for a telephone and made endless business calls, to banks and stock exchanges, I think, because he talked non-stop about shares, rates and interest. Then he answered telephone calls from brokers, jobbers and bank managers. They talked about selling and buying. Judging by Getty's tone, I guessed that something was amiss.

"It seems we have come at the wrong time," Steve whispered. "The old boy is irritated, which could mean that his oil shares are falling."

The only person who did not mind the distraction sat next to Paul Getty and smiled coquettishly at me. I had met her, a young Austrian, called Ilia, at the Astors'. Steve later told me that it was he who had introduced her to Getty. The young woman did not seem to be particularly interested in maintaining good relations with the oil tycoon. What she missed at the table was liquor. "Will somebody give me something to drink?" she complained to the maid.

Getty did not react at all. Seeing that she would get nothing here, Ilia called the host a miser and left the table as a sign of protest. Getty did not bat an eyelid. He was engrossed in a money discussion.

"Oh hell!" he exclaimed suddenly, slamming down the

receiver. "Unbelievable! They ask for a loan, as if they are poor! They think that I have money to hand out left and right. But I can't! Every pound has been invested. I would like to be as carefree as they are for just a day, without counting every penny, spending money in whatever way I want, hoping for help from my friends and not afraid of going broke. How spoiled they are!"

"Do you want a loan, Paul?" Steve asked with a sly smile. "I have about a hundred pounds tucked away for a rainy day. Take it, if you want."

"Joking all the time, my dear," Getty replied reprovingly. "Do you think that since I live in this luxurious mansion I have champagne baths and light candles with bank notes? I have become rich because I could *make* money, I repeat, *make*, not squander. More than that, I have learned to value money. I know a fool who sent his father's millions down the drain and who dares despise me for my moderation and carefulness. Well, it is I who despise him, because it is easy to spend money you have not earned. I earned every penny I have."

Feeling tension at the table, I attempted to change the subject of conversation, talking about investment in the British armaments industries, Anglo-American programmes designed for decades to come, guaranteed orders and profits. Silence fell heavily on the guests, broken only by my lonely voice. My design was simple and primitive: I wanted to provoke a reaction from my host to these direct statements, to induce him to share his opinions with me about which armaments industries and plants to invest in. Even a tiny bit of information of this sort would have suited me, because it would have pointed to the priority areas of British military development. I hoped he would continue the conversation. I could not have been more wrong. It turned out that Getty had listened to me merely for form's sake. Hardly had I stopped when he excused himself, pleading business, and called it a day. I could not hide my disappointment.

Later, I reconstructed that speech of mine, which was regrettably too direct, and tried to understand where I had gone wrong. Was it because I had made a genuine mistake? Or were the circumstances wrong? Or was my plan concerning the billionaire simply impractical? I came to different conclusions every time I thought about it, but all the same, I accused myself of undue haste and of being a damned nuisance.

When we were leaving the house, not without reason, Steve complained about my behaviour at the table: "Why did you decide to talk with the old man about what is profitable and what is not in this country, Eugene? Do you think he didn't understand what you meant when you started talking about military matters? If you wanted to learn something, you should have asked me first."

He was right, of course. And I was disappointed. However, Ward's proposal was a nice surprise, and I hurried to accept it.

"I take you at your word, Steve," I told him. "Next time I shall co-ordinate my actions with you."

Ilia, irritated, was waiting for us by our car. "Boys, do you have anything to drink?" she asked in a funereal tone. "I am dying for one."

Who could have left such a beautiful girl in trouble? Steve suggested that we visit his friend, Lord Harrington, who lived nearby. Ilia would find a well-stocked bar there, and we good bridge partners.

On our way there Getty's girlfriend complained to us about the old miser. "I wish you hadn't introduced me to him, Steve," she said. "He is not a man but a box. He lives here only to save on taxes back in the US. He goes only to day performances, because they are cheaper. And this does not happen often. He keeps his driver only till five o'clock, so we cannot go anywhere from the house in the evening."

We sympathised with the unlucky girl.

At Lord Harrington's she made a beeline for the bar, intent on drowning her misery in liquor. Steve introduced me to his friends and, after a short talk, we played a game of bridge. During our first break we found Ilia was quite drunk and decided to send her home. Steve called a taxi and told the driver to take the girl to Getty's home, cash on delivery. We resumed our bridge but were soon interrupted by a knock on the door. It was the taxi driver. Embarrassed, he said: "Excuse me, gentlemen, but Mr Getty refused to pay for the lady, and sent me back for my money here."

Steve cursed but paid the driver.

The Portsmouth Recruit

During the course of my eight years abroad, first in Norway and then in Britain, I recruited three agents, who continued working for the Soviet secret service after I left Oslo and London. Recruiting and controlling an agent is an extremely complicated, tiresome and risky business, so my first foreign posting, five years without leave, spent controlling two officers from Norwegian Navy Headquarters, wore me out completely. I begged for a short vacation, but was turned down repeatedly. So one day I sent everything to hell and returned to Moscow without permission, leaving my agents in the control of my chief, Captain 1st Rank Pakhomov, naval attaché of the Soviet Embassy in Norway.

The recruiting of agents and the creation of an agent network were among the most responsible and close-guarded activities of Moscow Centre and its *rezidenturas* abroad. For understandable reasons, such efforts were undertaken above all in NATO countries. The results differed from country to country, of course, success coming in some and failure in others.

Comparing my experience in Britain and Norway, it is clear that the GRU had many more difficulties in the former than in the latter, and, despite the smaller military and political weight of Norway, that our agents there provided a considerable amount of information, which included

NATO, American and British secrets. My Norwegian experiences will be related in Part Three of this book, "Mission to Oslo", but it is time to relate the story of my British "catch". I have changed the name of this English agent and some other related information – for obvious reasons, since I do not want to bring down the wrath of British counter-intelligence on him. By all accounts my protégé is still alive and active and hence may still be working for the GRU.

Of all the methods of recruiting I know, it was the best one possible, "love at first sight", as we call it, that brought him to me. He himself offered me his services, although not for nothing, of course. At that time he was "small fry" to us, although I don't know about now; the young officer could well have made it to the upper echelons.

As I mentioned earlier, I met him in Portsmouth, at one of the lectures I gave on my tours of Britain in compliance with the orders of General Pavlov. "Captain Souls" served in HM Navy's Coast Guard. He was very interesting as he disputed some of the points I had made at the lecture and he asked me some tricky questions about the foreign policies of both the Soviet Union and the US. Eventually, our debate developed into an ordinary, more general conversation in the bar, over a tot of whisky. We became acquainted, exchanging telephone numbers and addresses. The captain was a newly-wed and had a small house outside Portsmouth, bought on a mortgage. He said he had to save every penny to be able to pay his monthly instalments.

We then lost touch with each other for some time. In a few months, however, I was again in Portsmouth, and again met Captain Souls. Again we talked. The young

Portrait of the author as a young naval officer. Ivanov joined the Soviet Navy during World War II and was rapidly promoted to Group Commander.

Portrait of a party animal. With his charm, his ready laugh and a seemingly endless supply of vodka, Ivanov was the life and soul of every London society party.

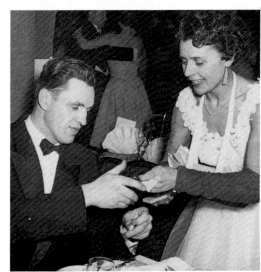

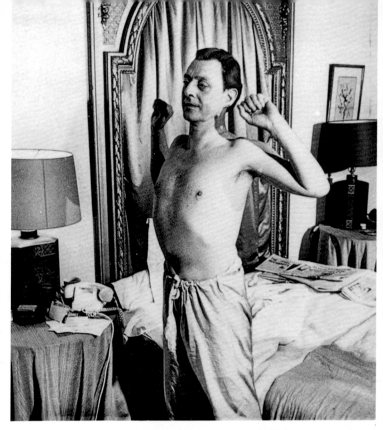

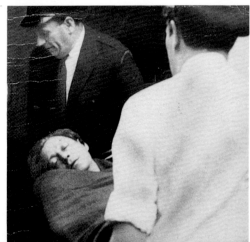

From dandy to disaster. Stephen Ward was dropped by all his society friends when the scandal broke. After Ivanov fled to the USSR and Profumo had been disgraced Ward killed himself.

Top: Yevgeny Ivanov at the wheel of a vintage Rolls-Royce owned by his friend Paul Richey.

Above: Ivanov knew no fear. Here he cheekily poses for a snap beside a British Fighter aircraft at Lossiemouth.

Left: 1955. Laying a wreath at the monument to Soviet soldiers who perished during the liberation of Norway. First left is Yevgeny Ivanov. Colonel Fursov, his GRU colleague and deputy military attaché, is in the foreground.

Top: 1957. On a Sunday outing in Holmenkollen, Norway.

Above: 1954. Captain-Lieutenant Yevgeny Ivanov assistant naval attaché in Norway - with his Pontiac on the Oslo-Bodø highway.

Left: 1992. Portrait of a retired spy. Captain Yevgeny Ivanov lived quietly in a small flat in Moscow.

Below: Yevgeny Ivanov with author Gennady Sokolov.

Englishman was leaving for a holiday, so I gave him a camera, which I had prudently brought along with me from London. He accepted it gratefully.

Next there was a pause. I had a great deal to do and quite forgot about my visit to Portsmouth. I did not call my new friend, since this could have meant trouble for him. I knew that if he wanted to, he would find me himself. I was right: we met in London, where the captain had come on business. He called me at home. We had a quiet evening in a restaurant, where he offered certain information as a form of payment for the camera which I had presented to him. It was a nice surprise. To be honest, I had not expected that the young captain would want to work for the Soviet secret services. We decided to meet again in two weeks' time.

"The first thing you should worry about is your safety," I told him. "You must never again call me at home or at the embassy. And no unplanned meetings."

I taught Captain Souls the secrets of conspiracy, on which his life – and mine, too – as well as the success of our future work, depended from then on. My keywords were harsh discipline, self-control and safety.

I had with me an address of a safe house in London, one of several which the *rezidentura* hired specially for meetings with its agents and which were used only for short periods. We agreed that the captain should come to that flat. We also discussed the usual and reserve times for our meetings, and the place we would use for the captain's possible contacts with our courier in Portsmouth.

I turned over the first material which I had received from the captain to the *rezident* later in the day. Specialists would determine its worth. I could not exclude the possibility of a fake or foul play from the British secret services. However, a cursory analysis suggested that the information was sound. It was data on the latest British mines, the sensitivity of new modifications to them, the reaction of acoustics to their presence, etc. Moscow Centre did not have this information before. Of course, it was not of vital strategic importance, merely concerning tactical and technical characteristics of new sea mines. But well begun is half done, and later the captain supplied us with more, and better information. We also had promising ideas about further work with him.

During our first secret meetings I asked the captain about his connections, acquaintances and their interests. It seemed that one such connection could lead our intelligence to the British research centre at the Portland naval base. For several years our agents at the base had been controlled by my old acquaintance from the Academy of the Soviet Army, Gordon Lonsdale, who had been hired by the KGB and sent for undercover work to Britain in the 1950s. A series of arrests by British intelligence in 1961, however, liquidated the KGB's network of agents in Dorset. The captain's contacts there could therefore help us launch a new GRU-controlled game.

"What specifically does your friend do there?" I asked the captain repeatedly.

"He once told me about the creation of an improved sonar for the latest classes of submarines."

My report on the meeting with the captain, which I presented to the *rezident*, outlined possible ways of developing this promising source.

"You must learn as much as you can about that friend of

Captain Souls's, his income, their relations with each other, his weaknesses, his likes and dislikes," General Pavlov instructed me.

Our further meetings with Captain Souls in London and the information we received via the courier, who regularly went to Portsmouth, brought more and more additional information about the potential possibilities of my protégé.

The *rezident* and Moscow Centre were not in a hurry to take the final decision. They were checking up on the new agent and his possibilities, analysing potential risks and the possible results of various modes of operation. I was not unduly pestered, yet time was pressing.

I think that by the end of 1962 Moscow Centre had exhaustive information on my contact and was prepared to offer me a detailed plan of action. Regrettably, I could not carry it out, because in January 1963 I was recalled from Britain as a result of the major scandal which was triggered off by the shots fired by Lucky Gordon in Wimpole Mews. Police investigations yielded ever more sensational results, and a political scandal of the first magnitude was brewing. I could not return to Britain.

During a subsequent meeting in Portsmouth, our courier relayed to Captain Souls the news of the return home of Captain Ivanov because of his mother's illness. I don't know anything else about the operation which was to involve Souls's friend in the research centre. In the GRU, such things are not discussed even among friends.

Paul Richey's Basement

Stephen Ward was not the only man in London who helped me. One of my contacts was made courtesy of Prince Philip. At the party I have already described, at the Royal Geographical Society in honour of Mikhail Mikhailovich Somov, His Royal Highness introduced me to Paul Richey: "I think you would be interested in getting to know this gentleman, who has long been trying to join our conversation." The Duke of Edinburgh pointed out an energetic man who, judging by his behaviour, was trying to find a suitable pretext for getting acquainted with us.

"Are you a traveller, too, Captain, like your famous compatriot Mr Somov?" this gentleman asked. "Allow me to introduce myself: Paul Richey, pilot and writer."

We had a glass of wine to celebrate our acquaintance and soon talked as if we had known each other for years.

"I must tell you that I don't travel much and not to such crazy distances as Mikhail Somov," I confessed to Mr Richey. "But I always set out on a journey with the inspiration of a traveller of long standing."

"Where have you been, if I may ask?"

"Well, to begin with, I have crisscrossed a sixth of the world's dry land, the Soviet Union. I have lived in the Baltic republics, in Siberia which is beyond the Urals, in the Far East, and in the south, by the Black Sea. I fought against the Japanese in the Pacific. I studied in Moscow, and I've worked in Scandinavia. Now I'm settling in London."

"I travelled a lot, too, Mr Ivanov," Paul Richey said. "I've been to Europe, Asia and America. I also fought the fascists, although not in the navy like you, but in the air force. So, we are allies, Captain, because we fought the same enemy for our common victory. Am I right?"

"Let's drink to our comradeship in arms," I suggested, touched by the veteran's sincerity.

"No, wine is not good enough for military men," the ex-pilot said, downing his glass of wine. "But they won't offer us anything else here. You know what we'll do, Captain? Come to my place when you have a minute to spare. I always have something good to drink for real men."

We became friends from the very first minutes of our acquaintance in the Royal Geographical Society. This sometimes happens in life: two people, who did not know each other one minute, can become lifelong friends the next. That is how it was with me and Stephen Ward and Sir Colin Coote, and that is how it was with Paul Richey. A few days afterwards, I went to his place, and it was not for the booze – although I took along two bottles of Russian vodka and several cans of Beluga caviar. The appeal of the former RAF pilot lay in his sincerity as a professional serviceman and the optimism of an experienced journalist who loved life and never succumbed to worries.

It turned out that he was also well-to-do, as evidenced by his two-storey house in London and his collection of vintage cars.

"This Rolls-Royce will soon turn fifty," Richey said, driving me in the star of his collection around London. "Do you want to give it a try, Captain?"

I could not turn down such a tempting invitation. I had loved cars since I was a boy; indeed I could drive not just cars but also five-ton lorries before I was not even seven years old, in the military garrisons where my father served before the war. My feet could hardly reach the pedals, yet I clung to the wheel with the passion of a born driver. That is why Richey's invitation to drive his car was an honour and joy for me.

It was not without apprehension, however, that I took the wheel of that beautiful car. Despite its age, it was in wonderful shape and easy to drive. We went via Piccadilly to Oxford Street and back.

"This car is just fantastic!" I could not help telling Richey.

"Yes, it was made to last," the owner of the Rolls-Royce agreed. "Imagine, Captain, that throughout all these years I have not had to change a single part. I just give it a once-over from time to time."

Paul Richey proved to be not only car-crazy but an expert on military hardware, with which he had worked during the Second World War in the RAF. He knew all the latest models of aircraft, too, both of Western and Soviet make. This is why I was interested in his opinions. Gradually, sitting by the fireplace in his cosy basement, we moved from one story to another, eventually ending by discussing the drawbacks of the British V-type bomber, or – which was much more interesting for me – the technical complications involved in the creation of the new US strategic bomber, the B-70.

"I don't think the plane will ever be built," I said. "So much money has been spent in the seven years to improve its first modification, and it's all been in vain."

"Not at all," Mr Richey insisted. "All the main problems have been resolved. The plane is as good as ready. They have to overcome only the slightest technical complications to make the fuel tanks air-tight and to find the best way of mounting the wing on the body, and that's it!"

The knowledge demonstrated by my host and his interest in military hardware and politics made me his frequent guest. Paul Richey's basement incorporated a bar, a billiards room and a small office with heaps of documents and papers lying on the table, which immediately attracted my attention, for among them were confidential papers on military matters of great interest to me.

I copied what I thought to be the most important ones. I remember one interesting document on the US programme of deploying tactical nuclear weapons in West Germany and other European NATO countries. It was the latest major military-political plan from the Pentagon, to be launched in 1961–2. Interestingly, it concerned more than just central Europe, because it provided for deploying tactical nuclear warheads also in Italy, Greece and Turkey. Under the plan, in three or four years, the number of tactical nuclear warheads in Europe was to double. My Minox camera copied that document while Paul Richey went to answer the door.

"Do you say that the document mentions both the yields of the warheads and their deployment sites at military bases and units?" General Pavlov asked me after reading my report on the visit to Mr Richey. "Interesting information, as you well know yourself. But please be careful while taking photographs, Zhenya. Don't risk your neck needlessly. We don't want parliamentary accounts and reports from the Ministry of Defence. We can get them from other sources.

"Last time you copied some trivial report from Chatham House, which might be useful to journalists, but not to Moscow Centre. Don't take risks like this again."

My chief was right, of course. In my haste I sometimes failed to make the correct choice.

"I would like to get some fresh information about Soviet aircraft and missiles," I told the general. "Of course, I mean declassified information. I'm afraid I have lagged behind in this sphere. I can't keep silent when Richey is discussing aircraft. It would be good if I could match his stories about NATO's air force."

"Have a word with Belousov," the general replied. "He will bring you up to date. Mr Richey must believe that you are sincere and well-informed. We must keep up his interest in meetings with you, but don't overdo it with questions about politics and weapons. There can be no more than one or two of them to a dozen others. You say that Mr Richey has lots of albums with erotic photographs and Thai love sculptures? Wonderful. Talk to him about sex."

I carried out General Pavlov's recommendations for about a year, until I left Britain. I was successful enough; Paul Richey proved to be an expert in that delicate sphere of human knowledge. I also found time to peruse more documents on the table of the former RAF fighter pilot and air correspondent.

Before my return to the USSR Paul gave me a book he had written. I still have it here, in Moscow. It's called

Fighter Pilot and it bears the following inscription on the flyleaf: "To Eugene, with whom we fought side by side, I in the Air Force, and he in the Navy."

I also still have a knife which Paul Richey gave to me. It has become dangerous in Moscow's streets at night. So, when I go out, I take Paul's knife with me, and this always reminds me of him.

MI5 Hand Out a Fighter

God forbid that you should ever have to deal with British counter-intelligence! They will turn your life upside down – and I know what I am talking about. Why didn't they catch me red-handed, then?

Indeed, this question is quite logical and obvious. I would answer it in this way: had it not been for the daily monitoring of British counter-intelligence, I would have accomplished much more. But I was bound hand and foot by MI5, who followed me everywhere, and it was difficult to shake them off.

Few GRU agents would question the following truth: Britain and the USA are the most difficult countries for our profession, with Britain having the indisputable lead in this sphere. Why? Because the high professional skills of its secret agents and the rigid control system of both the CIA and MI5 are complemented by old unsettled scores between the secret services of Britain and the Soviet Union, and the painful betrayals of their agents (the Big Five on the one hand, Penkovsky and Gordiyevsky on the other).

These betrayals remain open wounds in both the Soviet and British secret services to this day, preventing them from establishing gentlemanly relations, although since the August 1991 failed coup, Gordiyevsky's family has now been allowed to join him in the UK.

But back in the early 1960s, I had to overcome suspicion

every day in Britain. The head of counter-intelligence himself was concerned with my humble person at that time, so after I met him at a party in the Soviet Embassy, I tried to maintain business relations with him. By all accounts, he was interested in doing this, too, since it is always better for warring sides to keep each other in sight.

On one occasion I decided to make a trip to Lossiemouth in Scotland, where a major British air force base was situated. Demonstration flights of the carrier-based aircraft, the Buccaneer, then one of the best of its kind, were planned. Naturally enough, I wanted to see the plane in action in order to present my considerations about both it and the base to Moscow Centre. Aware of the delicate nature of my request, I filed my application to travel out of the thirty-five-mile limit ten days in advance. Two or three days before my intended departure, I had still received no answer.

I called my acquaintance, the counter-intelligence chief: "Excuse me, but what is the matter with my application?" I asked. "If you do not want to let me go, then say so outright. Why keep silent? But remember that you have your naval attaché in Moscow and he may want to travel around the Soviet Union, too. Reciprocity is very important in such matters."

Apparently accepting my reasoning, the chief eventually gave me permission for the trip. "No problem, Captain," he said. "You can fly to Edinburgh and from there to Lossiemouth. Good luck!"

I booked tickets to Edinburgh, but it was impossible to book tickets on to Lossiemouth. I had to phone the chief again: "There are no tickets to Lossiemouth, and it's your fault, because I had to wait so long. Now I shall have to cancel my trip. I can only sympathise with your attaché in Moscow. He might find himself without tickets at a crucial moment, too."

"Don't worry, Captain," he replied. "Go to Edinburgh and we shall think of something."

And so we flew to Edinburgh, my assistant, Pasha Shevelev, and I. In Edinburgh we were met at the plane: "Captain Ivanov? These planes have been ordered specially for you."

Pasha and I looked at the airstrip and could not believe our eyes: some fifty yards from us stood two Hunter fighters, both seating two, which meant that they were trainers.

I climbed into one Hunter, and Pasha into the other, and off we went to the Lossiemouth air force base. When we were about to land, I even asked the pilot to make another round of the base, so that I could have a better look at it. He complied.

We landed at Lossiemouth, thanked the pilots and went to the airstrip where the demonstration flights were to be held. The Buccaneers were in the air, and what wonderful birds they were! They flew at an altitude of fifty metres and turned in the air! Fantastic – or at least for that time it was. I watched the demonstration and simultaneously looked around me cautiously. And what did I see? On my left and right I saw two people who were not so much watching the demonstration as watching me, taking notice of what I did and with whom I talked, and if I had a camera. I recognised them as MI5.

To check the correctness of this diagnosis, I went to the

bar during a break in the demonstration and ordered a whisky and soda. I looked around, and again saw the same men. So, MI5 had provided a top-class service for me throughout my trip. I had to forget about my cameras.

I often went to Scotland, because there were so many facilities there that interested me, especially the Holy Loch base for US submarines armed with Polaris missiles. Moscow Centre requested information about it, and so I asked the chief of counter-intelligence for permission to visit the base.

He had a wonderful sense of humour: "You must just love fresh air, Captain. Are you going to tell me yet again how Scottish nature moves you?"

"You have very beautiful spots indeed there," I replied.

Despite my clear interest in military facilities, I hardly ever had a trip application turned down. But I had to put up with the constant presence of MI5, assigned to me by the aforementioned chief. As a result, my opportunities for espionage were considerably limited. It was like that at Holy Loch. The only thing I could clearly see for myself was the type of base it was. I had expected to see armoured pens for submarines, such as they had in Norway, but I did not see anything of the kind at Holy Loch.

At that time space and aerial reconnaissance was not so well developed as it is today. That is why we had to make these "on-site" inspections to gain a general opinion of military facilities. That is why I travelled a lot around Britain. MI5 men followed me everywhere. Sometimes the teams changed, but they never left me alone for a minute, and were not ashamed to tail me openly. I behaved quite insolently sometimes. For example, I used to give them a twenty-four-hour race from London to Edinburgh and back. Outside Edinburgh there was a repair base for Polaris-armed submarines, which is why I wanted to visit the area so much. I would take along sandwiches and drive non-stop. I did not even stop for a cup of coffee, which meant that my followers could not have a rest or a snack, either. They were put out by that.

Once, when I stopped at a filling station, they asked me: "When are you going to lunch, sir?"

"I'm not hungry," I replied curtly.

However, I did not keep them hungry for long. I stopped at a bar to have a pint of beer, while they had something to eat at a nearby table.

There were also more complicated situations. MI5 did not limit its activities to observation. They tapped my telephone – an understandable precaution. We listened to their conversations, too, over the radio and telephone. My wife Maya worked in the radio intercept group at the embassy, so in the afternoons I was usually told about how the MI5 men tailed me and with what results. As soon as I left Kensington Palace Gardens, our intercept group tuned in to the radio of the MI5 agents, who reported to each other, for example: "Ivanov is heading towards Oxford Street." It was a routine cat-and-mouse game, but it had its moments of suspense.

One of my duties in Britain was acting as chairman of a co-operative, which ran a small shop for embassy staff selling goods at low prices. As chairman of that co-operative I maintained relations with a businessman who sold batches of goods for the shop. Once that man said to me: "Eugene, we have worked wonderfully together. I want to give you a present."

It was a walkie-talkie.

"Take it," he said. "It's from the heart."

Indeed, it was a fantastic present, and very costly at that time. Who would turn it down? MI5's plan was clearly to encourage me to use it, which would have greatly simplified their work. I turned it down, of course, and changed the company that supplied goods to the embassy shop. I found an agency that appeared to be less interested in collaboration with the British secret services.

MI5 made one more attempt to gain control over me. Once I was invited to a party, but when I arrived, there was nobody but the host in the apartment. He showed me around, eventually leading me to a bedroom door with a peephole in it. "Soon a wonderful spectacle will begin here. Would you care to watch it?"

I did not say a word, just walked out, banging the door behind me. MI5 missed me that time. They must have thought me a fool who would not recognise a compromising situation. MI5 expected me to watch through the peephole as somebody made love, but I was an ace at collecting compromising materials myself, and so easily avoided cheap bait.

A Flirtation with Mariella Novotny

One day I was getting ready for a meeting with Lord Arran and Sir Godfrey Nicholson. Political tension was at its highest that day: 27 October 1962 was the worst day of the Cuban crisis. Steve was trying to help me set in motion London's mediatory mechanism in the Kremlin–White House conflict that threatened to develop into a world war.

Ward, however, who up till then had done everything in his power to help me get in contact with the political leadership of Britain, just as he had during the Berlin crisis, suddenly lost all interest in our efforts. "It's no use, Eugene, and besides, nobody needs it," he told me that day. "What mediation? Who needs it? Khrushchev? Kennedy? They are fighting each other like a cobra and a mongoose! I wouldn't try to pull them apart, not me."

Actually, Steve was right. He didn't believe that London's mediation could settle the Cuban crisis. I didn't either. But, actually, I was less interested than he was in bringing about a positive result for our mission.

How could I tell Steve that such a complicated game was being played with the sole purpose of undermining the resolve of the US President in his apparent determination to bring confrontation with Moscow to a victorious, if bloody, end? London's peace-making mediation was designed to distract and disarm Washington. The consent of the British to act as mediators would have given the

Kremlin the possibility of driving a wedge into London–Washington unity as NATO allies.

"Enough about the Cuban crisis," Steve suddenly said. "Tell me, did you manage to help Mariella Novotny?

That question reminded me of an affair which I had not finished. But I was not to blame.

It began in the summer of 1961. At a bridge party, Ward told me about a girlfriend of his, Mariella Novotny, who had recently come from the USA. Her husband, a certain Horace Hod Dibben, was an old friend of Stephen's. Hod and Mariella were married shortly before I came to London. Mariella was not yet twenty, while Hod was twice her age. In short, it was a typical marriage of convenience.

I would have forgotten about this girl, had it not been for an article in the *News of the World*, with Mariella as the star of a scandal. It turned out that back in New York Mariella had been a lover of the US President and of his brother, and she confessed this to the newspaper, although without providing much detail or any proof. This is probably why the item caused little uproar either in Britain or across the ocean: everybody thought that it was just another fabrication. I noticed the item only because I remembered what Stephen Ward had told me about Mariella.

She was born and grew up in Sheffield, without a father. Just like Christine Keeler and Mandy Rice-Davies, she started working in a London striptease cabaret, earning her living with her good figure. There was nothing unusual about her fate, had it not been for one thing: Mariella's father was the brother of the Czechoslovak President, Antonin Novotny. He had emigrated from Czechoslovakia and even served in the RAF during the war.

"You must help Mariella get a visa to her father's homeland," Ward once told me. "I know that you could do it, if you wanted."

I tried to convince Steve that the Czechs would not listen to me, but on the sly I thought about what would suit me better.

"Do you want to meet her?" Ward asked me one day.

I again voiced my doubts concerning the possibility of helping Mariella Novotny, but I agreed to meet her. Steve brought her to Spring Cottage for dinner. He left us alone to talk. Mariella was a charming blonde who, despite being a married woman, had no inhibitions in the company of strange men. She attacked me with all her charms. I did my best to resist her.

"Mr Ivanov," she whispered, her eyes downcast. "You will not refuse my little request. I have heard so many commendable things about you. Please, help me. I want so much to visit Prague, but I cannot get a visa."

All the while, Mariella's hands were playing a sort of kittenish game on my military jacket, although she was tring to get her claws into me. It resembled a scene from a vulgar novel.

"Madame," I replied with no less sugar in my voice, "if somebody advised you to seduce me in return for a visa to Prague, it was a silly joke. I'm afraid I cannot help you."

"I never do anything that I don't want to do, Mr Ivanov," she answered slyly. "It was that fool Christine who advised me to seduce you. She, for one, is convinced that you can do anything. And Steve assured me of the same."

"Alas, Madame, I cannot help you." I finished our conversation abruptly, bowed and tried to leave the room.

"You are a nice person, Mr Ivanov," I heard her say, "but why are you in such a hurry to finish our conversation? Please, give me another minute. I want to tell you something."

"What is it, Madame? Shall we continue our conversation in the garden?"

We went out into the garden and settled on a bench under a large, sprawling elm.

"Well, what did you want to tell me, Mariella – if you will permit me?"

"Of course, Eugene," she agreed immediately. "Why be unnecessarily formal?" She was no longer coquettish or flirty. "Please, help me, Captain, and I shall tell you something that you don't know but would be very glad to learn."

"Don't talk in riddles, Mariella," I replied, sensing that our conversation was leading nowhere.

"I shall not tell you more now," she said. "Let's return to the cottage. It is not convenient to be late for dinner here."

What information was Mariella dangling before my nose? I couldn't help thinking about it. Besides, I sensed that her proposal and even her request for a visa were just a pretext, and not a very good one at that. Her behaviour was not at all convincing.

Yet upon my return to London I wrote a report and handed it to the *rezident*. General Pavlov read it and said: "Yevgeny Mikhailovich, we shall ask Moscow Centre about Mariella Novotny, of course. In the meantime, I shall discuss the problem with our colleagues from the Czechoslovak Embassy. You have too much to do without this lady now."

Neither Mariella nor Steve returned to the subject of the visa after that meeting in Cliveden. Instructed by my chief to stay away, I soon forgot about my conversation with the charming blonde feigning love for me in Spring Cottage.

More than a year passed, and suddenly Steve had now reminded me about Mariella Novotny at the height of the Cuban crisis. Why? I was confused. Maybe Mariella had phoned him or called on him in Cliveden?

After I reported to the general about my meeting with Lord Arran (London's mediation in the Cuban crisis being my basic task in the autumn of 1962), I asked: "Anatoly Georgiyevich, do you remember my request concerning Mariella Novotny?"

"You've chosen the wrong moment for this, Zhenya. Don't you see what's going on? It smells of war. Better stick to Cuban affairs."

"Don't I do my work properly?" I was offended.

The general noticed my irritation and tried to calm me down. "Zhenya, do you think that I would not have informed you if Mariella Novotny's proposal had been accepted by Moscow Centre?"

"So, it was turned down?"

"Not quite."

"What do you mean 'not quite'?"

"It means what I said. You are a military man, Zhenya, and should understand. Besides, I cannot tell you everything. I can only add that somebody is already working with your Mariella Novotny. And don't meddle."

I did not ask any more questions. Back in Moscow, after I retired, I learned about the tragic death of Mariella.

Who knows, maybe it was that affair in which the general warned me not to meddle that cost Mariella her life twenty years later? I can't tell because I don't have the necessary information. I only know that before her death Mariella Novotny was going to make public some important information. But she was found dead of an overdose before she could do so.

The Cuban Crisis and the
Lost Wager

Just after midnight of 28 October 1962 I was speeding along an empty road to London, angry as hell and feeling totally humiliated. I blew off at my six-cylinder Humber Super Snipe by pressing the accelerator into the floor. Every fifteen minutes the radio reported that the Cuba-bound Soviet ships had turned back, while Khrushchev made a statement agreeing to remove Soviet missiles from the island. I turned the radio off in disgust.

"Our ships have always gone – and will always go – wherever they want," I had told Lord Astor several hours before, at a party in Cliveden. "I tell you that the Soviet ships will not change their course. Anybody want a bet?"

That evening the cream of London society had gathered in Cliveden: Lord Astor, Lord Arran and Lord Packenham, as well as Sir Godfrey Nicholson. We had dinner with the TV on, impatiently waiting for the evening news. The situation around Cuba was red-hot, extremely tense. US air defence facilities on the eastern coast were put on combat duty. Strategic bombers armed with thermonuclear bombs were in the air around the clock. A US naval armada of 200 ships and nearly 100,000 Marines was encircling Cuba. The armed forces of the Soviet Union and other Warsaw Pact countries were on red alert.

Shortly before, I had toured the main US and British air force bases, using the car of my Bulgarian colleague,

Nikolai Ivanovich Krivlev. I had seen pilots mindlessly drinking beer and flirting with local girls. I did not detect any alarming signals, and duly reported this to Moscow Centre. This tranquil situation in Britain, however, contrasted sharply with what was happening to worsening Soviet–US relations.

Early in the week I was summoned by my chief, alarmed by recent developments. He ordered me to establish unofficial contacts with the British political leadership with the aim of settling the Cuban crisis. "Nothing will come of London's mediation, of course," General Pavlov told me. "The British will never undertake actions on the sly from the Americans, even with the noblest peace-making aims."

"Why bother, then?"

"Don't ask idiotic questions, Zhenya," was the reply which did not explain anything. "Just do what you are told."

Khrushchev's Caribbean adventure did not please anybody in the USSR. The military complained that the country's leadership had not listened to their advice. The GRU and the General Staff warned Khrushchev that it would be naïve to think that the transfer of bulky missile systems to Cuba would remain undetected. Diplomats were outraged that Khrushchev's agreement with Castro on the delivery of missiles to Cuba was kept secret from both friend and foe. It can be imagined how difficult it was for them to avoid answering direct questions about the presence of Soviet missiles on Cuba, when photographs of them had been shown at the Security Council by Adlai Stevenson, the US Ambassador to the UN.

Party apparatchiks did not like the dictatorial actions of

Khrushchev, who had not even informed them about his dubious and highly risky plans. They were worried by the prospects of the growing split with Mao and by the militarisation of Germany. In these conditions, confrontation with the US was untimely at best, and downright dangerous at worst. Eventually, the Cuban crisis cost Khrushchev his Kremlin throne. Eighteen months later, Leonid Brezhnev easily knocked together a group of conspirators who helped him replace the conceited Khrushchev.

However, far from everybody was dissatisfied with his adventurist policy. Some empty heads were turned by it – mine included. Khrushchev's phrase, "frighten the hedgehog with the bare arse", was my favourite. I was a daredevil then, just like Khrushchev. The most important thing was impudence and self-confidence, I thought. This would teach the Americans not to encircle us with their bases! Deploying missiles right in their underbelly meant that no early-warning system would save them from a missile attack, because the missiles' flight time would be no more than three or four minutes. It would force them to remove their missiles from Turkey!

That confrontational ideology poisoned my brains so thoroughly that it even affected my work. Stephen Ward, who had to listen to my frequent lectures on the correctness of the Kremlin's foreign policy, came to believe in the possibility of nuclear war in that October 1962. But this suited me well, because I then did not have to convince Ward of the importance of his co-operation in securing London's conciliatory mediation in the Cuban crisis. In five days of one crucial week, he organised my meetings with

Lord Astor, Lord Arran and Sir Godfrey Nicholson.

"Prime Minister Harold Macmillan could make a major step towards peace if he suggested a Soviet–American summit with the aim of settling the Cuban crisis," I assured them. "Khrushchev will be prepared to accept this proposition. Peace is endangered, and you can save it."

I was politely promised that the Prime Minister would be informed of my proposition, but my initiative was never accepted, and I was not the only one who was turned down. The Soviet Foreign Ministry instructed its London-based diplomats to act in similar fashion. Vitaly Loginov, then *chargé d'affaires* in the Soviet Embassy in London, twice tried to induce Sir Alec Douglas-Home to undertake the conciliatory mission, to no avail, as General Pavlov had predicted. The British did not want to make any *démarches* without Washington's consent. And, in any case, the White House was carrying on a difficult but persistent dialogue with the Kremlin.

The official dialogue went through the Soviet Ambassador in Washington, Anatoly Dobrynin, while an unofficial one was conducted by Georgy Bolshakov, a KGB man and editor of the Novosti magazine *Soviet Life*. He established contacts with the brother of the US President, Robert, and set up the aforementioned hot line between Nikita Khrushchev and John Kennedy. I was told about the operation of that hot line when I returned to Moscow. I also learned from my friends in the General Staff that we had actually been on the brink of launching hostilities, but that a fragile peace had been established on the evening of 26 October, when President Kennedy received Premier Khrushchev's agreement to withdraw all missiles from the island in return for US guarantees not to interfere in the internal affairs of Cuba.

On the morning of 27 October a Soviet surface-to-air missile shot down a US U-2 reconnaissance plane over Cuba. Its pilot became the first victim of the blockade. The Pentagon was outraged. The generals demanded that the President authorise a retaliatory attack against the Communists. John Kennedy did his best to keep the generals at bay. The same day, the US President said over the hot line established by Georgy Bolshakov that he was being pressurised so heavily that it could lead to war. Having received this information from Washington, Khrushchev ordered the Soviet ships to return home in the late hours of 27 October. The missiles were to be withdrawn, too. The clock of war was turned back and started counting the first minutes of peace.

I was black with fury. I felt humiliated and wounded. How could I have been so taken in by my leader! How could Khrushchev have given in to the Americans! He was frightened! He had ordered our boys to withdraw! These bitter thoughts were seething in my brain. I cursed the Macmillan government, which had backed Washington and thus won, too. We had been defeated by both the Americans and the British. The humiliation was difficult to stand.

I returned from Cliveden to London in the early hours of 28 October and went straight to the embassy. The military section was abuzz. Everybody was working through the night. General Pavlov told me: "Go home and have a rest, Zhenya. I don't want your reports today. You know how it is."

I went home, downed a glass of vodka in order to damp down my anger and humiliation, and went to sleep.

It should be said that October 1962 came to symbolise damnation not only for me but for many Soviet officers. It graphically showed our weakness in the face of US might. The Cuban crisis precipitated the large-scale build-up of Soviet nuclear forces. The military-industrial complex, with its new leader Leonid Brezhnev, aimed at strategic parity with the US. Khrushchev's optimistic plans for catching up and overtaking America in the production of meat, milk and butter were put on ice by Brezhnev. The arms race was given a powerful boost.

But even after we had, at long last, attained military strategic parity with the US, the ambitious Soviet Party apparatus set themselves a higher goal: attaining military superiority over the USA. As a result, by the late 1980s, the USSR was in the throes of the severest economic crisis, which led to the collapse of the communist regimes in Europe and, eventually, in the USSR itself.

Christmas in the Country

The turbulent year of 1962 was drawing to its end. It was my third Christmas in Britain – and the last, although I did not know it then, for within a month I would be back in snowy Moscow, a city maimed by Khrushchev's horrible five-storey blocks.

The 650 white lamps on the giant fir tree in Trafalgar Square were ablaze again. That fir tree was a guest there, just like the thousands of tourists who came to London to celebrate Christmas. Ever since the war, giant fir trees have been delivered to London from Oslo, a sign of the Norwegians' gratitude for British assistance in the struggle against fascism. Radio was broadcasting Christmas carols. Children with money boxes were collecting donations, competing against energetic nuns doing the same. But the best "donations" were collected by the owners of the London shops which sold Christmas gifts.

I had a Christmas gift, too: old Russian vodka in a crystal carafe, which I had bought well in advance in Moscow's Yeliseyev shop. This gift was destined for the Earl of Dudley, who had invited Stephen Ward and myself to his country villa for Christmas. Steve was moody in those days. Even the merry celebration of his fiftieth birthday in late October had not cheered him up or made him more self-confident. Ten days before Christmas, Lucky Gordon, who never tired of besieging Christine Keeler, fired the ill-fated shots in

Wimpole Mews. The yellow press immediately plunged its teeth into the scandal. The police were investigating it, too. This did not bode well, either for Ward or for myself. We were both aware of this, which explained our gloomy disposition.

There was nobody in the earl's mansion apart from a woman called Anne-Marie, who had come over from Paris for Christmas. Like most French women, she spoke English with a noticeable but pleasant accent.

"Well, and where is the Earl of Dudley?" we asked her after we had introduced ourselves.

"I think he is having a ride," the charming guest from France replied.

The earl soon appeared, merry and hot after a jolly ride on a crisp December day. Dressed for a white-tie reception, Steve and I looked like outsiders in the company of our host and Anne-Marie. The latter was dressed in a woollen skirt and a warm jumper, while he sported a dirty shirt and well-worn trousers. It was hard to believe in the sanctity of British traditions and etiquette after witnessing this. However, Lord Dudley soon changed his shirt when the other guests were due. One of them was Sir Godfrey Nicholson, my recent partner in London's failed Moscow–Washington mediation.

"Anything new in Parliament?" I asked him.

"Anything new in the Kremlin?" he parried.

Those were the only two phrases we exchanged that Christmas night. Sir Godfrey apparently wanted to talk with Steve, eager for news about Christine Keeler's behaviour in the past few days; he did not leave Steve for a minute, pestering him in the hall, at the table, and during the game of bridge. I think that they even left together for London the next day. My conversation partners were the earl, Anne-Marie and Sir Edward Tomkins. The latter spoke Russian rather well: he had learned it during the Second World War, when he had been on the staff of the British Embassy in Moscow. Sir Edward and Lord Dudley joined forces against me in our verbal battle over political matters, while the charming Anne-Marie took my side. I think she was my Christmas present from my host and my relations with her grew warmer with lightning speed. She buttressed my every argument – as in the good old days of the Entente.

The Christmas table was exceedingly rich, with vintage French cognacs, old Scotch whisky, and good Spanish wines – and my carafe with Yubileinaya vodka from Yeliseyev. The traditional Russian spirit was the first to be tried and finished. Understandably, it was a smashing success with ladies and gentlemen alike.

Anne-Marie noted with regret that she had had only one tot. "Fantastic," she twittered ecstatically, reminding me of Valerie Hobson for some strange reason.

Pride of place on the table was occupied by the traditional Christmas turkey, served on a silver tray. It looked tender and pink, but the loud admiration of the guests was cut short by a remark from Steve Ward: "Your Grace, everybody knows that you are not just an aristocrat but a businessman. In the latter capacity you own a farm that grows turkeys. In this connection I have only one question: Is this a turkey from your farm?"

The guests fell silent, because far from all of them understood the secret meaning of this question.

"Don't bother, Steve," Sir Godfrey Nicholson replied.

"Everybody knows that Lord Dudley breeds turkeys only for sale. That is why they are fed growth hormones."

"Ladies and gentlemen, this turkey was raised on natural feed," the host assured us. "Do you think that I would dare treat you – and myself – to a turkey that grew up on my farm? God forbid!"

The guests happily returned to their meal. The dinner ended with the traditional game of bridge, with Anne-Marie my admiring fan, probably accounting for my winning against the earl and Sir Edward, with whom we talked after the game long into the night. In the small hours of the morning the guests went to their bedrooms. I have never seen a more luxurious room in my life, before or since.

The morning was sparkling white: it was a white Christmas. The landscape around the mansion reminded me of Russia.

After a light breakfast the host went for a ride, as was his habit, while his guests worried about getting back to London in all that snow. Some of them decided to take their host at his word and stay for another day or two, but I had to return to London. The Earl of Dudley's servants helped me to get my car out of the garage.

"Eugene, will you take me along?" Anne-Marie asked.

Of course I did, gladly. The snowed-over roads presented a miserable picture. Lots of cars were standing idle at the kerb because many Englishmen, unaccustomed to snow, preferred to freeze rather than drive. But for me, snow and ice were old acquaintances, both from Russia and Norway. I felt wonderful, enjoying the snow, the beautiful woman at my side, and the Christmas morning.

Anne-Marie babbled about Paris and even recited some

French verses. She also tried learning some Russian words. "Eugene, how do you say 'dear' in Russian?" she asked, studiously repeating the difficult Russian word. "And 'love'?"

We arrived in London in double-quick time. As far as I could see, nobody had followed us. The men from British counter-intelligence must have taken the day off to enjoy the company of their families around Christmas tables. I stopped at Anne-Marie's hotel in central London.

"Would you care for a cup of coffee?" she asked me, the invitation in her tone unmistakable.

We went to her room, and had not only coffee but also something stronger than that. The eyes of my new acquaintance lit up with devilish sparkles.

A week later a postcard from Paris arrived at the Soviet Embassy.

"I went to a performance of the Russian ballet yesterday," Anne-Marie wrote. "It is the best in the world. I have never seen anything like it." There was a P.S.: "The postcard shows the house where I live. Drop by, when you are in Paris." There was an X-mark on the second building to the left of the Arc de Triomphe.

Today, many years later, I still cannot say whether it was an innocent rendezvous or a trap. It does not matter, however, because there was no time left either for an MI5 trap or for another meeting with Anne-Marie. My days in the West were numbered.

Kim Philby's Dispatch

My last month in London was filled with unpleasant weather. At first the capital was shrouded in a thick fog, resulting in the inevitable car crashes that claimed about two hundred lives. Cars stood at the kerb like so many tons of scrap metal. Next followed heavy snow and severe – for Britain – frosts, which lasted about three weeks in January. Specialists say that the weather was the worst in 150 years. Temperatures dropped to minus five Centigrade, causing genuine chaos. Railway points froze stiff. Roads were covered with deep snow, with no machinery available to clean it away. Even the radar station in Fylingdales, designed to detect Soviet missiles four minutes before their arrival in Britain, was rendered inoperative. Sappers were specially flown in by helicopter to free it from snow.

Despite bad weather, I had work to do – at least I thought so when planning my operations for 1963. But I was in for a nasty surprise. My plans were cut short by a shrill telephone ring. "Come to my office. At the double." I heard the dry and nervous voice of Anatoly Georgiyevich.

I felt foreboding in the pit of my stomach.

"I know you will be disappointed, Zhenya," General Pavlov told me, "but I have received an order recalling you to Moscow immediately."

"What a nice Christmas surprise from Moscow Centre!" I tried to joke, although it was not a joking matter at all.

"It is not a nice surprise for me either," the chief replied. "I wanted you to help me here. Besides, we had planned so many joint operations."

"What has happened then?" I asked impatiently. "Is it my fault?"

"God forbid, Zhenya! Not at all. Moscow Centre believes that you would do better to return home. According to their information, a major political scandal is brewing here, involving Christine Keeler, Profumo and yourself. In short, start packing."

"Anatoly Georgiyevich, nothing ventured nothing gained, as they say here." I attempted to overrule the decision of Moscow Centre. "We are going to have a scandal, so what? I can make scandal, too, and you know it better than anyone."

"No, Zhenya, an order is an order. Start packing," the general repeated, this time in a commanding voice.

"Yes, Comrade General," I replied curtly, understanding that it was absolutely useless to argue.

I returned to my office and ordered my aide to prepare all the materials needed for the handing-over ceremony. He mumbled some condolences, but I did not listen to him. My head was filled with different kinds of thoughts. "Now wait a minute, Yevgeny Mikhailovich," I told myself, "this is a crash, pure and simple. If a scandal breaks out, your connections with Ward, Keeler, Profumo and Astor will eventually be revealed. You will be put in the limelight and revealed for what you are. This means a fat cross on all your future trips abroad."

I called Ward and we arranged a meeting. Several hours later, we were silently walking in snowed-over Hyde Park.

Neither could find suitable words for the occasion. I could not tell Steve the true reason for my recall. I lied to him, telling him that my mother was seriously ill. I think he understood that my mother had nothing to do with it, that I was leaving because of the scandal; he had sensed the dangers of this scandal already in the autumn, but he could do nothing to stop it. Before parting, we kissed each other three times, Russian style.

"Eugene, you are my friend. You know this. And you will remain my friend for ever. Good luck to you," Ward told me.

"It's very difficult to part with you, Steve. Please, take care of yourself," I replied and turned away, trying to hide my nervousness.

The last few days before my departure flew by. The farewell ceremony was sponsored by the London association of naval attachés. Their farewell presents – a silver cigarette-holder and tray – still stand on my working table in Moscow. On the tray are inscribed the names of all the twenty-eight members of the association. The men from the military section of the Soviet Embassy gave me a farewell dinner. I bade goodbye to Sir Colin Coote and Paul Richey, Sir Godfrey Nicholson and Lord Astor, Lord Ednam... I did not manage to say goodbye to many more people.

Farewell ceremonies and lunches followed one another. I listened to many sympathetic words from my acquaintances on account of my mother's illness. They wished me health and good luck. Yet I could not get used to the idea of losing. I had hardly started working, I had found my way to influential people and acquired access to fantastic sources of information. I had breathtaking plans for the future.

I understood the decision of Moscow Centre, but I could not accept it.

Only my wife was happy to return to Moscow. She rushed about London, buying household appliances difficult to come by in Moscow: a dishwasher, a fridge, a radio set, a stove, and what not. They were ordered from different companies, delivered, packed and sent to Moscow on a freighter. I booked Aeroflot tickets for 29 January by telephone, knowing that it was tapped. After that I went to the railway terminal by underground – making sure that nobody followed me – and bought two tickets to Chatham. The air tickets had been ordered as a kind of a diversion, and my caution was later vindicated: as my colleagues told me, on the day of my departure, about twenty reporters, armed with cameras and tape-recorders, gathered at Heathrow. They waited for me in vain. MI5 must have alerted them. But I deceived them; I left by train. In Chatham I took a Dutch ferry, which on the night of 29 January 1963 left for the Hook of Holland.

The ferry was leaving the foggy British coast behind. The lights of Chatham were becoming dimmer against the dark blue background. I stood at the stern, looking at the receding coast. The cold wind was tearing at my overcoat. That's it, I thought. *Finita la commedia*. I shall never return to this country.

Maya came up to me silently. "How good!" she said happily. "Yes, Zhenya? In two days we shall be home."

But I was not happy at all. I went to the bar and ordered three double brandies.

Moscow met us with the rush of the railway terminal and biting frost, temperature about twenty-five degrees below zero Centigrade. I was happy, yet at the same time sad, to be back home again. I felt that I had never really parted from my homeland. It had always lived inside me, and now it was also all around me.

A new life, strong and overpowering, snatched us up on to its carousel, without giving us a chance to look around. I was summoned to the directorate to make my report. Soon, too soon, it seemed to me that I had never been to Britain at all. I might have dreamed all those people whom I had met on those far-away islands.

Some time later General Pavlov returned to Moscow, too, promoted to deputy chief of the GRU. One day, he summoned me to his office, asked about my wife's health and my work; he spoke about our work in Britain, and a little about himself. Then he said: "You know who reported to Moscow about the impending Profumo scandal?"

"Who?" Not that I was particularly interested.

"Kim Philby. When the KGB received this information from him, they decided to make a fine gesture and relayed it to the leadership of the General Staff and the GRU. Our superiors were advised to save Ivanov before it was too late. That's why you were recalled."

"I see now. And who is this Kim Philby?"

"An interesting person, Zhenya. Few people know him, but judging by what they tell me, he is a living legend. You can meet him, if you want."

But honestly, I did not want to meet the person who had advised my superiors to recall me from Britain.

PART TWO

The Way to the Top

My Nomadic Childhood

Now that the story of my life in Britain has been told, it is time to explain where I come from and why I chose to become a professional spy.

I was born on 11 January 1926 in the old Russian town of Pskov. My mother, Maria Leonidovna Kaurova, came from the old ducal family of Golenishchev-Kutuzov, which included the famous Field Marshal Mikhail Illarionovich Kutuzov, whom Emperor Alexander I placed at the head of the Russian army in the 1812 war against Napoleon, and which eventually defeated the invader.

My mother was born in 1900, which means that she was one of the nobility for a short time. The Bolshevik 1917 October Revolution deprived her of this rank, leaving her, young and inexperienced, without parents or means of subsistence. Unlike her, my father was a simple peasant lad from Mytishchi, a small village outside Moscow. Mikhail Parmenovich Ivanov was a recruit in the First World War, joined the Red Army after the October Revolution and was eventually given a command.

His unit was billeted in Pskov, where he met my mother. An orphan, she worked at the local tobacco factory, trying to earn a living for herself and her younger sister Anna. It was at that factory that she learned to smoke, and she was unable to break this habit till her dying day. My father never smoked or drank.

Although my parents came from widely different sections of society, they made a peaceful and happy couple. I never saw them quarrel, or heard Father say a rude word to Mother. They never banged doors or shouted, although they had quite a few problems.

My childhood was composed of endless roaming around the country, from Pskov to Vitebsk, from Bely to Grodno, from Kaunas to Riga. We changed cities and flats, I changed schools and friends, yet everywhere my favourite occupation was playing at war or telling other boys about the films I had seen.

My favourite hero was the Baltic seaman Andrey Balashov, from the film *We are from Kronstadt*. I would inevitably end my story about it by quoting the following words from the film: "Well, who else will rise for Soviet power?!" It was not just a phrase for me; I was prepared to rise with the Red Baltic seaman Balashov against anyone who dared to fight Soviet government. I was a child, of course, but a dedicated one, like the millions of adults who believed in Stalin despite the endless night-time arrests of "enemies of the people". We all – including myself – lived as if in a dream at that time.

Since my father was a military man and we often moved, I learned to speak several languages. When we lived in Vitebsk and Grodno, for example, I learned to speak Byelorussian. In Kaunas and Riga I picked up Lithuanian and Latvian, respectively. In addition, I studied German at school. This talent for languages later helped me a great deal, both in Norway, where I went without knowing any Norwegian, and in Britain, where I had to pick up colloquial English because I had not had any practice at speaking the language before.

My life in military settlements taught me to love machinery. When I was still a small boy, I learned to drive my father's Emka car and the lorry ZiS-5, which brought provisions for the mess. I also learned to operate a radio station. I could shoot a gun or a carbine, throw anti-tank grenades and use a gas mask as efficiently as the ordinary soldiers.

In those days radio quite often broadcast live from the trials in the Supreme Court in Moscow. I listened to the speeches of Procurator General Vyshinsky and was as eager as he was to fight the enemies of the people. I did not understand what was going on around me; I was taught to think that groups of murderers and spies were all around us and that we had to fight them like mad dogs. This was the subject of the radio broadcasts and of many meetings at school.

No wonder my parents were gloomy. And when Uborevich, commander of the Byelorussian military district and my father's old friend, shot himself without waiting to be shot after the verdict of the court in 1937, an oppressive silence filled our flat. My parents seemed to be waiting for something terrible and unavoidable to happen.

Father hardly spoke at all. Mother chain-smoked and froze every time a car passed by our house. Father was saved from arrest by his transfer to the Baltics. Mother calmed down a little only after Father was promoted to major in Riga. Promotion meant that he would not be arrested, she thought. Yet arrests continued in the Baltics, too.

"What's going on?! Imagine, they have taken Blukher!"

Father told Mother. "They claim he is a German spy! Masha, please, be very careful. And don't go to that Razumovskaya, because her husband is NKVD. They can tell such dirty things about us that we would never exculpate ourselves."

Thank God, that terrible storm blew over without touching us, although my mother's noble rank could have cost Major Ivanov dearly. That fact alone was enough to condemn him by association with a counter-revolutionary underground group or with émigré White Guards. But we were lucky, and escaped tragedy.

In 1938 my brother Vitya was born. Mother did not want a second child, because it was a troubled time, but abortions were prohibited by a decree from Stalin, which Mother cursed: "Hang that decree! I simply refuse to have this child!"

"Shush, you silly woman," Father entreated her. "Don't shout so loudly, the whole settlement will hear. I shall be fired and shot!"

And so she gave birth to my brother Vitya, and I looked after him and taught him a boy's tricks when he grew a little. I liked helping Mother. Besides, Vitya was a nice boy, and clever. Regrettably, he died of scarlet fever in the difficult year of 1942. Father was in the hospital then, too, convalescing from a heavy wound he had received during the battle of Moscow. Nearly every Soviet family was scarred by the war. We were no exception.

On 22 June 1941, I lived near Riga. Father was serving in the headquarters of the Baltic Military District, while Mother, Vitya and I lived in a *dacha* in Bulduri, a resort outside Riga. It was a hot day and I took my brother for a swim in the sea. We were returning home, walking between the rows of *dachas*, when we heard Molotov saying over the radio that Hitler had treacherously attacked the Soviet Union. The word "war" caught my breath; I thought: "At long last I shall show those fascists!" We ran from *dacha* to *dacha*, shouting "War!" like crazy.

Father soon came back from the city: "Pack quickly," he told us. "We are going to Riga."

When we were safely in the car, he told us, seriously and confidently: "Hitler has had enough of Europe. He has decided to test us. But we'll soon show him."

Like many other people, Father was convinced that the war would not last long, that the Red Army would defeat the enemy in two or three months at the most. In the meantime, he ordered us to go and stay with Auntie Anna, Mother's sister, who lived in Sverdlovsk. On 23 June we joined a trainload of other evacuees. Father remained behind, to fight the enemy.

I remember that shortly before our departure I heard shots at the bridge over the Daugava, fired by Aisergs, members of the Latvian fascist organisation. I grabbed Father's handgun, which he kept at home, and ran to the bridge. Suddenly somebody snatched me by the collar: "Are you crazy, Zhenka?!"

It was Father. He had come to fetch us because the Germans were already bombing the port. The city was filled with the whining of air alarm sirens.

"Into the shelter, immediately," Mother ordered.

"No, everybody remain here," Father retorted. "Should the bomb hit the neighbouring room, we shall all be buried in that shelter. We have more chance for survival where we are."

Father was right. The shelter was bombed but we remained alive.

At the railway terminal Father embraced us: "Take care of Mother, Zhenka. You are responsible for her now."

He came back to us six months later, with two of the then most highly valued combat decorations, the Order of Lenin and the Order of the Red Banner. He was also shell-shocked and lived for barely eight years afterwards.

Life in the Urals, during the war, was very difficult and marked by hunger. Mother and Auntie Anna worked at a plant, while Father was pensioned off after he was wounded and given a job at the Sverdlovsk recruitment office. I went to school, and for the first time tried to understand what was going on around me. It turned out that the war would not be so amusing and quick as we had imagined. I saw the pain and suffering of the war only in the hinterland, but it was enough. I knocked on the doors of many a recruitment office, begging to send me to the front, but they told me I was too young.

Father sent me to school when I was seven, to keep me off the streets in Vitebsk, where we lived before the war. When I was in the tenth form in Sverdlovsk, all of my classmates were called up – but not me. I was a year their junior. And so I went to school with girls, and fell in love with one of them, Galka Zhigareva. I could not have imagined then that thirty years later, I would meet her in London, the wife of Anatoly Belousov, a friend of mine and assistant air force attaché. But back in 1942–4 I often visited her at home. Her father, the future Marshal and then General Zhigarev (air force), had been sent to

Sverdlovsk by Stalin himself, to monitor the transfer of American lend-lease aircraft.

Once, when I was visiting Galina, I saw another girl there, whom I did not know.

"Come in, Zhenya." I heard the voice of the head of the family. "We are going to have tea."

I went up to the girl and introduced myself. She shook hands with me and said: "Nice to meet you. Svetlana Alliluyeva." After a moment's pause, she added: "That is, Svetlana Stalina." My feet nearly gave way under me. My heart was in my mouth.

General Zhigarev noticed this and said: "Well, Zhenka, did Svetlana frighten you? Now, this will not do for a boy your age."

We settled down at the table for tea and talk. My embarrassment soon disappeared. It turned out that Svetlana had come from Kuibyshev to live with the Zhigarevs for some time. Galina and she had been acquainted since before the war, when they had studied at the same school. I looked at Stalin's daughter and could not believe that the daughter of such a great man could be so ordinary and modest. Did this mean that Stalin was an ordinary mortal man, too?

Svetlana gave me her Moscow address and telephone number. "Drop by when you are in Moscow," she told me. "I will be glad to see you."

I would have done it, if fate had taken me to Moscow. And who knows what would have become of me then? But I was destined to move to the east first, and when I travelled to Moscow after the war, I met not Svetlana but Vassily, Stalin's son. The full story of this encounter will be told later.

Cadet at the Red Navy School

In my teens, I would spend my free time in the Sverdlovsk officers' club. There were old billiard tables there. They were a fixture at all the military settlements where Father took us. I wanted to play like a pro. In the officers' club I was even called the Prince of Sverdlovsk Billiards. The King was an air force lieutenant. I sometimes even beat him, thus earning me the respect and admiration of the numerous billiards fans of Sverdlovsk.

I have loved sport and games since my childhood, and strove to be first in every sport I took up. By the age of twenty I had acquired sports degrees in skiing and boxing (the latter leaving me with a broken nose), volleyball and chess, swimming and water polo, yachting and tennis. I remember one game, played simultaneously on twenty boards in the Soviet Embassy in London, where I was the only player to win from Mikhail Botvinnik, then the world chess champion – infuriating him and surprising my friends.

It was in the billiards hall of the Sverdlovsk officers' club in the spring of 1943 that my fate was sealed. Sanya Kruglov, a friend and peer, and the son of a senior officer on the staff of the Urals Military District, used to come to the officers' club, too. One day he rushed in, happily waving an envelope with the stamp of the Pacific Higher Naval School on it. He showed the envelope to one and all, shouting in a voice crazy with happiness: "Zhenka, I've been admitted! They accept seventeen-year-olds! Got it?!"

I took the envelope with trembling hands, read the letter of admission, and ran out of the room without looking back. That same day, I requested an appointment with the chief of the local naval unit. Without so much as saying hello to him, I proclaimed: "If you don't want to send me to the front line, then send me to a naval school. You helped Sanya Kruglov. I'm as good as him."

I returned home happy beyond description, clutching a letter of introduction to the Vladivostok naval school. Mother wept when she learned about my impending departure, but Father said: "Help him to pack, Masha. His turn to fight must have come."

Mother helped me to pack my meagre belongings and gave me a thousand roubles. I bade goodbye to my parents, promised them I'd write, and left for the Far East.

My independent life began. On arrival in Vladivostok, I immediately went to the school, where the entrance exams were in full swing. Some applicants had already passed two or three exams, while the unlucky ones had been turned down. I had finished my general education with good marks, and hence passed all the examinations with flying colours in three days. I was enrolled, just like Sanya Kruglov, who had come to Vladivostok a day before me.

A year later I turned eighteen, like many others in my class. We could have been admitted to the navy, yet we sat over textbooks. After a short discussion one evening in the spring of 1944, we all decided to fail in the coming examinations so that they would send us to the front line.

The war was drawing to its close and we were in a hurry to do our bit.

But you have to know how to fail. I did my best. The first exam was in applied geography. For example, they asked me what "cumulonimbus" meant, and I answered that it meant cirrus. Or what "cirrostratus" was, and I said, rain clouds. In short, I gave answers exactly opposite to the right ones. Others tried to do the same, but the school's teachers soon saw through our ruse.

My examiner laid out my future for me, missing out all my hopes of getting to the front: "Stop pretending to be a fool, Ivanov. You hope that I will send you to the front line? Nope. I shall order you to clean the toilets instead, together with all your friends. You can tell them that." What could we do?

Eighteen months later, after tiresome training in schoolrooms and on training grounds, we were sent for combat training to the Pacific Fleet. I was detailed to the training ship *Smolensk*, and Sanya to the transport *Transbalt*.

Sanya's and my war started only when the war in Europe was finished. In August I underwent my first trial by fire, in an operation against the Japanese navy. Our ships left Vladivostok and headed for the open seas. It was an ordinary operation, but we youngsters thought it difficult, probably because this time the enemy were real, flesh-and-blood people, and we had to kill them, or they would have killed us. But they did not want to die either, and showered us with mines and shells, torpedoes and kamikazes.

One August day we were given a combat mission in the Sea of Okhotsk, Sanya's *Transbalt* leading the formation, and my ship behind it. But on the second day of the mission my ship was recalled to Vladivostok. When we returned to the port we learned that the *Transbalt* had been attacked and sunk by a Japanese submarine. Some members of the crew had been saved, but Sanya had perished. My heart bled; I wanted to throw myself into battle and take revenge on the Japanese. But there were no more combat missions because Japan capitulated. The school was transferred to Baku, on the Caspian Sea, where I passed out two years later with flying colours.

The most difficult of wars was over, leaving the country ruined. Many people lacked such bare necessities as shelter and bread. What we had in abundance was Stalin's love of the people and Stalin's hatred of our enemies. The great leader taught us that the class enemy would never stop its attacks, and that the closer we were to communism, the more fierce class struggle would become. Party propagandists called on each and every one of us to fight resolutely the remnants of capitalism in our minds and to crush those who did not want to live by Stalin's laws.

The war had ended not long before, yet the air smelled of gunpowder again. The newspapers were filled with cartoons of a militant Uncle Sam preparing to attack the Soviet Union. Recruitment offices sent out thousands of summonses. Soldiers were re-enlisted. The officials of the most peaceful ministries donned a kind of uniform. Military departments at higher schools were enlarged and ordered to train officers in different military skills.

On graduation day we stood on the parade ground, listening to our appointments. Rear Admiral Golubev-Manatkin announced: "Ivanov Yevgeny Mikhailovich is appointed group commander of the largest guns on the battleship *Sevastopol* of the Order of the Red Banner Black Sea Fleet."

This is how I was posted to Sevastopol, to the flagship *Sevastopol*. I had always wanted to be a naval artillery man, because I thought it more interesting to deal with guns than with maps. I told everybody on the battleship: "You all are working for me, so that my twelve guns can cruise the seas."

During the first exercises, I hit all the targets and was graded the top naval artillery men of the squadron. At that time, the captured ships of the Italian navy were distributed among Soviet fleets, and the squadron commander sent me to examine the artillery guns of the Italian destroyer, the *Napoli*. It had been brought to Odessa by Italian civilian sailors. It is not difficult to examine guns that are in good condition; the only problem was that the *Sevastopol* had 305mm guns, while the *Napoli* was equipped with 405mm guns, which meant that our shells could not be fired from the *Napoli*'s guns. The essence of my first naval-diplomatic mission was therefore to point out this major difference.

Having examined the guns, I went around the ship, looking into its cabins. There, I was surprised to see ancient aluminium handwashing cans hanging in nearly every cabin. An accompanying Italian sailor explained in faulty Russian: "This is not for washing hands... This is for drinking."

Indeed, the cans were filled with grape wine. The Italian poured me a glass of wine and raised his glass to peace and friendship. We drank. I raised my glass to co-operation and mutual understanding. Then the Italian said that we should drink to the ship, so that it should fare well. We had one glass of wine more, from another can, because there was no wine left in the first one. By the end of the day I had visited nearly all the cabins; my first international diplomatic mission was a huge success.

Next day the commander listened to my report and commended me on my performance. At that time the commander of the Black Sea squadron was Vice Admiral Sergey Gorshkov, later an admiral and commander in chief of the Soviet Navy. His staff was stationed on the *Sevastopol*. They were as inefficient as the commander himself. I was to witness the results of their poor skills. When approaching the pier, one of the Italian ships hit a mine. The ship should have been ordered to slow down and dock, because it was close to the shore; instead, Comrade Gorshkov's staff attempted to steady the ship by filling its sections with water. As a result, the ship overturned, killing many seamen in the process. But Sergey Georgievich Gorshkov did not punish his staff. He put the blame on the dead seamen.

Want to Become a Spy?

Two years of service on the battleship *Sevastopol* flew by, taken up by short voyages and exercises. In the spring of 1949 the ship's commander relayed to me a summons from the chief of the Black Sea Red Navy headquarters, in Sevastopol.

Captain 1st Rank Karpets was friendly; he even offered me a cup of lemon tea and asked me how I was doing. Next he took my personal file and asked me several questions. I answered them calmly, unsure what to make of this summons.

"Well, and what would you say if we offered to get you a good higher education?"

"I already have one diploma, Comrade Colonel. It is enough for me."

"What about a diploma from the military academy? Want it?"

"Yes, sir," I replied after a while.

"Then here's your letter of introduction, Lieutenant. Go to Moscow."

That same day I went to the capital, to unit number 35576. There I was presented to the members of a military commission. I had never seen so many hero's stars and other decorations. I was asked questions, both from the file and concerning my views. I answered without much enthusiasm, sometimes even insolently, because I did not

understand what was going on. At the end of the
"interrogation" a lieutenant-general asked the other
members of the commission: "Well, what do you say,
comrades? Shall we take him on?"

Everybody nodded.

"Comrade Ivanov, by decision of the state commission
you have been admitted to the military diplomatic academy."

I mumbled something incoherent and left the room with
the heap of papers they gave me. Only when I looked at
the papers did I understand that my life had just taken an
incredible turn. I had become a Muscovite. I was going
to study at an élite academy. In store for me was the
promising career of a military diplomat. My head span.

It took me several days to understand just what sort of
an academy it was and what profession I had agreed to
enter. The military diplomatic academy, later renamed the
Academy of the Soviet Army to conceal its true nature,
was a department of military intelligence for training secret
service personnel. The strange name of the academy was
a longstanding joke. Designed to camouflage the true
character of the academy, it revealed it with great clarity.
As a result, it was clear even to laymen that if one studied
in that academy, one became a military spy.

The chief of the academy was simultaneously deputy
head of the Main Intelligence Directorate (GRU) of the
General Staff. The academy's operation was kept top
secret, never to be made public. Its graduates became
cadre spies in legal and semi-legal GRU *rezidenturas*
abroad, head officers of secret services in military units,
and provided the personnel of the central apparatus of
the GRU.

In short, I had entered a spying academy and was to become a spy myself.

The academic year began in autumn with lectures on the history of diplomacy, seminars on regional geography, language lessons in small groups. I took up English to complement my German. The curriculum included a course of Marxist-Leninist philosophy and political economy, guaranteed to paralyse the brain completely. But there were also new subjects, to which much attention was paid: how to shake off followers, how to recruit an agent, how to organise a secret meeting, how to transfer and receive secret information and the like.

We even set up mock exercises, dividing ourselves into spies and counter-spies. The teams did not know each other. One team had to prepare a safe meeting with an agent, shake off watchers and safely hand over information. The other had to watch and follow, reveal the enemy's plans and provide the fullest possible information about its actions. We played these "games" in the busy streets of Moscow or in quiet small towns outside it. Such games were held throughout the four years of the course. Their results were analysed in great detail to reveal the weak points in the operation of the teams. These short-comings were never to be repeated. Those games taught me the skills which I later used during my work in Norway and Britain.

In this situation our personal lives were bound to change. More responsibility and self-discipline made me behave cautiously even outside the academy. Hardly any of the academy's cadets allowed themselves drinking bouts with girls, for instance. Besides, we had to choose friends and acquaintances carefully. Gradually, with the help of my new friends from the academy, I made my way into the Moscow élite of the early 1950s.

They were mostly military people, like General Vassily Stalin (air force), chief of the Moscow Military District, a fighting pilot and the son of "the great helmsman" and "father of the nations". We met at a party in the Kremlin on the occasion of the anniversary of the October Revolution. I had been sent there by my academy superiors. At that party, General Stalin drank so much that he nearly fell from the parade staircase. Happily, I was at hand and helped him to his car. Our acquaintance continued at football matches, concerts and parties.

Vassily Stalin hated Lavrenty Beria, chief of the security service, and did not conceal this animosity. They never stopped fighting, even during football matches. Vassily was a fan of the Central Army Club, and Beria's favourite team was Moscow Dynamo. Lavrenty arrested the best players of the Central Army Club, while Vassily did every-thing to save them. He even hid Andrey Starostin, a famous forward from the Central Army Club, in his Moscow flat in order to prevent his arrest.

At this time I witnessed one of Beria's dirty tricks. He used to pick up girls from the streets, ordering his aide to bring the girl he liked to his house. On the way, the aide would explain to the poor victim what was expected of her. Resistance was tantamount to signing her own death warrant. Sofia Gorskaya was one of such victims. She was taken from the street when she was still a schoolgirl. Beria gave her a flat in Tverskaya-Yamskaya and used to visit her there. The girl hoped that the visits would stop after she got married, but Beria was unwilling to quit. She therefore decided to commit suicide and once cried on the shoulder of her friend Sasha Nagiba, who was my girlfriend. That's how I knew all about this sordid business. Outraged by what I had learned, I decided to help Sofia. I wrote a letter to Stalin, telling him about the dirty life led by Beria. I had decided to give the letter to Vassily Stalin, but before I did so, I asked the opinion of my classmate Anatoly Konstantinov. He was older and hence more experienced than I. Three years later we even became brothers-in-law by marrying sisters, as I have mentioned in an earlier chapter.

When he learned of my plan, he shouted: "Are you crazy?! This letter will never reach the father of the nations. But it *will* get to Beria, and this will be the end of you."

"And if I give the letter to Vassily Stalin?"

"And what if Beria learns of it?"

I was still a naïve boy then, who believed in ideals and lived by slogans about truth and justice. Thank God, Tolya managed to dissuade me. Had it not been for him, you would have not been reading this book. Young people are naïve, but this is also their strength. Cynicism, pragmatism, does not enter into their calculations, which is probably why young people never doubt – and are generally happy as a result.

I was really happy during my academic years in Moscow. It seemed to me that I could do anything, could set myself any goal and reach it. I could talk philosophy for hours, bathing in the admiration of pretty girls who would succumb when they heard the sacramental phrase, "the law of the negation of negation is the essence of existence". But I could not understand then that, although other people could see me as a wise Hegel-quoting young man, I was nevertheless a naïve metaphysician. When I look back now, I see that I myself was a graphic example of the law of the negation of negation, because throughout my life I changed constantly, trying to find my true self.

Shortly before the end of my first year at the academy my mother wrote to me, telling me that Father had died. I was given several days' leave to attend his funeral in Krasnodar. After the war, retiring combat officers were each given a hectare of land by Stalin's order. Father could get his hectare, too, but he refused. He could not have tilled it due to shell-shock. He took Mother and they headed for the south, where it was warmer and quieter. They settled in Krasnodar, but even the mild southern climate did not help Father. The shell-shock he received on the Valdai in 1941 eventually killed him. Mother did not want to remain in Krasnodar after Father's death; she went to her sister Anna, who lived in Grozny. The two sisters then lived quietly there on the banks of the Sungja.

In 1953 I was to graduate. Soon after Stalin's death, Beria was arrested, tried and shot. Many graduates of the academy were sent to the KGB, which was purged after the death of its chief. In June, shortly before the graduation exams, I was summoned before my superiors. Anatoly Konstantinov, who had passed the same trial before me and was already preparing for his first posting to Britain as deputy air force attaché, gave me some advice: "Zhenya, don't agree if they ask you to become an under-cover agent. They will try to talk you into it, but just don't budge. What they need is your agreement. If you give it, they'll keep you abroad till you crumble."

He was right again: I was invited to become an undercover agent but managed to refuse.

I defended my graduation thesis and passed all my exams with flying colours, got the honorary gold medal and was sent to work in the GRU. The first question in the personnel department was: "Why don't you marry, Comrade Ivanov? We must send you abroad, but you are single. Get married immediately."

Again it was Anatoly Konstantinov who helped me. He introduced me to his wife's sister, Maya Gorkina, who had just graduated from Moscow State University. We got married without thinking twice. Her mother, using the connections of her husband Alexander Fedorovich Gorkin, then secretary of the Presidium of the USSR Supreme Soviet, arranged a trip to a Scandinavian country for us. My kinship with the Gorkins had yielded its first fruit, although I did not marry Maya for that reason.

I was given three months to get ready for my posting to Norway. Maya and I celebrated Christmas in Oslo, where I worked as deputy naval attaché to the Soviet Embassy. My first trip abroad began.

PART THREE

Mission to Oslo

Visiting Haakon VII

A first posting abroad was regarded as a kind of training, and did not usually yield great results. Moscow Centre did not expect effective and immediate action; the main task of such missions was to take root and put out feelers. If one managed to do this, Moscow Centre predicted positive results.

These tactics may have been justified for beginners, but some of my colleagues were so demoralised by them that they did not produce any results in a year, or even four years. I thought that the best tactics for me would be to launch a resolute offensive in all the key directions, without special preparations. For me, the preparation period ended in Moscow. Young people tend to be conceited and over-active, but it was thanks to these traits that my mission to Norway was successful.

When I look back at my work for the GRU, I see a glaring paradox in it. My mission in Britain was not successful: much of what Moscow Centre planned for me did not come to fruition. Yet journalists used reams of newsprint describing it in detail. True, readers' interest was piqued by the Profumo scandal. As for my mission to Oslo, it provided a steady stream of secret information, including data of vital strategic importance obtained from the staff of the Norwegian navy. Yet the Western press, including that of Norway, have hardly ever mentioned this in the nearly forty years that have passed since then. Perhaps there is nothing strange in this: during my five years in Norway, the local secret services did not expose either of the agents I recruited, or any connections, safe houses and flats. They still don't know anything about them. I shall raise the veil of secrecy a little.

My office was situated in the Soviet Embassy in Oslo, in 74 Drammensveien, a short walk from the city centre and the royal palace. The building was surrounded by a beautiful park, with the ambassador's villa deep in its inner recesses. I hired a flat in Bugdei, close to the summer residence of the king and the yachting club, the district of the local bourgeoisie. My villa, which I rented from Fru Orum, stood close to the sea and Oslo Fjord. I often invited guests there and we went on sea voyages together. The embassy gave me a speedboat for this purpose, which I registered at the local yachting club.

To travel around the country, I bought a Pontiac, then considered a powerful and fast American car. I made improvements to it, however, by putting a heavy stone slab in the boot, to facilitate purchase between the back wheels and the roads, which in northern Norway are often covered with snow and sleet. As a result, the car was one of the best in the Soviet colony. Low and fast, it helped me more than once to escape the watchers of Norwegian counter-intelligence, the Overvakningspoliti.

My GRU chief in Norway was naval attaché Captain 1st Rank Pakhomov. Regrettably, one is unable to choose one's chiefs. Mikhail Mikhailovich Pakhomov was an experienced serviceman, but he knew little about intelligence; he could not give good professional advice even if he tried. The only

thing he could do wonderfully well was relay Moscow
Centre orders and monitor their fulfilment. Not much for
a military spy, and a commander to boot. I therefore had
only myself to rely on. But perhaps this was all for the best.

I did not know Norwegian when I first came to Oslo;
I made do with my German and English, but it was not
enough, so I soon found a teacher for my wife Maya and
myself. This teacher was called Siri Svedrup Lunden, and
she was the daughter of Mimi Lunden, the head of the
women's democratic movement in Norway. Lessons lasted
two hours every other day. My other teacher was Knut
Oversen. Recruited into the German army during the war
– against his will, of course – he surrendered to the Red
Army in his very first battle. As a result, he had learned
Russian, which greatly helped me during my lessons. And
yet my greatest teachers were the Norwegians themselves.
I sometimes spent days, and even nights, in company with
various different people. Naturally, we talked.

In three months I no longer needed a teacher. During our
years in Norway, Maya learned the language so well that
back in Moscow she was hired as a teacher of Norwegian
by the Moscow State Institute of International Relations at
the Soviet Foreign Ministry. She is still considered one of
the best Norwegian experts in Russia.

It was my first spring in Norway. Fru Orum was digging
in her garden till late at night – not that darkness ever came,
because it was the time of white nights. Chestnut trees
sprouted candles. Lily bushes were in blossom. Apricot and
almond trees in neighbouring gardens were covered with
fragile pink flowers. The heavy smell of snow-white cherry
trees hung over the street. Almond and cherry trees do not

usually grow side by side, because they belong to different climatic zones, yet they do so in Oslo, because north and south meet there, courtesy of the Gulfstream. Norwegians have calculated that every second this stream brings four million tons of warm water to their shores, four times more than all the world's rivers taken together. The Gulfstream thus gives Norway as much warmth a minute as would the burning of 100,000 tonnes of oil. That is why almond trees bloom there.

By the spring of 1954 I no longer felt handicapped because I had learned about Norway, the Norwegian language and the Norwegians well – or at least so I thought. Parties in the embassy, talks with members of the government, holidays and sports competitions which I attended, all had helped me to establish the necessary contacts and meet the necessary people. I even met the royal family. I was surprised to find that they drove about Oslo without bodyguards. King Olof V was then the crown prince. He himself drove his Simca, which was far from my ideal for a future king's car. He often took along his son Harold, who became King in January 1991, after his father's death. His grandfather, the legendary Haakon VII, did not look like a king at all. We often attended competitions in Holmenkollen. The old man loved skiing and tried to attend the less important competitions. He would come to Holmenkollen in a modest short jacket and a cap with mufflers. You would never have imagined that he was a king. But he was a wise and far-sighted politician. I shall never forget my talks with him.

"I do not share your beliefs, Mr Ivanov," he once told me over a cup of coffee in his palace, where I had been officially invited. "But this does not mean that we should be enemies. Do you agree?"

I could not but agree with him. What we lacked on both sides of the political barrier in Europe then was tolerance.

"Our right-wingers are pressurising me," he went on. "They want me to ban the Norwegian Communist Party and to bring Communists to court for their views."

"What will you do, Your Majesty?"

"A very simple thing, Mr Ivanov. Aren't the Communists of this country my subjects? They are. Hence, nobody can prohibit them to live how they want and to believe what they want."

I lived in Norway during the last years of Haakon VII's reign. He died in 1957, fifty years after proclaiming the "Everything for Norway!" slogan, which symbolised Norway's independence from Sweden and Denmark. Olof V then became King.

Before his coronation, Crown Prince Olof often attended parties in the Soviet Embassy, and I was invariably assigned to him. Diplomatic and military contacts were important then, especially in Norway. After the tragic events in Hungary in 1956, it was rumoured that NATO's nuclear weapons were to be deployed in Norway. And although the Norwegian royal family did not rule the country (just as in Britain), the monarch's opinion with regard to this deployment was taken into account by the government and the Storting.

Moscow Centre therefore ordered me to maintain contact with Haakon VII and his son, Crown Prince Olof, in order to explain Moscow's attitude to this problem, which had great importance for national security, as well as to learn the opinion of the royal family. The cautious and sober policy of the King and the Storting saved Norway from becoming yet another nuclear bridgehead in the struggle against the Soviet Union. This decision was in a way precipitated by Soviet military intelligence, which had contacts in the Norwegian army and in the higher echelons of power. We did everything we could to turn the "silent discontent" in the Norwegian government and military quarters over dependence on the USA into an insurmountable barrier to the deployment of American nuclear bases in Norway. Olof V often invited me to his palace. We would talk about family problems and life in general, but invariably we would turn to this key political problem of nuclear weapons. Despite certain difficulties in understanding each other, we found a common language with regard to one question: Norway must not become anybody's military appendage, or worse still, a nuclear hostage.

Sometimes Harold attended these evening talks. At that time he was still a boy. Olof V once told me the following story about him: "Once a teacher, who thought that Harold was not diligent enough, asked him: 'What are you doing? Harold! What will become of you?' The boy replied: 'I don't know what will become of me, sir, but I know for sure that I will be King.'"

He was crowned in 1991. During the ceremony, the new King of Norway, Harold III, repeated the famous words of his grandfather: "Everything for Norway!"

The Febs

In late 1954 I recruited two senior officers from Norwegian naval headquarters. I shall not reveal their names, of course, but I shall tell you about my work with them. Moscow Centre's work names for them were Feb One and Feb Two, because the first agent suggested calling himself Feb, and I did not object, and so later the second officer I recruited was called Feb Two. They were largely similar, which is why it seemed proper to give them the same names. I don't know what the name means. Maybe it is short for February. Maybe the first recruit was born in February or an important event happened in his life in that month.

I met Feb One in Horten, where the Norwegian naval base is situated. They once held an open day there, which I naturally attended. We were attracted to each other because we had similar interests. I was ferreting out information about NATO's bases in Norway, while Feb One was not averse to selling me this information. We thus easily agreed on the conditions governing our co-operation and on the procedure of working together.

I met Feb Two, who headed a department in the naval headquarters, later. I was in the headquarters on the eve of an impending visit by Soviet warships; the embassy's military mission had ordered me to co-ordinate details with my Norwegian counterparts. Our official conversation in the headquarters continued in a quiet restaurant in Oslo, where we agreed to co-operate.

It was love at first sight in both cases, as I have already explained it is called in the vocabulary. My interest in delicate information, suitable to my position as deputy naval attaché, was apparent to both officers; their desire for money was equally transparent. Both Febs gave me to understand soon enough that they had information from NATO sources and were prepared to share it with me – for payment. To all appearances, they had no conscience about this, probably because the information they supplied concerned not Norwegian but American and NATO forces.

At our second meetings the Febs delivered heaps of top-secret information. I could barely conceal my surprise at their eagerness to please. I gave them both large sums of money – accepted with gratitude – and told them where and how we would meet next. After that I hurried back to the embassy. Naturally, my Febs did not know about each other's existence. Each believed himself to be the only one in my employ.

I maintained regular contacts with the Febs throughout my four years in Norway. They supplied me with NATO documents once or twice a month, and these were immediately forwarded to Moscow Centre by diplomatic courier. The strain of those four years – Moscow Centre did not allow me to leave Norway even for a week, in order to keep the trail warm – wore me out completely. Eventually, as I have said, I chose to return to Moscow without permission. The physical exertion and psychological strain had proved impossible to bear.

A layman may wonder that my work should be so

exhausting. Meet an agent, get information, hand it over. That's it, you might say. But it isn't. In order to meet Feb One more or less safely, I had to take my wife to Holmenkollen every weekend, allegedly for a good rest. Norwegian counter-intelligence naturally assumed that it was monitoring all my movements; my task was to lull its vigilance with these regular visits to Holmenkollen, always taking the same route and leaving at the same time. We either skied all day, for everybody to see, or lay in the sun, depending on the weather. We always lunched in the same restaurant, and never tried to shake off our watchers.

These routine visits continued from the moment of my arrival in Norway till the day I left. And I succeeded so well in lulling the vigilance of Norwegian counter-intelligence that there were moments when I could safely turn off the main road and meet my agents. If I failed to shake off my followers – this happened only twice in the four years of running the two Febs – I always turned up at the fallback rendezvous. I would turn off the road every third Sunday, but my watchers did not even notice my ten-minute disappearances on our way back to Oslo. I usually left Maya in a cafe, went out by the back door and retrieved a parcel from Feb One from a prearranged place exactly on time. It was all rather undramatic. I would put a roll of money and instructions safely hidden in the package with the remains of what I had eaten in the cafe into a garbage can. Simultaneously, I picked up the package left for me by one of the Febs minutes before. To minimise risks, my agent usually watched me from the window of a hotel across the road. A lamp on the windowsill meant that he had put the package in the prearranged place.

To guarantee safe and regular meetings with Feb Two, I would leave the embassy at 1.30 sharp every day and head home for lunch. There were no exceptions from this rule: I took the same route every day, from the embassy home and back. I think that in this way, just as with the visits to Holmenkollen, I managed to lull the Norwegian secret service; they would either slacken control over me, or have lunch themselves. This apparently dull routine had one aim: to guarantee a safe meeting with the agent. Every other Tuesday I left home, ten minutes after I arrived, by the back door, into the neighbouring street. At 1.50 sharp, I would meet Feb Two and exchange parcels, his full of documents and mine containing money and instructions. It was the perfect place for a secret meeting, quiet and unobtrusive, with hardly any passers-by, it being the lunch hour.

Far from all meetings, however, fitted into this pre-arranged framework. We quite often had to have an unscheduled meeting because I needed information immediately. In those cases the risk was great. Once, it nearly cost me my head. It was at the beginning of Norwegian navy manoeuvres, and Feb One was summoned to the exercise headquarters in Kristiansand, in southern Norway. I went there to meet him. At that time Norway did not have distance limits for diplomats from socialist countries, which meant that I did not have to get permission to travel from the Foreign Ministry. The Norwegians were therefore in the dark concerning my plans. As a result, I often toured Norway without watchers, in contrast to my experiences in Britain. But this time, my Pontiac was followed. It took me much time and effort to shake them off, call my Feb and arrange a short rendezvous in a nearby restaurant. I got the papers about the exercises and was leaving Kristiansand when I encountered a police car blocking the road.

A policeman came up to me and asked: "Where have you been? What were you doing here?"

If that policeman had looked into the boot of my car, my mission in Norway would have ended there and then. I could not allow this and so counter-attacked: "How dare you stop a diplomatic car? Who gave you the right to question me?! I just like this town. I didn't enter closed areas. Stop questioning me, or I'll lodge a complaint!"

The policeman backed down. Sighing with relief, I sped to the Soviet Embassy in Oslo.

Naturally, I wanted to know how my agents acquired their information. It turned out that since both were senior staff officers, they had access to secrets. In other countries, I would have had to supply them with miniature cameras, dictaphones and mini-copiers, or debrief them, although this takes a great deal of time and involves great risks. But in the 1950s the Norwegian naval headquarters had a procedure for the destruction of secret materials that greatly simplified their work. Believe it or not, the headquarters' officers themselves filled in the forms concerning the destruction of such materials and themselves signed them. In the Soviet army and navy this negligence in security matters would be impossible. In the Soviet General Staff, for example, the destruction of secret documents was supervised by three specially appointed officers, who filled in special forms together and burned the documents together. This guaranteed reliable control and safety.

The Norwegian rules were actually one big loophole. No wonder my Febs both exploited it. From time to time, they would fill in the form and sign it, but not destroy the documents. There was nobody to check up on them. As a result, I received a wealth of top-secret information from the two leading departments of Norwegian naval headquarters. Information did not trickle but flowed to Moscow Centre in a powerful stream.

In their work with me, however, the Febs had to follow strict security regulations, which called for unflagging attention, maximum concentration and caution. I did not have any difficulty writing instructions for the Febs, which I geared to the demands of Moscow Centre, because both agents were top-notch professionals and knew what information would interest Moscow. For example, they knew that Norway, with its three divisions, would not interest our secret services. But NATO plans, especially those that concerned actions on the northern flank in case of war against the USSR, were another matter.

Norway was a participant in and a potential executor of these plans. Suppose NATO headquarters decided to create a front of fifteen divisions. Although only three Norwegian regiments would be involved, they had to co-ordinate their actions with other units and to know their tasks and targets (what and where to bypass, where to deliver the strike, etc). It was this information that the Febs provided to Moscow Centre.

My main task was to deliver payment on time. On an average, the Febs received monthly from me a sum of money three times larger than their salary. I could also give them bonuses for most important documents, and did this quite regularly. Their foreign trips were also paid for by the Oslo *rezidentura*.

It was Feb Two who most often travelled to Belgium, Britain and the USA, usually to attend NATO conferences. Before each trip he received a lump sum of money from me in the currency of the country of destination. Upon his return, Moscow Centre received a package of secret documents from the latest NATO expert meeting. There were rare pearls in that sea of secret information, materials that were of special importance for the Soviet Union. While working in Norway I could not correctly assess their importance, and was not supposed to anyway, but when I returned to Moscow, I asked my superiors' opinion of the Febs' work. Lieutenant General Konovalov, then chief of the GRU European Department, told me: "I cannot tell you about all the materials you delivered because they were divided between departments. But I remember one document, from Feb One, I think. It concerned the noise level of our submarines. It was very important for our strategic defence. It saved the designers and producers of missile submarines quite a few million roubles."

I remembered that document, too. Feb One had drawn my attention to it himself. He said that it had been drafted by the Americans. The thing was that Soviet designers did not know when and how our submarines made noise, but the smart Americans had learned this. The document they drafted pointed out what noise a water pump or any other part of Soviet submarines made, and provided appropriate tables and charts. This information might seem mundane to a layman, but experts regarded it as a godsend. It showed that an American submarine could safely follow ours, while the commander of our submarine plodded on without ever suspecting that his ship was shadowed by a potential enemy that could destroy it any moment – thanks to the huge amount of noise our submarines made.

Having received those American reports, our designers started working to eliminate this shortcoming. Eventually, the noise became less, which for a certain period protected our strategic forces from a potential pre-emptive strike. In other words, the Febs' reports eliminated a part of the risk of quick destruction of Soviet submarines by the Americans. But the noise made by our submarines remains a problem to this day. Regrettably, my information from Oslo did not help eliminate the shortcoming completely. Just as they were three or four decades ago, modern Russian submarines are little more than heaps of scrap metal.

Here is just one piece of shocking information: according to expert opinion, our submarines would be destroyed in twelve days in the event of a conventional war. Why? Because the main task of anti-submarine warfare is to detect the enemy. The rest is simple: guided torpedoes will not miss. Modern Russian missile submarines can be detected at a distance of 500 miles, while American boats of the same class can be detected only when they are twenty miles away. That damn noise is giving our submarines away. One of the reasons for it is that our submarines have very light bodies, which rumble like a tin can. American submarines are nearly noiseless because they have a sensible body design.

Information about the noise made by Soviet submarines arrived in Moscow from several sources. Feb One provided it to me in the late 1950s. But today, thirty years later, our submarines are still rumbling all over the world's oceans because the monopoly of the Soviet military-industrial complex on the production of hardware seldom guarantees quality, to put it mildly. In short, despite the great importance of the information I provided, the combat-readiness of Russian submarines remains sub-standard. Maybe this is why defence plants are turning out so many of them, as if making up with quantity for poor quality. As a result, the Russian navy has the world's largest fleet of nuclear submarines. Only the economic and financial crisis of the early 1990s helped radically to cut their production.

Had it not been for my "escape" from Norway, I would have been moved up another rung and given an order for that information from Feb One. Instead, I was punished for returning to Moscow without permission. I never regretted this, because I never cared that much about my career.

The Bodø Theft

Apart from monitoring the Febs, my other important task in Norway was to watch NATO military bases. That is why visits to Kristiansund, Kolsas, Orlando, Bardufoss and Bodø were more or less routine for me. Besides, I often visited Kirkenes, which borders on the Soviet Union. Moscow Centre wanted to know about the situation there. Kirkenes lies nearly two and a half thousand kilometres from the capital by mountain roads and ferry crossings.

In short, I travelled a lot. Most of my so-called inspection trips led me to the north, along the famous Highway 50, which links Oslo with Finnmark. A part of this road in northern Norway, as well as several military bases which now belong to NATO, was built by thousands of Soviet POWs interned in Norway by the Germans in 1941–4.

Stills and cine cameras were my main weapons. If I could not use them, I tried to remember whatever I saw in order to be able to report it to Moscow Centre. But sometimes Lady Luck smiled on me, and I brought back from those trips more than just impressions. Something of this sort happened during one of my visits to Bodø, where NATO aircraft were taking part in the Main Embrace exercises.

These exercises were designed to test new methods of defence for NATO's Northern Fleet against a potential attack from the USSR, as well as variants of a counter-offensive. At that time the Americans believed that the main aim of the Soviet Union in case of war would be to provide access to the Northern Sea and the Atlantic for its Baltic Fleet. Consequently, they thought that this aim could be attained either by forcing their way through the Danish straits or by seizing submarine bases situated on the western shore of Norway.

The simplest way of defending Norway was therefore to fortify that area, while the landing of Marines from several aircraft-carriers, supported by a naval task force, and active use of military aerodromes in northern Norway, in particular those such as Bodø, were considered the most probable method of US involvement in the defence of Norway. Naturally, NATO aviation was to be used not only for defending Norway against the potential enemy, but also for attacking Soviet military bases on the Kola Peninsula and in the Baltic.

No wonder Moscow Centre wanted to know everything about Main Embrace. I filled up the tanks of my Pontiac at a Mobil Oil filling station in Oslo and headed for the north, towards Bodø, where the exercises were to be held. The Old Norwegian phrase *Nord vegr*, which gave Norway its present name, means "road to the north". It is a most beautiful route running across the vast expanses of three regions, Nordland, Troms and Finnmark, complete with mountain roads over which rises the ice cap of Sulitelma, shining nearly two kilometres above you.

It was a long way along the seashore, which brought the salty breath of the fjords. Row upon row of aspen, alder, birch and fir trees grew along the road, almost sweeping the bonnet of my Pontiac. On the second day of my trip, the narrow strip of the Salt Fjord to the left of the road became broader, and two islands, Strom and Knaplund, appeared on the surface of the sea, as if protecting the southern entry into the fjord. On the northern shore, at the foot of fantastic mountains, lay a small town dotted with bright houses, Bodø. The aerodrome, which was a NATO military base, was situated in the centre of the town.

I stopped at a hotel across from the aerodrome and asked the manager: "Do you have rooms on the upper floor looking out north?"

"Yes. Would you like to see one?" The manager was very polite.

We went up to the third floor. The window looked out on to the aerodrome. I rented the room and tipped the manager. As soon as he left, I took out my cine camera with its powerful zoom lens and settled at the window. Aircraft were taking off and landing right in front of me. Aircraft-carriers and auxiliary ships rocked on the waves farther out in the sea. Moscow Centre would love this film. My job done, I went for a walk.

I circled the base, carefully noting what cars and lorries entered and left it, what hardware stood in the hangars and on the take-off strips, and how the auxiliary services worked. Then I headed for the seashore and settled there in a place protected from prying eyes. I targeted my binoculars on the naval force, and wrote down the details of it, so as not to miss something important when writing my report. Then I took out a stills camera with a telephoto lens and took several pictures. When I had finished working there, I returned to the hotel. Before supper I went into the bar. Two US air force officers, a colonel and a captain, sat at a table. They must have dropped in for a drink after their flights.

I ordered a whisky and settled near them. I sipped my drink and looked at the Americans. They were discussing something, probably what happened at the base that day, rather loudly. They finished their drinks and went to the bar to order more. I looked at their table and saw on it a yellowish paper, folded in two. It was not a letter, more likely an official paper. I rose quietly and, keeping the Americans in sight, put my hat near the paper. The Americans remained at the bar, unaware of my movements. I took the paper and left. Since I had paid for my room in advance, I immediately took my bag and looked at the paper in the bathroom on the way out.

My God! It was a NATO plan of action in case of war, which was being tested in Bodø, marked "Top Secret". The loss of this paper would cost the colonel dearly, but that was his problem. My task was to deliver it to Oslo as soon as possible, because it enumerated the combat tasks of the allied air force and navy. Ships would guarantee protection from this to that latitude; aircraft-carriers would deliver strikes at this or that target in the Soviet Union.

It was a formidable piece of luck. I put the paper into my sock and went downstairs. Everything was quiet, but it was too dangerous to remain in the hotel. Although it was growing dark, I headed for my car. I would stay overnight in a small hotel along the road to the south, I thought.

My Pontiac revved up. At the crossroads I saw a police Opel. We saw each other. Was the Opel following me? Yes. What should I do? The police car gathered speed and quickly caught up with me. Yes, it was after me. The policeman signalled for me to stop. That American colonel in the bar must have tricked me, I thought. I stopped the Pontiac.

The policeman from the Opel came up to me and said: "Your left light isn't working. Change the lamp."

I sighed with relief but couldn't utter a word.

"Do you understand me?"

"Yes, yes, of course, I do," I replied at long last, regaining control of my senses. "Thank you. You are very kind. I shall do this at the nearest filling station."

My journey back to Oslo passed off without a hitch. Several days later the document I had stolen in Bodø was analysed by our experts on the General Staff. It helped the Soviet military leadership to specify priority directions and targets of NATO's air force and navy in the north, and hence to strengthen our defences where massive enemy strikes were to be expected.

Picnics in Oslo Fjord

I had two great helpers in Norway: the Pontiac, which speedily delivered me to meetings with agents and to NATO military bases, and the speedboat *Elma*, made of mahogany. Those who live, or at least work, in Norway are bound to spend some time on the water, in the fairy-tale kingdom of the fjords. Their attraction is irresistible, and few can resist the temptations offered by Norwegian nature. I was no exception.

I still remember Oslo Fjord, both as I saw it from the hills surrounding Oslo, and from the boat, with the outlines of the city rising from the sea like a mirage. Words fail me when I try to describe the beauty of that view: a caressing summer sun overhead, the azure expanses of the fjord below me, the hot air that breaks up the geometrical outlines of the town hall, and my *Elma* speeding on the water, leaving a long white trail.

What luminaries my *Elma* carried! For example, there was the then chess champion Mikhail Tal, who played a blitz with me, without a bishop. I remember that I could not outplay him even though the young chess king was so severely handicapped. Mikhail Sholokhov, of *Quiet Flows the Don* fame, came to Norway after he got his Nobel Prize in Stockholm, and told me about his plans on the *Elma*. Comrade Itskov, USSR Minister of Fisheries, sent by Khrushchev to Norway to settle a dispute concerning the catch of herring by Soviet fishermen in Norwegian territorial waters, pondered possible changes to the Soviet position to the quiet rumble of the boat engine. I remember that he paid 700,000 kronen to settle the dispute, and that only after he treated his Norwegian counterparts to lots of vodka and caviar at the Soviet Embassy. The thing was that for the Norwegians, fishing was not just an economic undertaking, fish was their bread, because Norwegian nature is like a foster mother, and only the sea is generous. That is why the wellbeing of Norwegians largely depends on successful fishing off Bergen and Lofoten, or far away in the open seas. Norwegians used to say that herring was their queen and cod their crown princess. But times change, bringing new monarchs. The Norwegian economy is now ruled by a new king, who pushed aside the queen herring and the crown princess cod. I mean oil, of course. "Black gold" earned Norway new income and confronted the country with new problems.

But back to my story: my *Elma* also carried simpler people, like athletes and actors, workers and servicemen, who were in Oslo for a few days. Chance brought us together for a day or two, only to separate us again for the rest of our lives, but however good or bad those people might be, my beautiful *Elma* was meant not for them but for such people as Vice Admiral Kristiansen.

I met Bjorn Kristiansen not by chance, or rather by chance prepared in advance. At that time Kristiansen was a leading officer in the Norwegian navy; for many years he had been head of the navy's personnel department. Acquaintance with him promised an interesting exchange of opinions. Moscow Centre even thought about recruiting him. Although I was merely a captain lieutenant then, I had two agents working for me in Mr Kristiansen's agency: the Febs. My position at the embassy and my knowledge in the sphere of naval politics attracted a number of Norwegians, including Mr Kristiansen, to my humble person. We were attracted to each other. Besides, we were not dissimilar: both naval officers, direct and open, who liked to eat and drink heartily. My *Elma* was always well stocked with caviar and vodka. Even in the hottest weather ice preserved the food and kept the Russian vodka cool. As for subjects of conversation, there were more than enough of them.

Leaving the shores of Oslo far behind us, we would sometimes drop anchor in a bay deep in the Oslo Fjord, where the air was always clear and fragrant, the water from a spring was tasty and cool, and the wind brought to you the bittersweet smell of the pines. I would make a fire and, when the wood burnt to coals, cook aromatic pieces of shashlik, marinated with salt, pepper and vinegar, over them. The tender and juicy lamb pieces went well with cold Pshenichnaya wheat vodka, followed with velvety caviar, which filled your throat with its salty and spicy, absolutely inimitable, taste.

Politics and military matters did not dominate our talks. We talked more about life and nature, hobbies and disappointments, vices and talents. It was easy for us to find a common language, because we were so much alike. But even if we hadn't been, it was my task to become friendly with Mr Kristiansen – and possibly to recruit him. Aware of the complexity of the task, my superiors did not hurry me. I studied my new acquaintance at leisure, asking myself one and the same question over and over again: should I try to recruit him now? Is the time right?

The touchstone was our talks about Norwegian membership of NATO. I seldom began this conversation, but when I did, I listened to Bjorn's answers very carefully. "Like you, Captain, I am against too close association with NATO," he told me, "or nuclear weapons in our fjords. But, I am not against NATO as such. Some politicians claim that ours is a small country on which nothing depends. Nuts! Even a small nation can do a lot."

We agreed on some topics and differed on others, but we always came to terms over toasts for Norway. Once I tried to play the German card: "They have forced on you an alliance with former Nazi criminals. Have you forgotten the lessons of the war so quickly? Didn't you suffer in those years? It was a miracle that your Premier Einar Gerhardsen survived the Nazi death camp Sachsenhausen. Do you remember that King Haakon VII had to flee to the British Isles? And now Hitlerites are again bossing around your military bases. Is this the alliance Norway needs?"

Several years later this approach swept Sir Colin Coote off his feet. But Bjorn Kristiansen did not budge. The picnics in Oslo Fjord, however, continued and bore some fruit. I sometimes ferreted out interesting information from my companion; at other times I "leaked" secret information to him from my directorate. But I never dared try to recruit Bjorn. I think this was wise, because it could have resulted only in a scandal. The Norwegian was a hard nut to crack, and I had no reason to suspect this wholehearted dedication to his country's welfare was anything but totally sincere. Besides, did I really need Bjorn Kristiansen when two of his senior headquarters officers were already working for me?

Yet another regular "customer" of the *Elma* was Kalle Rog, a businessman of high standing who loved cars and horses. He was the man who opened the doors of Norwegian high society to me. When I think of him, I always look at the bronze figurine of the horse who won many a race in Norway and abroad, which he presented to me. He was a giant of a man, weighing 160 kilogrammes, who could eat a whole lamb and drink a barrel of beer, but despite his bulk, he was active and energetic.

Once I met him at the airport upon his return from a London trip. Kalle walked towards me, happy and content. "Hullo, Eugene!" he shouted so loudly that everybody around him looked up involuntarily. "I fooled them all. Three bottles of whisky I carried through!"

"How could you?" I wondered. "The customs allow only two bottles."

Kalle patted his big belly and bellowed: "The third one is already here!"

It appears that before passing through customs he drank a whole bottle of whisky, which was for him what a glass was for me.

Kalle Rog was an invaluable friend. All doors opened before his massive hulk. He introduced me to nearly everybody I needed, and this saved me a lot of time, which I always lacked in Norway. Besides, he was a walking encyclopaedia on all business matters: shares, investment policies, debts, interest rates or taxes. With a head like his one did not need a computer.

"Eugene, do you want to become rich?" he once asked

me. "I can help you. You need only to invest in a joint stock company, say, Cosmos, and reap the coupons in two or three years."

"Looks too simple for me," I replied. "There must be a hitch somewhere. What about the law on excess profits? Doesn't it limit interest from joint stock capital to six per cent?"

"You don't understand anything!" Kalle was outraged. "Any law has exceptions! In some cases dividends can reach fifteen per cent!"

"Well, one cannot get rich on exceptions," I retorted.

"Wrong again. You can have as many exceptions as you like! A dozen a day! But you have to use your brains. Well, why am I trying to convince you? If you don't want to get rich, don't. You Russians are all set against capitalists," he said with obvious disappointment. He never returned to that subject again.

But one of *Elma*'s passengers – let's call him Lieutenant Emmy – would not have missed that chance. This young man worked for a NATO country embassy in Oslo. He really wanted to get rich. If his information had not been so shallow, he could have made a good profit, but he knew little and hence his revenues from co-operation with me were not big. Who could pay well for trifles? Yet thanks to him our *rezidentura* in Norway knew about all the reshuffles and the more or less important developments in his embassy. Picnics in Oslo Fjord were my expressions of gratitude to Lieutenant Emmy. When cold weather set in, we would meet in a pub called the Golden Cockerel, where we could talk safely. I paid, of course, for what the lieutenant told me about the goings-on in the embassy. It is possible that the modest yet interesting information from Lieutenant Emmy helped considerably in my career.

By the end of 1958 the endless meetings, fallbacks, and talks, all undertaken without leave and practically without weekends, had worn me out completely. Maya and I decided to return to Moscow; we just bought air tickets and left.

My reception at the directorate was more than cool. "When are you going back?" Vice Admiral Yakovlev, then GRU chief of strategic intelligence, asked severely.

"Never."

"What?!" the admiral bellowed. "I'll have you demoted!"

He would have, had it not been for the boys from the English section. Having learned about my predicament, they offered me a job in their office and helped me to get it quickly. Moscow Centre had to hand the Febs over to Captain 1st Rank Pakhomov, the naval attaché in Oslo. I started preparing for a new posting, to London.

As I have already related, that mission ended in disaster: I had to return to Moscow without finishing a number of promising deals there. I had, however, a last test to pass on my return: my last one, as I thought then.

PART FOUR

Working for the GRU

Test by Returning

I returned from Britain in January 1963 with a heavy heart. A premonition of trouble would not leave me for a moment. I hungrily read every despatch from London on the hearing of the case of John Edgecombe and Aloysius "Lucky" Gordon, boyfriends of Christine Keeler, in the Old Bailey. Tension increased as more and more witnesses provided information on Christine's scandalous connections.

On 22 March Jack Profumo made his statement in the House of Commons. Trying hard to avoid a scandal, he decided to deceive Parliament, saying that he had never had any relations with Christine Keeler. He and his friends hoped that they could induce her to keep silent, but she was promised good money by newspapers and publishers and decided to profit from the political scandal. She revealed everything, or nearly everything, and even recalled some things that had never happened.

Profumo was forced to resign. In his 4 June letter to Prime Minister Harold Macmillan, he admitted that he had lied to Parliament and to his colleagues in the Conservative Party on 22 March. It was a suicidal admission. One of the leading members of the ruling party was proved to have lied, and, of all places, in Westminster itself. The Tory government was living through its last days, gradually ceding its position to the Labour Party and losing the confidence of its voters.

The hearing of Stephen Ward's case began in the Old Bailey on 22 July. He was accused of supplying girls like Christine Keeler and Mandy Rice-Davies to rich clients for money. This was an outrageous lie, yet it was an accusation which successfully distracted the attention of the public from high-ranking officials who did not want to be involved in a public scandal. Stephen could not stand the treachery of his ex-friends who had made a scapegoat of him. He would not defend himself by accusing others, or even wait for the verdict. He committed suicide on 30 July 1963 by taking an overdose of sleeping pills. It was a shock for me. They had killed my friend. They had actually forced him to die simply because he was in the way. They feared his revelations. He knew too much, things that must never be revealed. And so he was removed from life, for ever.

I promised myself that if I ever visited the British Isles again, my first trip there would be to Steve's grave.

In the summer of 1963 Lord Denning was working on his report on the Profumo scandal, at the request of the Prime Minister. This report was published in the autumn of 1963 and concluded that the connection of Ward, Profumo, Keeler and others with Captain Ivanov, who was probably an agent of the Soviet secret services, had not damaged British security. But even that, far from true, conclusion by Lord Denning, who clearly did not know everything, did not save the Conservative government. At the 1964 parliamentary elections the Tories were defeated by the Labour Party, and the government of Harold Wilson came to power.

A no less serious scandal was brewing in Moscow, too, although the newspapers did not write about it, and the

Supreme Soviet did not discuss reports about damage to national security. *Glasnost* was not even in the making then. Nevertheless, the hearing of the case of Colonel Oleg Penkovsky, who had been working for the British and American secret services, shook the GRU to its foundations.

At that time Marshal Biryuzov, Chief of the General Staff, sent me to study at the Academy of the General Staff. Its diploma was a coveted prize for any Soviet officer. Education at that élite academy was the apogee of professional military training in the Soviet Union. But for me it was actually an exile. I did not need a third diploma.

"Can't you understand that you should get out of the directorate for some time?" Marshal Biryuzov tried to explain the situation to me. "Keep a low profile, so to speak."

The marshal, who had always liked me, wanted to help me get out of the line of fire of both my superiors and many rank-and-file GRU members. Penkovsky's treason, just like the Profumo affair, had cost many people their posts and even their lives. The marshal was well aware of its implications and so he found a good refuge for me in the academy. I think old man Gorkin had also had a hand in saving me.

Marshal Biryuzov was right: we were in for a dark age, and not only in the GRU. Personnel were reshuffled nearly everywhere. Khrushchev's economic reforms engendered covert but widespread discontent in the Party apparatus. The military did not like his foreign policy. Leonid Brezhnev, then an influential member of the Party and second secretary of its Central Committee, had been covertly engineering a coup since the spring of 1964. Indeed in 1964, KGB chief Vladimir Semichastny was offered several scenarios for assassinating Khrushchev. The future leader of the Party and the country advocated an air crash during one of the premier's foreign visits. Semichastny did not like the idea, arguing that the crew of Khrushchev's plane was loyal to him and hence that the scenario was doomed to failure. Brezhnev then suggested poison or a car crash. But Semichastny told him assassination was too risky; they could do away with Khrushchev without resorting to such drastic measures. He was right.

At the October 1964 plenary meeting of the Party Central Committee, Brezhnev launched a quiet but effective offensive against Khrushchev, utilising the support of all his opponents. They did not even let the premier have a last word: he was forced to resign from all his posts.

A new era began in Soviet history. Following the advice of my wise relatives and superiors, I sat out the storm over staff games in the spacious halls of the old building of the Academy of the General Staff in Kholzunov Pereulok. (At that time the General Staff did not occupy its later site, a big monster of a building in south-west Moscow.)

Marshal Biryuzov had been right; it had been better for me to keep a low profile in the wake of the Profumo scandal.

"Wait till the dust settles, Zhenya," he told me. "Both in Britain and here."

Indeed, my involvement with Christine Keeler, which became known to all and sundry after the publication of the Denning report, did not do credit to me as a GRU officer. At that time only the KGB was believed to use such "dirty" methods, while the GRU pretended to be orthodox and "clean". I could have blamed the lying bourgeois press for the scandal, of course, and I did. But this did not deceive my superiors. Nobody was bothered by my love affair with Christine Keeler, because it was not proved, after all, but rumours about my amoral goings-on did not help improve my standing with the GRU leaders. Why did Ivanov have that affair? they asked themselves. And he did not even inform Moscow Centre! If he had been more discreet, there would have been no scandal. In that case all the planned operations involving Jack Profumo could have been carried out, most probably successfully. Some GRU superiors must have thought these arguments convincing, but everybody who really knew the situation realised that it had not been my affair with Christine Keeler that had caused the scandal and wrecked Moscow Centre's operation.

Nobody blamed me in earnest, but nobody thanked me for my efforts in London either. Some people surreptitiously used the results of my work to their benefit, while I was seen as an obscure and not always disciplined maverick who had worked in London under somebody else's steadying command. While those smart people wrote their fine reports, exploiting the results of my work, I was offered a chance to gain credits in a race for yet another *cum laude* diploma. I got that diploma, complete with the stripes of Captain 1st Rank, in 1968.

My years at the academy were not all spent in vain, though. I recruited for the GRU one of its best students, General Nikolai Chervov, who was being persuaded to become a graduate student at the academy and defend a doctor's thesis there. We were in the same group and often sat side by side over our maps. We would even go together for a swift drink to a cafe at Frunzenskaya underground station after classes. In a word, we became friends.

Once Kolya was reporting the situation of an exercise. His commanding voice carried well: "The group of ... Mind that the left flank is weak... It seems expedient to deliver the strike bypassing the fortifications..." Kolya's voice echoed in our ears.

Such exercises were always attended by General of the Army Ivashutin, the new GRU chief. He spotted Chervov and ordered the personnel department men to recruit him. They started working, promising him a high salary and a top post. He would not budge: he wanted to become a military scientist.

The superiors then asked me to take him on. Eventually, I recruited Nikolai Chervov; he became head of GRU operational intelligence, and later headed the GRU information department.

Another of my achievements during my years at the academy was the construction of a fireplace in the Moscow flat of German Titov, cosmonaut number two, who was also upgrading his knowledge at the academy. German and his family had left Star Town, where all cosmonauts lived, and settled in Mosfilmovskaya Street in Moscow, where academy students were given flats. He chose a flat on an upper floor, close to the stars, and decided to add some conveniences. And who could advise him better how to make a chimney than myself, who had spent some time in Britain? As a result, the ceiling of his flat was broken open, and a chimney and a fireplace were fitted. We used to spend long winter evenings there, by the fire over a glass of brandy.

While I was playing military games, recruiting General Chervov and building fireplaces, the GRU was cleansed of the bad influence of Penkovsky. The country's new leader, Leonid Brezhnev, appointed Sergei Ivanovich Izotov, a Party apparatchik, as head of the GRU personnel department. He was given the rank of colonel, and soon climbed the ladder to lieutenant general. Pyotr Ivanovich Ivashutin, Brezhnev's old pal, was appointed GRU chief. He used to work for the KGB, where he headed the sixth Main Directorate responsible for military intelligence. His first successful operation in the GRU was to remove all those who were associated with Ivan Serov and Oleg Penkovsky.

But corruption was something he was not going to combat: it had sprouted under Serov and was blossoming under Ivashutin. I was foolish enough to emulate Don Quixote and attempt to fight it.

The Corrosion of Corruption

My new jacket of Captain 1st Rank was decorated with a third rhombic sign. The first two denoted my graduation from the Frunze Higher Naval School and the Military Diplomatic Academy. The third said that I had graduated from the Academy of the General Staff. Many of the workers in the GRU office in Gogolevsky Boulevard, where I was given a new post, looked at it with envy.

The GRU chief General Ivashutin promptly signed an order appointing me head of the analysis department. I was given a leather folder with an inscription in gold on it, "Main Intelligence Directorate", which I was to take every other day to the GRU chief, alternating with one of my subordinates. This went on till 1981, when I retired.

At first I thought that it would be a temporary job. It was an admiral's post yet I was not promoted to that rank. I was expected to work hard to get an admiral's stripes, and I worked like a galley slave. I honestly wanted to become an admiral.

I would sift, study and analyse the mass of daily information, sum it up on five typed pages for the chief of the General Staff, the Defence Minister, chief of the main operations department of the General Staff, and the GRU chief. General Ivashutin would read the pages in my presence, ask questions, listen to my answers, thank me for my work. My temporary job became permanent.

Everything would have been all right had not my

enterprising and ambitious deputy, Colonel Kishilov, wanted my job. He was prepared to use any means to get it. Clouds started gathering over my head. Kishilov began by fortifying his rear, befriending General Milevsky, head of the GRU's main command post which incorporated my department. The general proved to like toadies and soon started frequenting Kishilov's *dacha*. He also quickly grew used to accepting costly presents from my deputy, at first on special occasions, and then without any pretext at all. In return, General Milevsky helped Kishilov, advising him on ways to please the GRU chief and to spite me. Gradually, my demotion became their shared goal. Colonel Kishilov wanted to climb another rung, get a new post and general's stars, and some of my superiors obviously wanted to get rid of the principled and honest Ivanov, who simply did not fit into their team.

Colonel Kishilov soon saw that his friendship with General Milevsky was not enough, so he won over to his side General Izotov, head of the GRU personnel department, by means of small services, toadying and presents. To seal their newly-established coalition, the threesome spent their free days and holidays together. The untiring Kishilov undertook to provide them with the necessary comforts during their holiday on the Caucasus Black Sea coast. He clearly scored great successes in this undertaking; his return from leave was triumphal. He was so confident of his standing that he could not conceal from his colleagues that he had special, friendly relations with the GRU upper crust. He hinted to me, half jokingly and half seriously: "Yevgeny Mikhailovich, I hear that General Izotov wants to offer you an interesting posting abroad. You are clearly a preferable candidate, with your knowledge and experience. If I were you, I would not turn this offer down."

My friends warned me that my position was being undermined.

"Zhenya, maybe you should indeed go on a mission abroad in this situation," General Chervov told me. "Why the hell should you tolerate that deputy of yours? Go away and let him enjoy the crown."

General Izotov, bent on pleasing his new friend, was working on that idea. His team showered me with offers: "Yevgeny Mikhailovich, there is a military attaché vacancy in Sudan. Aren't you tired of sitting over books in Moscow? Would you like to go abroad?"

"My wife cannot stand heat. Her health is not that good," I replied without thinking twice.

Yet attempts to send me abroad did not stop. "Comrade Captain 1st Rank," the personnel rats would tell me, "we are offering you the job of military attaché in Indonesia. We hope you'll accept it."

"You know that my wife cannot live in a hot climate," I replied.

Sensing that I would not give up my post voluntarily, my enemies changed their tactics. "What does it mean, Comrade Captain 1st Rank? Why do you refuse all offers? Are only Rome and Paris good enough for you?" General Izotov's department, unable to remove me from Moscow – and the farther the better – was clearly trying to question my professional loyalty.

"Well, if you put it this way, then I have nothing to do but agree. But I shall go without my wife," I said.

They would not accept this, and I knew it. Besides, old

man Gorkin was still a deputy of the USSR Supreme Soviet and Chairman of the Supreme Court. He would not have let General Ivashutin rest if the latter had sent me to far-away lands for several years without my wife.

I won that battle against General Izotov and his team, but not the war. Colonel Kishilov did not lose heart: he formed another alliance, paying for it with more services and presents. His new ally was the GRU chief doctor, who signed health certificates for all officers and their families posted abroad. I was not much surprised when this new friend of Kishilov's stated that my wife was in perfect health. They wanted to deprive me of my best argument. An alternative examination outside the GRU was inadmissible. A new examination in the GRU, should I want it, would have been supervised by the same doctor and hence produced the same result. I was driven into a corner. Thank God, Maya still had a copy of a statement issued by the same doctor several months before, which said that she should not spend her leaves in the south for reasons of health, but should rather go to health resorts in central Russia. The defeated chief doctor had to admit that he had issued this recommendation. It was enough to give me breathing space in the protracted battle against Colonel Kishilov.

But this tactic of procrastination would not be successful for long. I had to attack, and soon Kishilov himself provided me with an opportunity. He was too demonstrative in displaying his friendship with General Izotov; he even showed me photographs of the two of them, taken in the south. On them, the tipsy general was surrounded by girls of dubious morals, supplied by Kishilov. The latter was foolish enough to joke about them. I decided to use my old skills. While my deputy described the benefits of vacationing in the south and the charms of local girls, I turned on the dictaphone which I had in my pocket. The skills I had acquired in Britain did not die easily. Later in the day I asked General Izotov for an audience. I did not have to explain the reason for my coming; I just turned the tape on and let Izotov listen to it. He soon turned off the dictaphone, removed the cassette and put it, together with the photographs, into a drawer.

"I just wanted to warn you, Sergei Ivanovich," I told him. "You've become too trustful."

Some time later General Milevsky and Colonel Kishilov resigned. As for me, I did not get the admiral's stripes; General Izotov clearly had not forgiven me. After I defeated Milevsky and Kishilov, the department's officers started fearing me.

As the Italians say, the Mafia never dies. I won only one battle, but it was impossible to combat the corruption which had reached unprecedented proportions in the GRU. Brezhnev's regime had turned breach of trust and abuse of power into a fact of life. Bribes and "presents" were used in the GRU to get a general's stars and admiral's stripes before time. It worked this way in the cases of some twenty such newly-created generals and admirals to my knowledge. Postings abroad were also handed out for money. I remember a sixty-one-year-old officer, who should have resigned long before, being sent abroad and given general's stars.

Superiors used such people abroad to carry through all kinds of schemes, including financial scams. With time, refusal to buy costly presents for superiors and their families came to be regarded as insubordination, and the culprit was soon recalled to Moscow. This meant that doing one's duty was not important any longer. Who needed good professional intelligence work? Toadying became the only way to succeed, although imagination was also necessary to guess what intelligence Party and state leaders wanted to see.

In the late 1970s toadying thus pushed aside professional work. There remained talented and loyal officers, of course, such as General Mamsurov and General Pavlov, deputy chiefs of the GRU (the latter being the man with whom I worked in London). But the corrupt triumvirate – the GRU chief General of the Army Ivashutin, head of the GRU political department General Dolin, and head of the GRU personnel department General Izotov – was weighing down on rank-and-file officers more and more heavily. As a result, during Brezhnev's rule Soviet military intelligence largely stopped functioning properly and lost its prestige, won by years of hard work. Some higher GRU officers offered their services to the enemy and were duly recruited by foreign secret services.

For years information leaked from the GRU, and the leakage was eventually stopped only by pure chance. But this revelation came too late: the damage done to the GRU was irreversible. It happened after I had resigned. Ex-KGB General Kalugin did not balk at making it public. If his KGB colleagues had not recruited a CIA agent, who revealed the names of the GRU officers working for his service, the leakage of vital information from Moscow Centre would have continued even longer.

The corrosion of corruption destroyed nearly all state structures during Brezhnev's rule. As a result, the most important military and political decisions were taken without a suitable, in-depth analysis of the situation. Instead of thorough analysis, the time-serving desires of Politburo members – and especially the General Secretary himself – determined state policy at that time. It was dominated solely by assigned ideology, while common sense went out of the window. The results were the criminal Afghan war, which lasted for ten long years and cost us tens of thousands of human lives, and the destruction of the economy in what should have been the world's richest state. Three hundred million Soviet people thus did not benefit from the promised prosperity. Poverty became a fact of life for every fourth citizen of our country. We could have hardly expected a different result. The totalitarian regime and its bankrupt immoral ideology were bound to lead Russia into a dead-end.

Disintegration

I resigned from the GRU as soon as I could, at fifty-five still Captain 1st Rank. Nobody tried to hold me back, because I was such an outsider in the organisation. By 1981 the GRU, just like nearly all other Soviet structures, was dominated by the all-powerful mafia of Brezhnev.

The pain of years wasted in the GRU was not easily dulled; I started to drink. Before this time, I used to have a drink or two at weekends, just like any other normal person. But when I retired I released all brakes. To add to my pain, my mother died and Maya asked for a divorce. We had been husband and wife for thirty years. We did not quarrel and parted amicably. Maya left because we did not have children, or because I started drinking; it's difficult to be certain as to the precise reason. In any case, we drifted apart, and I remained alone.

I had to do something to prevent myself going mad, and so I started working for a department at the Novosti Press Agency studying methods of effective propaganda. I was its consultant till 1989, writing backgrounds on military-political subjects and reports on Novosti's propaganda campaigns. I soon saw that the agency was fatally ill, too: it provided only information that suited the Party apparatus and its leaders. Gorbachev's *glasnost* offered only temporary release from censorship; nobody could voice opinions that differed from the position of the Kremlin élite.

The true-blue Party apparatchiks, such as the former Novosti board director Albert Vlasov and his deputies, were careful to prevent their subordinates trespassing into prohibited terrain. At least a third of Novosti's posts abroad were occupied by KGB and GRU men. The provision of legal cover for them was Novosti's second most important function, its first being the popularisation of the policy put forward by the country's leadership.

This sham Novosti journalism was bound to engender – and eventually did engender – time-serving and corruption. Even the rise of Mikhail Gorbachev could not erase this legacy of the totalitarian regime. Posts and trips abroad were handed out to relatives and friends, or simply sold. The non-conformist opinions voiced by a few honest journalists resulted in dressing-downs at board meetings, sackings, or their more civilised equivalent, resignations "of one's own free will". I would never have worked in such conditions had my pension not been so meagre. I sincerely sympathised with the many talented journalists I met at Zubovsky Boulevard. Their talents were forced to remain latent, while their objectivity and honesty were trampled underfoot by the absolute reign of the Party apparatus and its ideology.

After the adoption of the liberal Law on the Press in 1990, many free-thinking journalists left Novosti, despite difficulties on the job market. Indeed, it was not just futile but immoral to sell life, freedom and talent to the Party apparatus, which over the seven decades of its rule had learned how to do only one thing well: to brainwash and dupe millions of Soviet people. After the tragic events of August 1991, the agency was completely overhauled and ceased to be the mouthpiece of orthodoxy.

I resigned in the summer of 1989. I spend my days queueing in shops, for soap, matches. One cannot smoke without matches, and I cannot cut out this bad habit. At one time, even cigarettes disappeared from all the shops. I spend my days in queues, holding my food and tobacco ration cards. I listen to the Russian people, sick and tired of such a life, cursing the Communist Party which brought this great country to this humiliation. Sometimes I persuade an old lady to queue for me and buy me rationed vodka, for an additional payment, naturally.

On the eve of 1991, I, as a veteran of the Second World War, was given a "present" from Germany. The parcel contained nothing but several boxes of matches. Well, I had matches at least, thanks to my German benefactors. But it was extremely humiliating for me, a naval officer, to take such presents.

The main thing, though, was not that there was nothing to eat; the trouble was that innocent blood was being shed. The army had been transformed into an instrument of oppression turned on its own people. The army which liberated half of Europe from fascist slavery, which had suffered so much during the war, had been turned by the Kremlin into an instrument of tyranny. It was used first against Eastern European countries, next against Afghanistan, then under Gorbachev the army fought its own people, in Tbilisi and Baku, Vilnius and Riga.

The failed right-wing coup in Moscow in August 1991 crowned that neo-Bolshevik orgy. But by that time both the people and the army had changed irreversibly. Fear had given way to a firm resolve to fight the dictators. The élite army units, the KGB and GRU task forces, when they were ordered to storm the building of the Russian Parliament and to arrest the Russian President Boris Yeltsin on the first day of the coup, 19 August, simply did not obey orders. The split in the army and the KGB became one of the chief reasons for the coup's failure.

In those three days of the coup I, Captain 1st Rank (Rtd.) Ivanov, was on the barricades at Russia's White House, along with thousands of others. We won, we stopped the dark reactionary forces. Russia entered the way of democratic renewal.

My days are numbered. I'm afraid I shall not live to see a better life in my country, although it deserves it. I can only hope that the dying totalitarian regime will not dare unleash a bloody terror campaign in order to restore its diktat. New, young democratic forces are rising. The future belongs to them. Young people believe in them, because their souls and minds have not been poisoned by ideological demagogy.

It is with my belief in these growing forces and with penitence for what I have done in my life that I finish this story.

Moscow, 1992

Yevgeny Ivanov died in January 1994. He was aged 68.